BIG SCREAM
IN A
SMALL TOWN

BIG SCREAM
IN A
SMALL TOWN

The Nic Knuckles Collection

NIC KNUCKLES, PI

LEVEL
BEST BOOKS

First published by Level Best Books 2023

This novel is entirely a work of fiction. The names, characters and incidents portrayed in it are the work of the author's imagination. Any resemblance to actual persons, living or dead, events or localities is entirely coincidental.

Nic Knuckles, PI asserts the moral right to be identified as the author of this work.

Author Photo Credit: Jonathan Ade

First edition

ISBN: 978-1-68512-522-6

Cover art by Robert Allen

This book was professionally typeset on Reedsy.
Find out more at reedsy.com

James Lee Hoot Jon Spear
Sandy Falenski Brendan Hanlon

Praise for Big Scream in a Small Town

"*Big Scream in a Small Town*, by William Ade, is a fast and clever (and often funny) read that neatly spans a couple of common mystery categories. On one level, it's a private-eye novel, but at the same time, it includes many of the elements of a more traditional "cozy," e.g., small town setting, multiple—often eccentric—suspects with bizarre motives, shaky alibis, and often contradictory clues that must be put together in the right sequence to solve the mystery. The story revolves around wisecracking New York-based PI Nic Knuckles, who is hired by a mysterious client to travel to Kleinstadt, Indiana, to find evidence that will free a man wrongfully convicted and imprisoned for a murder that took place several years earlier. In the end, of course, the intrepid Nic cracks the case, taking readers on an unforgettable stay in a small town with secrets a-plenty to hide. I unreservedly recommend this book."—Gregory Stout, author of *Lost Little Girl* and *The Gone Man*

"If you like your mystery with a heaping helping of humor, then Nic Knuckles is your kind of private eye, and *Big Scream in a Small Town* is your kind of book! This one will keep you guessing—and laughing—all the way until the final reveal!"—Alan Orloff, Anthony, Agatha, Derringer, and two-time Thriller Award-winning author of *Sanctuary Motel*

"William Ade, writing as Nic Knuckles, introduces the reader to the wackiest Private Eye you won't soon forget. If you enjoy laugh-a-minute humor and zany action, this book is for you."—Harriette Sackler, Agatha Award-nominated short story Writer

Prologue

The murder could've happened in any small town in the USA. Kleinstadt wasn't any different from the other aging communities peppering the midsection of Indiana. Its population peaked in the mid-sixties just before its manufacturing sector left for China, then Viet Nam, on into Bangladesh, before the inevitable next desperate place where people worked for pennies.

Main Street, which once hosted fine family restaurants, a movie theater, and two department stores, now gave up the space to taverns, tattoo emporiums, and consignment shops. Some said Kleinstadt was a busted, rundown little burg full of broken, rundown people.

But not all was as dismal as it may seem. The social nexus for Kleinstadt was the high school football team. In the autumn chill, Friday nights drew the locals to cheer the Fightin' Diphthongs. Everyone loved seeing a star quarterback, his girl, the prettiest cheerleader, rooting from the sidelines as he led the hometown team to glory. Unfortunately, the Kleinstadt High QB couldn't heave the pigskin more than twenty yards. The players performed so poorly that no young lady with self-esteem would lift a pom-pom for them. Nonetheless, it was still the best entertainment value in town.

Which made you wonder what was wrong that October evening in 2005 as a small, dispirited crowd of locals watched their gridiron heroes steamrolled by their visiting opponent. In the quiet of the night, how'd people fail to hear that bloodcurdling scream coming out of Stickerbacker's Woods no more than 300 feet away? Yes, it was very odd. Unless everyone in attendance had hearing impairments, which was possible since the mean age of Kleinstadt was fifty-three years.

Nonetheless, the citizens woke the following day to the shocking news that one of their own had met a gruesome death. The local sheriff moved quickly and arrested Timmy Hanlon, an oily-skinned teenager with a weak alibi and a killer's cold eyes. A handful of months later, the county prosecutor convinced a jury to remove Hanlon from polite society. It took less than an hour to condemn the young man to a lifetime of making license plates in the state penitentiary.

While the capture of a killer brought relief to most folks in town, some questioned the fairness of the whole process. Timmy Hanlon was a poor boy from the outskirts of town who lacked the finances and the intellect to mount a worthy defense. Nobody seemed to care enough to contest the verdict, however. Only fifteen years later did someone with a conscience feel it was time for the people of Kleinstadt to take a good look in the mirror. Revisiting the crime would, without a doubt, resurrect old feelings and heartbreak. But it might also generate new leads and a different outcome for Timmy Hanlon. Whatever the prospects, those small-town folks, with their willingness to take secrets to the grave, would make it a challenge. But the residents of Kleinstadt, Indiana, had never dealt with someone like me. I'm Nic Knuckles, Private Eye and the revealer of truth.

Chapter One

I t all started on a September afternoon as I sat in my office, my rising intolerance for boredom intersecting with the falling balance in my checking account. The week had been the slowest in a month, already moving at a snail's pace. After calculating how much blood I could sell and still function, I was three pints short of covering next month's office rent.

Most self-employed individuals would be out hustling for work, but as Nic Knuckles had learned, that's not how private investigators operated. There'd be no promotions, ads, TV commercials, or flyers stapled to telephone poles. Any competent private eye would sit and wait and eventually hear from a mysterious client they'd regret taking on.

Sure enough, my cell phone buzzed like an enraged hornet. The conversation was textbook.

"Knuckles Investigations, how can I help you?"

"I'd like to talk to Nic Knuckles."

"You're talking to him."

"I need your services."

"I'm listening."

"There's a fifteen-year-old murder case I want you to give a second look."

"Fifteen years, huh? Give me the background."

"A small town in the Midwest and a young girl brutally murdered. You think you can handle it?"

"What part of the Midwest?"

"Indiana, the Hoosier State, Crossroads of America, State Bird, the Cardinal, State Flower, the Peony, known for limestone, and the Wabash

River. Is that enough background?"

"What about the victim? What's her story?"

"Sixteen-year-old female, blue eyes and auburn hair, braces like a car grill, five foot four inches tall and a hundred and five pounds."

"How'd the girl meet her demise?"

"Something sharp separated her head from her shoulders."

"Holy Manchego, that's gross. Did she have a name?"

"Her name was Mindy, Mindy Bauerman."

"Okay, sounds like a nice girl. I'll take the case."

"When can you start?"

"I'll be on an airplane to Indiana an hour after ten grand appears in my checking account."

"Pack your bags, Mr. Knuckles."

"Yeah, sure, my eager friend, but care to share your name?"

"Client. Just call me Mister Client."

Twelve hours later, that phone call lifted me out of my cozy walkup in Queens, NY, and deposited me in the Hoosier State, where I'd meet people who'd make my life a living hell, which was something I never understood. Are there different kinds of Hell other than the living one? Do the undead, like zombies, operate in another type of Hell than phone solicitors? More importantly, who makes up the entrance criteria, anyway?

Whatever the answer, Nic Knuckles wasn't going to resolve metaphysical questions about the nature of Satan's domain. A client was paying me good money to determine whether a dead sixteen-year-old girl had received justice. And no matter how many demons I'd face in Kleinstadt, Indiana, I'd solve every mystery and deliver the truth. The spirit of Mindy Bauerman could rest easy because Nic Knuckles was now on the case.

Chapter Two

My flight from LaGuardia airport dropped me at the closest municipal airstrip servicing Kleinstadt. After picking up a rental car, I drove seventy-five miles and arrived in town right before sundown. The signage outside a boarding house on the main street caught my eye. Miss Crumble's Cozy Lodge had rooms to let, so I stopped and took a look-see. The bed felt firm, the bathroom looked sanitary, and the decorations were inoffensive, the usual collection of dried flowers and framed TV Guide covers. It was a sweet deal for twenty-eight dollars a night and breakfast in the morning. I doubted there'd be too many options in the area, so I took the room.

Miss Crumble looked to be in her early fifties and carried herself with all the warmth of an ill-tempered librarian. Running a boarding house apparently exposed her to too many sad sacks and cheaters to give her a well-rounded personality. I'd call her attractive but in a tired, world-weary way.

"So, how many nights will you be staying, Mr. Knuckles?"

I explained the purpose of my visit and admitted my stay could extend into weeks. "It all depends on how quickly I get people to open up about a horrible crime."

A smile tried to form on her face, but she beat it back. I was curious to know if she thought I was on a fool's mission or if she was calculating the big boost in revenue my visit might give her. Maybe it was both.

"Have you lived in Kleinstadt all your life, Miss Crumble?"

"I'm born and bred and will be buried here."

A chill climbed up and down my spine before settling in my coccyx. How lucky was that? The first place that I stopped and my landlady was qualified to be the town's historian. I ripped off four crisp fifty-dollar bills and handed them to the woman. "Apply this to my first week's tab," I said. "I'd love to hear your take on Kleinstadt if you have the time."

Miss Crumble held the cash to her nose and sniffed. Apparently, the aroma of new currency affected her because her stern countenance melted away. "I'll happily do that," she said, her voice soft, almost sultry. "I serve afternoon wine and cheese on Tuesdays and Thursdays in the parlor. Come by then, and we can chat."

I smiled and told her to count on it, and I went into my room and unpacked, feeling more excited than I wanted to admit. It'd been two months since my last job, and that gig could have gone better. How'd I know a wild turkey could run twenty-five miles an hour and would peck your eyes out if you let it get too close? I swear I'll never investigate the working conditions at a children's zoo again. Starting tomorrow, Nic Knuckles would be back at the job I was born to do, probing the dark underbelly of humanity.

The word belly reminded me that I hadn't had a meal since leaving home that morning. I decided to stroll around town and get a feel for the community. With any luck, I'd find that quintessential small-town diner with a chatty waitress and a menu built around bacon and gravy.

Kleinstadt's nightlife, judging by what was open and operating after sunset, was limited to a small market and a diner called The Next to the Last Supper. As I'd predicted, the eatery had a special on biscuits and sausage gravy, served by a salty waitress. Where I was wrong, however, was about her being chatty. The woman snarled at me as she dropped my plate on the table. "Try not to make a mess," she said.

That's when an angel holding a cup of coffee in her hand plopped into my booth. Her name was Molly Spear, and her face conveyed a hard-living woman's wear and tear. "I can tell you're not from around here," she said. "What brings you to this small town in the heart of Indiana?"

"I'm Nic Knuckles, and I'm here on a mission to find truth and justice."

The woman slurped her coffee and smiled. "I think I can help you, Nic.

Buy me a donut to go along with my java, and I might be your new best friend."

Chapter Three

My first task that morning was to call the Kleinstadt Sheriff's Department and schedule an interview with the town's top cop. The woman who answered told me I had to be there immediately before the sheriff left to make his rounds. I hated skipping my all-inclusive breakfast at Miss Crumble's table, but I was on the clock, and duty called.

I motored my rental car over to a one-story brick building off of the town's main drag and found Kleinstadt's chief law enforcer, a ruddy-faced man who filled out his brown and tan uniform like a Bratwurst pressing against its casing. His name was Sheriff John Brown, and I had to ask him, "You ever heard that Bob Marley song?" Before I could finish, he replied, "I shot the sheriff? Yeah, I know it."

I suggested that he must duck and run whenever he heard someone singing those lyrics. My attempt at humor failed to elicit a smile, let alone a chuckle, so I pulled out my notebook and moved on to why I was there.

"I've been hired to look into a murder that occurred fifteen years ago. The victim was a sixteen-year-old girl named Mindy Bauerman, and she was savagely butchered. As a fellow crime fighter, I'd appreciate if you'd give me a little history lesson."

Brown hesitated, and his face twisted into what I thought was a masterful knot of exasperation. "First, let me clarify something. The victim was not savagely butchered, and using sensationalist words like those only fires up people, and I won't let you agitate my town."

"I was told by a local source, that it was a monstrous murder, something that shook Kleinstadt to its core. Are you saying I was misled?"

"I'm betting your source was some gossip-mongering, yellow journalist, so I'd have to say you'd definitely been steered wrong."

I didn't recall Molly Spear looking jaundiced, but Sheriff Brown had me there. She was a retired reporter for the Kleinstadt Klarion and that old rag, the newspaper, I mean, closed down last year. Molly, nonetheless, still remembered every word of her copy. She made it out that Mindy had been brutally murdered, and her graphic description of a beheading, pools of blood, and piles of gore, made it impossible for me to finish my biscuits and gravy.

"So, the murder wasn't savage, you say?"

Brown rolled a fat bottom lip and yupped me. "The victim was found fully dressed in a blue sweater and freshly ironed jeans. She had shiny new shoes on her feet and a silver charm bracelet on her right wrist. The only unnatural thing was the wound atop her head, created by the fatal blow of a meat cleaver."

"You telling me Mindy's head wasn't found fifteen feet from the rest of her body?"

Brown bellowed. "No, no, no, it was no dang fifteen feet." He squirted a stream of chocolate-colored tobacco juice into a Mason jar sitting on his desk. "It was more like two, maybe three feet."

"So, she *was* decapitated."

"Naw, my predecessor, Sheriff Feif, suspected that wild critters found the remains and, you know, pulled it apart. That happens all the time when a corpse is left out in the woods."

"But wasn't Mindy's body discovered the next morning, less than ten hours after her murder?"

Brown shrugged. "The feral cats around here get awful aggressive, so we still think it was the conk on the head that did her in, not a beheading."

I had reason to suspect the quality of the sheriff's thinking. Last night's chat with Molly gave me some background on John Brown that helped me understand his peculiar opinion. Brownie was a student intern working for Sheriff Feif when Mindy Bauerman died. As a teenage boy, violent video games must've filled his time. How many hours of thumbing Mario and Luigi into a murderous rampage had numbed the young man's sensitivity to mayhem? No wonder he was oblivious to the hideous aggression of Mindy's murder.

I jotted down in my notebook what I'd heard and added a notation at the end. Brownie not 2 bright.

"How'd the investigation move so quickly? It seemed Hanlon was picked up within days."

"Good old, dogged police work," Brown said, rubbing his palms like he relished sharing the scoop. "Sheriff Feif always suspected Timmy Hanlon was responsible and focused on him. Eventually, he found a meat cleaver in Timmy's school locker. Later, they heard from a jailhouse snitch that Timmy bragged about killing a pretty little girl back a while ago."

"That does sound like rock solid proof," I said, suddenly wondering what I would do for income if this Bauerman gig wrapped up too quickly. "Why do you think Hanlon would do such a terrible thing?"

Sheriff Brown cocked his eye and grumbled. "Who can explain evil? The poor girl was in the wrong place at the wrong time with the wrong guy holding a meat cleaver."

As much as I like simple answers, and believe me, as a kid, I loved true and false tests, what Brownie said didn't sit right with me. "If Timmy Hanlon's conviction was such a slam dunk, why did someone doubt it enough to hire me to investigate the case?"

The corn-fed visage of Sheriff Brown went flat, and he rumbled in a voice with all the lightness of a distant freight train. "Why don't you tell me? I'd love to know who hired you to come to my town and create a ruckus."

I shook my head. "All I can say is that my client paid me to get answers to questions, and if I created some waves, so be it."

"Let me make a prediction, Mr. Knuckles," Sheriff Brown said as he tilted back in his chair, a massive plug of tobacco pushing out his right cheek. "When you finally end your little wild goose chase, you'll have more questions than answers."

"Let me return the favor, Sheriff Brown. When Nic Knuckles takes a case, the only unanswered question is, why didn't we hire that guy weeks ago? He's brilliant."

I usually kept my braggadocio under tight control because I liked appearing calm and calculating. However, the sheriff's hint that Nic Knuckles would fail triggered the memory of my mother telling me I wouldn't be toilet-trained by the third grade. Maybe it took me until that summer before, but I *showed* her, and I'll show John Brown what Nic Knuckles can and can't do.

"You can waste your time if you want," Brown said. "But I won't tolerate you ruining the reputation of my mentor, the legendary Sheriff Feif."

I stretched my lips into a big grin. "I'm sure Sheriff Feif can teach me a lot about this case. I'm looking forward to meeting him."

John Brown responded with a sneer. "Just watch yourself, Knuckles."

I closed my notebook and stood to leave, figuring that Brownie and I would butt heads many more times before my Indiana visit ended. It would be a classic story of the clever and tenacious big-city investigator going against the truculent small-town lawman. Our animosity went beyond incompatible Myers-Briggs personality types, however. I suspected shoddy police work was behind Timmy Hanlon's conviction, and John Brown knew it. I felt he'd do everything to prevent me from proving how badly his predecessor had screwed up.

After returning to my car, I flipped open my notebook and read Brown's comment about Sheriff Feif believing wild critters had pulled apart the victim's corpse. How could a competent investigator find a head separated from the body and not think it wasn't a crime of passion? In my experience, such brutality came from rage fueled by hate. They were mistaken if old Sheriff Feif and new Sheriff Brown thought Mindy's fatal walk in the woods was lousy timing. How badly mistaken? Maybe enough to convict an innocent kid and leave a killer running free.

I now had to assume that I'd work the Bauerman case without the support of the local law. Not surprising, I guessed. If I found the true culprit and exposed the Kleinstadt Sheriff's Department's incompetence, Brown's beloved Sheriff Feif would look the fool. Equally alarming was if

I determined that the jury had correctly convicted Timmy Hanlon. Then I'd spend weeks swimming against John Brown's tide of resentment and ill will, listening to him calling me stupid. It'd be like living with my mother again, down to the same brand of chewing tobacco.

Chapter Four

In a lovely part of town, between two churches and a block from a funeral facility, was the Ever-Last Nursing Home. It was Kleinstadt's attempt at one-stop shopping for the terminally ill. The attendant who greeted me at the door gave off a cool suspicion like I was trying to sell her a golf magazine subscription. She glared when I asked for Mr. Feif, ran a painted fingernail down a spreadsheet, and asked, "Do you mean Mr. Fie, as in pie?"

"No, madam, I meant Mr. Feif, as in beef."

Her eyebrows edged closer together as she studied my face. "Okay, come with me."

I followed her down a hallway stinking of antiseptic and into a small room that smelled like rotten bananas. In a wheelchair sat a shriveled older man, all the color bleached from his body by age and illness. He greeted me with a toothy grin.

"Here you go," the attendant said, "Mr. Fee at your disposal."

"Fee, I wanted to meet Mr. Feif, not Fee."

"Oh, I thought you said Fee, as in disagree."

I heaved a breath and asked, "I don't suppose Sheriff John Brown happened to call you about my visit, did he?"

Placing her hands on her hips, the attendant bounced her head in rhythm with her words. "Now, why would our sheriff warn me about some big city know-it-all messing with one of my patients?"

Ah, another dose of unadorned Kleinstadt hostility. "I'm not messing with anyone," I said, "I just want a few minutes of Mr. Feif's time." I spun my head as I scanned the room. "And, judging by the absence of any activities going on in this place, Mr. Feif has plenty of time to spare."

The woman stared at me another minute before turning and leading me down the hallway and onto a sunny patio. "There you go." the attendant announced, pointing at a bandy-legged silver-haired man standing in the corner and gazing at his slippers. "That's your man, Barney Feif."

"Good afternoon, Barney," I said, offering a handshake, "I'm Nic Knuckles."

The man slapped my hand away. "Just because my name is Barney Feif," he said, his voice almost uncomfortably high-pitched, "don't ask me if I'd grown up in Mayberry. I'm Feif, not Fife. You got it?"

"Yes, sir, I hear you loud and clear."

The attendant reinforced the obvious. "He's very sensitive about his name, so don't rile him up."

"Oh, I know how Mr. Feif feels. When you're born with a name like Nic Knuckles, you appreciate the burden of being tagged with a peculiar moniker. I can't tell you how many times someone called me Nickels or Noodles or Numbnuts. Nonetheless, I didn't come here to compare a lifetime of grievances about how our mothers named us."

I turned to Feif and smiled. "No, I'm here to tap the great mind of Kleinstadt's legendary former sheriff."

The attendant snorted and wished me luck, and I grunted right back. Who did she think she was talking with, some Nancy Drew wannabe? Nic Knuckles didn't need luck interrogating anyone because I could smooth talk a confession from the Sphinx.

"Sheriff Feif, my fellow champion of justice, I've come a long way to meet with Indiana's iconic law enforcement professional."

"Who?"

"You, sir," I said. "I need your help in understanding the Mindy Bauerman murder investigation."

"Who?"

"Mindy, Mindy Bauerman, the girl murdered fifteen years ago. It was your most celebrated case."

Feif flicked his lower lip and slowly nodded. "Yeah, okay, if you say so."

"Did you have any other suspects other than Timmy Hanlon?"

"Who?"

For five minutes, I felt like I was debating an owl. Feif met every name I threw out with the same confused grimace and the question, who? I swore the man didn't know what I was talking about. I lowered my head and slipped closer to him. "You know Barney, as an out-of-town guest, I've yet to experience that famous Hoosier hospitality. I'd hate to go back to New York City and bad mouth the fine folks in Indiana."

Feif's face sagged, and he looked at me with watery eyes. "Well, okay, I don't want that. What do you want from me?"

"Was there anyone other than Timmy Hanlon who might've had a reason to kill Mindy?"

"Who?'

I threw my hands in the air and felt my face flush hot. "Okay, Feif, stop screwing with me, tell me how you solved the greatest criminal case of your career?"

The good news was that Feif responded to my new approach. The bad news was him babbling about how he'd solved the crime of the century by proving it was the head nurse hiding his bedpan, not the afternoon attendant.

"Listen up, buddy," I said. "I'm working for a client with an interest in the Mindy Bauerman murder case. That client is paying good money for answers, and I intend to get them. So, knock off your crazy old coot act, and tell me why you thought Timmy Hanlon murdered Mindy Bauerman."

The old sheriff twisted his sunken face around on his scraggly neck and snapped like a crisp green bean. "Leave me alone. I ain't talkin', and you can't make me."

Nic Knuckles had dealt with more than a few characters who didn't want to answer my questions. I might've incorporated the old phone book method to get the guy to talk, but not anymore. With all my valuable phone numbers on my cellphone, whacking a creep got me nothing but a cracked screen. I'd have to go hardcore verbal on the older man until he broke.

Standing taller to look more intimidating, I raised my voice and waved my hands. I called Feif names and insulted his family, but the man didn't react. After ten minutes of ranting like a lunatic talk radio host, I realized that I didn't need a Ph.D. in neurology to know something wasn't right with the man. The legendary lawman's brain had turned to mush, and he had no memory of a cold-blooded murderer named Timmy Hanlon or the young victim, Mindy Bauerman.

"Barney, do you know where you are?"

Feif sputtered and spat. "I'm running a speed trap. I swear, I'll stop those scoundrels from Peckersville from using my street to drag race their hot rods."

I sighed and slowly shook my head. I wouldn't be writing any observations into my notebook on Barney Feif. I would never learn his thoughts on what motivated someone to murder a sixteen-year-old high schooler or if he considered any other suspects. Instead of tapping a critical primary source in Sheriff Feif, I'd hit a dead end. Barney's cognitive derailment would now force me to crack the hard shells of Kleinstadt's citizenry for any answers.

I patted Feif on the shoulder. "Barney, I hope you find some peace inside your scrambled mind."

Feif cussed, pointed a shaky finger in my face, and cried out. "So, it's you stealing my bedpan. I'm calling the sheriff, and don't think I won't. Sheriff Feif will make you pay, you hooligan."

"Yeah, he will," I said in a whisper. "I wish I could hang around and meet the guy."

Chapter Five

George and Mary Jane Bauerman invited me into their home, a place that put the ram into ramshackle. I sat in a chair George pulled in from the kitchen while he and his wife rested on a tattered sofa. They gave off an appearance of weary acceptance, but Mary Jane couldn't hide the grief behind her faint smile. She had to be hurting because Mindy had been their only child, their baby, as she called her.

"How did you and Mindy get along?" I asked, not being one to dillydally when trying to solve a long-ago murder. Mary Jane's lips quivered, and she dabbed an embroidered hankie under her thick-lens eyewear.

"Mindy and me never shared a cross word," she said. "The last time we talked was when she came home from school to get dressed for the football game."

"Can you recall what was said?"

"Oh, you know how teenage girls can be."

Actually, I knew nothing about teenage girls because when I was a teenager, I was a boy and a lonely one at that. "I can't say I do, Mrs. Bauerman. Why don't you enlighten me?"

Mary Jane pressed her hands together, and her eyes misted. "Oh, she fussed with her hair, whined about her best friend, and cried over her complexion, you know, the usual girl stuff."

"Bad hair, mean friends, and zits, I got it," I said. Young Mindy's concerns didn't sound that different than mine when I was a kid. And not just me but my mother also fretted over my face. She claimed I didn't look like my siblings and wondered if someone had switched me at birth. I don't know why she thought that. My birth records showed that a midwife named Stretch McAuliffe delivered me on the bowling alley floor. My mom bragged she'd rolled a 750 series that night despite contractions.

"Do you happen to have any photographs of your daughter?" I asked. "I'd like to see who I'm working for."

When I investigated a murder case, and things got complicated, it helped to have an image of the victim to keep me motivated. Without one, I had to imagine what they looked like, and my mind tended toward the Mona Lisa. Please don't ask me why, maybe because her sly grin made me wonder if she'd shoplifted cannoli.

Mary Jane walked to a bookcase and pulled a fat binder from a shelf. "Oh dear, I have a lot of pictures of Mindy," she said, juggling the photographs cascading from the brown leather covers. "Let me show you."

And show me she did. The woman shuffled photos like a Vegas card dealer, rapidly handing me one after another. There were pictures of Mindy as a baby and every birthday until we got to her sweet sixteen celebration.

"Wasn't she a beauty?" Mary Jane asked.

"Yeah, your kid was a cutie."

What could I say? On her best days, Baby Mindy looked as plain as a bowl of oatmeal. Usually, I'd have no qualms running over people's feelings because only brutally honest characters survived in the private eye business. But I wouldn't go that route at the expense of some grieving mother. Not today, anyway.

"Did she ever tell you that someone was causing her troubles?" I asked. "You know, at school, on the playground, while she was running the streets?"

Mary Jane's eyes dropped toward my shoes, danced around my ankles, and slowly worked their way up my leg. They stayed uncomfortably focused on my thigh until I shifted in my seat, forcing her to look me in the face. "Boys were always vying for her affection, and they might've given her troubles," she said.

"Anyone in particular?"

Mary Jane shook her head. "I trust that Sheriff Feif caught the right fella, so it doesn't matter, does it?"

"So, you're telling me you're satisfied that the right man was sent to prison?"

Mary Jane looked at George, and after he growled, she said, "Yes, we are."

That comment squashed the tiny chance that the Bauermans had hired me.

"Those are all the questions I have right now," I said. "I'm sorry I had to resurrect such sad memories."

Mary Jane sniffled, and her mouth worked hard, denying our conversation had been painful. I mumbled a farewell and walked out of the rundown little house and its wretched atmosphere of sorrow. After starting my car, I saw the needle flickering near the big E on the gas gauge. Recalling seeing a service station on the town's outskirts when driving in from the airport, I headed in that direction. After pulling up to the pumps, a bent, older man came out and asked me how much fuel I wanted. "Thirty bucks should do it," I said.

My mind was as disheveled as the gas jockey pumping the fuel into my tank as I recalled today's interviews. Sheriff John Brown swore that Timmy Hanlon was the killer, and now Mr. and Mrs. Bauerman appeared equally convinced. Not that Brown's and Bauerman's opinions would deter me. A seasoned investigator learned early on that the first murder suspect is rarely the actual killer. If that weren't true, Agatha Christie would've been known only for her short story mysteries, not novels. The other question bothering me was, who'd be interested in examining the Bauerman murder investigation? Why did someone hire me to rattle a small town in Indiana in the hopes of shaking loose the truth and maybe freeing Timmy Hanlon?

I must've been loudly talking because the stooped man fueling my car offered an answer. He said some folks living on the edge of town, down by the dump, might be eager to prove Timmy Hanlon's virtue.

"Well, thanks, my friend," I said as I paid him for the gas. "I'll make my way down the road to check out those people."

The local purveyor of gasoline stuffed his hands into the pockets of his stained coveralls and dropped his head. "You know, business has been mighty slow around here."

I took the hint. Nic Knuckles was from New York City, where you couldn't cross a street without someone throwing a palm up for a tip or handout. I followed the man into the tiny concession area of the station and bought a moon pie and a bottle of cola to show my gratitude. After I opened the bottle and drank, he said he couldn't break the fifty I used to pay for the gas and snacks, so I had to give him a fifteen-dollar tip. I knew that old timer thought he'd played the city slicker, but no small-town hustler pulled one on Nic Knuckles. I shoplifted a couple of oil filters on my way out.

Chapter Six

The folks I met outside the town dump had every reason to finance an investigation of the Mindy Bauerman murder. They were Timmy Hanlon's parents. His dad was a skinny little fellow, and the mother didn't have much heft to her either. They insisted I address them as Pa and Ma, just like their boy had once done before being sent to prison.

The smells waffling from the dump next door and into their humble abode made me doubt the Hanlons were the money behind my hire. However, I've had more destitute clients over the years, like the man who lived in a chicken coop and paid me in eggs, lots and lots of eggs.

"I've been hired to look at the Mindy Bauerman murder case," I said after handing out my card. "I'd like to learn something about your boy, Timmy."

"Ain't much to say," Pa said. "He wasn't the brightest knife in the drawer."

"Sharpest," Ma screamed. "He wasn't the sharpest knife in the drawer, not brightest."

Pa chuckled. "Oh yeah, I always screw that up."

"But he was hard-working," Ma said, her voice rising with her right hand to her heart. "That boy worked after school starting in the fourth grade, trying to help us out."

Pa nodded. "Yeah, that's right. Our son had ambition."

"And he was funny," Ma said. "He was always with the jokes, wanting me and Pa to laugh away our troubles."

"I didn't get 'em half the time," Pa said as his shoulders twitched. "But he tried to lift our spirits."

"It sounds like your son was a good kid, ambitious, helpful, and funny."

Pa and Ma looked at each other, shrugged, and turned back to me. "Yeah, he was a good boy," Ma said, "up until he murdered that girl."

Holy Gorgonzola, Nic Knuckles wasn't expecting that comment. Most parents of suspects I'd interviewed in the past swore on their kid's innocence. The mother could be on the floor with a smoking bullet hole in her chest, and she'd gasp that her boy hadn't done it, even though he stood over her with a hot pistol.

"It sounds like you have no doubt that Timmy committed the murder?"

Ma's eyes didn't water, and her voice didn't wobble as she answered. "As much as I wanted to think my boy hadn't done such a dastardly deed, the evidence convinced me."

"Me too," Pa added. "Timmy had done wrong, and he must serve his punishment. That's what's written in the bible. You know, eyeballs for eyeballs, tooth for teeth."

Ma bellowed loud enough to shake the windows. "It's tooth for a tooth. You can't knock out a bunch of teeth from another fellas' mouth when you only lost one."

Pa chuckled. "Oh yeah, I always get that confused."

If Timmy's blood thought he was guilty, I'd be wasting my breath pressing for any insights that might work in their son's favor. I thanked the Hanlon's for their time, and as a bonus for their straightforward honesty, I awarded them fifteen dollars' worth of oil filters. My gesture made their day, as Pa wished he had another child in prison so he might score a new air filter for his pickup truck.

I drove back toward town feeling depressed. I'd interviewed three sources on my first day and struck out on each one. Good thing I wasn't playing baseball, or I'd be sitting in the dugout with my head in my hands. That's why I loved the private eye game. You swung for the fences as many times as you wanted, and you only got out if you quit. Hopefully, my luck would turn with my last interview of the day. I wanted to see what my new best friend, Molly Spear, had to say about what I'd learned.

Chapter Seven

The sun had settled behind the Kleinstadt water tower by the time I found Molly Spear sipping a cup of coffee at The Next to Last Supper. A smile creased her thin lips when she saw me approaching. "So, you're back."

I plopped onto the bench across from her, and the cracked, red seat covering made a sound that suggested I might want to skip a few desserts.

"Yes, Molly, I'm back," I said. "I've met with a few of your fellow citizens and have to admit I'm more than a bit flummoxed."

The woman's laugh came from a throat that had taken in the smoke of a half-century of unfiltered cigarettes. I continued my whining. "Not only are the Bauermans quite convinced that Timmy Hanlon's jail time is justified, so are Timmy's folks."

Molly chuckled. "One's happy to be done with it, and the others are halfwits."

"Your sheriff, John Brown, is a disagreeable fellow who has no interest in helping me determine if justice had been done all those years ago."

"Don't let him fool you," she said. "John Brown has a great interest in the Mindy Bauerman case."

"Well, I hope so, because I discovered that old Sheriff Feif has left the room, so to speak."

Molly nodded. "He has good reason to block out his role in that investigation."

That comment twisted my upper esophageal sphincter. What did Molly mean by that? What did Feif do to earn her disdain? "Give me some insight,

21

sister," I said. "I'm dying here."

"I'm not your sister, buster, and you're not dying, but I'll share a vague rumor that might be more critical than you'd think and offer up one solid suggestion."

I whipped out my notebook and leaned in, pencil poised.

"Back then, the buzz was that Mindy had trouble with the IRS, and maybe they had a hand in the murder."

I didn't jot down Molly's rumor. What she said had to be small-town paranoia about the Deep State. Nic Knuckles had more than a few clients in hock to the government, and the tax man had better methods than breaking legs to collect debts. Hopefully, her second tip would make more sense.

"Okay, Molly, what else should I do?"

"You need to talk to Timmy Hanlon. He'd give you a different perspective on what went down fifteen years ago. I have some prison contacts I'll call to get you in there. After that, you're on your own."

After failing to squeeze much helpful information out of anyone I'd interviewed, I felt grateful for whatever Molly gave me. The speculation about the IRS sounded ridiculous, but if she could pull strings to get me a visit with Hanlon, she was golden in my mind.

"Molly, my friend. I know you swore you'd only give me two tips, but hopefully, you'll provide one more bit of insight."

The way the woman's eyes squeezed together suggested that an answer didn't look likely. I'd ask anyway because that's what Nic Knuckles did. "How's the pie in this place? Is it worthy of a fork?"

Chapter Eight

Timmy Hanlon looked like he'd spent the past fifteen years in prison. Skinny as a light pole with flesh haphazardly tattooed with farm animals in obscene poses, he had a mouthful of yellowed teeth that he flashed as I approached. The man seemed genuinely happy that I'd taken a half-day drive to the State's most notorious prison to talk with him.

"I've been trying, like forever, to get someone to listen to me," he said, the handcuffs preventing him from hugging me. "I swear, once I get my conviction overturned, I'll sue that damn town for a million dollars."

I didn't want to ruin Hanlon's dreams of a quick financial bonanza, but you could sell every asset in Kleinstadt and be lucky to clear a hundred grand. But still, I understood the man's thirst for revenge. There'd been times in my life when the goblet of justice ran dry, and I'd tell him about that one incident back in the nineties involving a squirrel and a bag of peanuts if I didn't have a parking meter running time.

"I have to say, Timmy, the evidence against you looked pretty convincing, with the murder weapon *and* a confession."

"What are you talkin' about, dude, that's all nothin'?"

Yeah, yeah, the old innocent-man-in-prison song and dance. Nic Knuckles had seen it performed plenty of times by jailbirds. No one, however, sang and dance it better than that Riker's Island Musical Troup. I loved their rendition of Hello Dolly, but, as much as I wanted to sing the finale, I had to stay focused on Hanlon.

"Did they not find a meat clever in your school locker?" I asked.

Hanlon chuckled. "I had an after-school job at the meat packing factory outside of town. What did they expect to find in my locker, a vegetable peeler?"

Whoa, my lower esophageal sphincter twanged. That made sense. Did I harbor false assumptions about Timmy just because he looked like the kind of fellow who'd chop off your head as to look at you?

"What about the confession you made to that cellmate? Was that not true?"

Hanlon hung his shoulders, and his mouth slid to one side. "No, man, I never told that idiot I killed Mindy Bauerman. The woman I killed was a buxom platinum blond with a wispy, baby girl voice named Marilyn."

I clasped my hands and begged. "Please don't tell me her last name was Monroe. I can't take another pop culture appropriation."

Hanlon laughed. "Naw, it was the kind of relationship where last names were never exchanged, you know what I mean?"

Did I know what he meant? Who did he think he was talking to, some novice straight out of the nunnery? Sure, I did. Nic Knuckles had a long history with women who refused to give me their names and forget about me getting their phone numbers.

"If you didn't kill Mindy, why tell the stoolie you killed a woman."

"Well, I did. I killed Marilyn."

There they went again, both of my esophageal sphincters plunking like guitar strings in the hands of a flamenco guitarist.

"So even though you didn't murder Mindy Bauerman, you're admitting you killed a woman named Marilyn."

A creepy grin rolled across Hanlon's face. "Yeah, and she loved it." He finished with a wink that made my skin want to crawl off my muscles and scurry from the room.

"So, you *did* murder a woman named Marilyn," I yelled, jabbing my finger at his sludge pile of a face.

"No, I didn't murder Marilyn, I killed her."

Now Nic Knuckles was a proud graduate of his hometown high school, good old Bernie Madoff Secondary, so I'm familiar with Webster's dictionary. In my well-thumbed copy of that famous book, *killing* and *murder* shared the exact definition of causing bodily harm that resulted in death.

"I think you might be placing your hopes of exoneration in the wrong hands, Mr. Hanlon," I said. "It doesn't matter if you didn't kill Mindy Bauerman, because I won't help a murderer get out of prison."

Hanlon looked at me with cold, reptilian eyes, and his pointed tongue flickered around his thin lips. Then the monster fell back in his chair, cackling. "What you talkin' about, man?"

"You're a pathological killer," I said. "I'm out of here."

I pulled away to make my escape when he grabbed my arm. "No, no, don't go. You got me all wrong."

While being touched by such a serpent as Hanlon made me shudder, I gave him a hearing. I had to since Nic Knuckles stood for truth, justice, and the integrity of a story's plot.

"My lifelong ambition had always been performing as a standup comedian," he said. "On weekends, I'd drop in at the open mic nights at the local dives."

"You don't say?"

"I do say. So, when I tell you I killed Marilyn, I'm usin' the term the way a comedian would if he brought the house down with his routine."

"You telling me this Marilyn thought you were hilarious?"

Hanlon's face lit up as he appeared to raise that memory from the dumpster of his mind. "Yeah, after a few knock-knock jokes, I had her willin' to let me touch her hand."

I was stunned. The two pieces of crucial evidence that put Timmy Hanlon behind bars for life were as flimsy as a ten-dollar parachute. The young man had been an industrious kid with show business ambitions, not a cold-blooded killer. Nic Knuckles had seen a few wrongly convicted people in his time, but none as severely cheated as Timmy Hanlon. Even though he was a man who looked like he could slither across the floor, he didn't deserve such treatment.

"I have to tell you, Timmy. You've given me a new way of thinking about this case. I was going in for a slam dunk, and you just bounced it off the back of the rim."

"Huh?"

The basketball metaphor didn't work with Hanlon. I didn't know why I used it. I guessed that since this was Indiana, I assumed everyone understood basketball terminology. "What I'm saying is that you've just made this investigation a lot more complicated."

"If it helps get me out of this hellhole, then I won't apologize for makin' your job harder."

"Not a problem, Timmy," I said. "My client wants to see justice served."

A tear formed in Halon's left eye, slipped down his pockmarked cheek, and dropped to the concrete floor. "Thanks, Mr. Nickels."

"Knuckles, it's Nic Knuckles."

"Okay, Nic, I'm countin' on you to get me my freedom."

I bade Hanlon farewell while promising him nothing but my best effort. I walked the dank prison corridor and out to my car, mulling a suspicion that had only grown stronger with that visit. Timmy Hanlon looked the part of a vicious, cold-blooded killer. Heck, even I would've put him away for life for a traffic violation. That's why all it took was lousy police work and a mob mentality running through the jury box to convict him. If it took a village to raise a child, they damn well could take him down.

I pulled my notebook from the coat pocket and added the notation. Kleinstadt justice stinks.

Chapter Nine

I t's almost mandatory that every murder victim have at least one best friend. Criminal investigations, without such a source, would be greatly hindered. How else would a detective ever learn the inner workings of a victim's mind without a best friend willing to talk?

You might think the easiest murders to solve would be the Prom Queen cases. With their tribe of gushing acolytes, those victims would have many juicy sources. However, that's not what Nic Knuckles had learned during my illustrious career. Think about it. How could a Prom Queen with so many adoring followers choose just one girl as her best friend? Her relationships with them had to be superficial to keep everyone happy and loyal. The Prom Queen would have no other choice.

I knew the girls with the most dope were those singular besties because when you had only one confidant, you were prone to share your deepest, darkest secrets. Ask my mother. Until she begged me to keep my personal life private, we were as close as cellophane on a slice of processed yellow cheese.

When Mary Jane Bauerman was rolling through her mountain of family photos, she identified the girl who appeared in half of Mindy's pictures as her childhood best friend. Her name was Sandi Fliminsky, and I called her yesterday after I'd returned from visiting Timmy Hanlon. She was eager to talk, so we agreed I'd come over for an early morning coffee before she left for work. I pulled up to her home address right at seven in the AM.

Fliminsky's house was an old Craftsman bungalow with a well-maintained exterior and a thick, trimmed lawn. Various shrubbery was rooted in the properties' corners and the house's foundation. Flowerbeds were tucked away for the approaching cold weather, although some hardy flowers still held on to their colorful blooms. As I walked by the driveway along the side of the house, I understood why Sandi's landscaping looked so professional. The words, Sandi's Dandi Lawn & Garden Service, were stenciled on the door of a yellow pickup truck.

"Good morning, Miss Fliminsky," I said after she answered my knocking on the front door. "I'm Nic Knuckles."

Fliminsky had thick brown hair crowning a round face punctuated with deep-set green eyes. "Come on in," she said, standing aside as I stepped into the living room. The woman had decorated with Peruvian minimalist furniture and painted the rooms in multiple shades of mauve. We sat on her living room sofa, where she'd served a nice coffee blend and homemade chocolate cookies.

"I loved Mindy," Fliminsky said, her eyes suddenly large and heavy, like a cloud saturated with rain. "We became best friends in second grade, and I swear we talked every day right up until the night she died."

I felt a smile dance across my face. Sandi was the kind of best friend that every investigator loved meeting. Hopefully, she had a memory like an elephant and could recall what was happening inside Mindy's mind back in 2005. If local law enforcement wouldn't cooperate with my investigation, then Sandi might have to serve as my go-to source.

"I know it's been more than fifteen years since Mindy's murder, but can you recall if she was having troubles with anyone around the time of her death?"

Sandi sighed, her whole body expanding and contracting. "When you're sixteen, aren't you always in trouble with someone?"

"True," I said. "But most teenage hassles don't end up getting you murdered."

Sandi's mouth puckered. "Yeah, but Mindy had more troubles than most people."

That response put a flutter in my chest, somewhere between the third and fourth rib. Sandi appeared to be holding high-value cards, and if I could get her talking, I'd be well on my way. I pulled my notebook from my pocket and poised my pencil over a blank page. "I'm listening, Sandi. Let it pop."

The woman ran her mouth almost too fast for me to record her comments, but I got lots of supremo scoop. Mindy had a boyfriend named Buddy, who her parents hated. A boy who lived across the street had a major crush on Mindy. His name was Buzz Rockwell, and Buzz's other fascination was with axes. And a mysterious salesman created some problems for the girl and her family.

"And you have to look closely at John Brown," she said. "He and Mindy had a history worth investigating."

"Sheriff John Brown?" I asked. "That's interesting. What was the attraction?"

"Mindy loved to dance. I know she and John did a mean tango until her father made her stop."

"Why'd Mr. Bauerman put the kibosh on it?"

"Mindy's old man thought dancing was sinful, you know, bodies rubbing up against each other, stuff like that."

Nic Knuckles knew a thing or two about how dancing could be the fast track to perdition. She was a young performer named Olga who was lithe and nimble, a low-rent Twyla Tharp. I watched her from afar, admiring how Olga balanced herself upside down on that pole. But a relationship wasn't meant to be, as one afternoon, she lost her grip, fell, and knocked herself into a different dimension. I've heard she lives in Vermont and writes cozy mysteries.

"What about the IRS," I asked. "Did she complain about the government being interested in her family?"

Sandi slowly rolled her head back and forth. "Oh no, no, no, you got that wrong."

"Come again."

"Mindy didn't have issues with the IRS. It was her daddy. He got himself in trouble with them."

I immediately flipped through my notebook until I came to the page with my Molly Spear scribblings. I crossed out Mindy + IRS = *Trouble!*

"One more question before I let you start your workday. Do you think Timmy Hanlon killed Mindy?"

Sandi's eyes lit up, and she dropped the cookie she'd been munching. "I'm glad you asked, Mr. Knuckles. I never thought Timmy Hanlon was capable of murder."

"How could you think that when so many other people in this town thought otherwise?"

"It was easy to think that," she said. "Timmy was a natural-born comedian. How could someone who had the courtroom falling out of their seats with his hilarious yet topical insights into everyday life chop off a young girl's head. That never made sense to me."

"So, you think Hanlon was innocent?"

"Yes, I do. Timmy was a classmate of mine and Mindy, and I knew him throughout my childhood. I always thought the old sheriff was lazy and went after Timmy because he was an easy target. Feif never seemed to have the desire to find the real killer."

I felt a sense of excitement bubbling in my gizzard. Not even Hanlon's parents thought he was innocent, and here was an old classmate who believed the trial was a miscarriage of justice. If Sandi proved to be the source, I thought she could be, I'd be stirring up many more people in this town than just John Brown.

"Do you have anyone in mind when you say the sheriff gave up too quickly trying to find the culprit?"

Sandi's lips gathered to one side of her mouth. "I think you should consider everyone a suspect in this garbage pit of a town." I nodded and replied. "Yeah, I will."

Sandi's suggestion was so indiscriminate and vague that it made me wonder. If she had such a low opinion of Kleinstadt, what kept her tied to the community? Did the woman who dished so quickly have mysteries of her own? That's the problem of relying on a dead girl's best friend. They'd willingly spill the details of their deceased friend's inner life but held on to their secrets.

"One last thing, Miss Fliminsky," I said. "There's one common thread to most small-town murders, and I wondered if it applied to Mindy's case."

"What's that?"

"Back during the time your best friend was killed, were you aware of any mysterious drifters passing through town?"

Sandi pressed her fingers against her lips, and her eyes seemed to cloud. "I don't know if he'd qualify as a drifter, but there was a rumor about a guy named Wayne who operated in the shadows."

"Did Wayne have a last name?"

"No, not that I'd ever heard," she said. "I guess that's what made him mysterious."

I added a few more lines to my notebook and closed it. "I appreciate the insights, Miss Fliminsky; you've been a big help."

"I'm happy to do what I can, Mr. Knuckles. I owe that to Mindy."

I thanked the woman and stood to leave. "Before I go, what's the best place to grab a meal here in Kleinstadt other than The Next to Last Supper?"

The woman hunched her shoulders. "I don't eat out much, but I've heard the bar food at Buddy's Tavern was edible."

Edible wasn't the roaring review I was looking for, but the owner's name did catch my interest. "Wait for a second. Did you say Buddy's Tavern?"

Sandi nodded.

"Would this be the Buddy who squired Mindy fifteen years ago?"

"The one and the same."

"Wow, a meal and a key witness, all in one place. Thanks, Miss Fliminsky, you're a doll."

I was now on my fourth day in Kleinstadt, and I had never spoken more appreciative words. Not only had Sandi proved to be a flowing spigot of information on Mindy Bauerman, but with all those new leads she provided, I'd be booking client hours well into next month. Woo hoo, this case could be the gravy train I'd needed for a long time. Maybe now I could afford to get my mother's teeth fixed. If her dentures didn't hurt her, she might be nicer to me. It'd be worth a try.

I stepped out of Fliminsky's house with two pages of notes and a big grin on my face. The smell of autumn filled the air, and as I strolled to my car, I again admired Sandi's tidy property. Being a big city boy who grew up in dense public housing, I'd never trimmed a lawn or planted a flower. We had people like Sandi doing those things.

Looking up across the street, I saw a red-headed older woman standing in her yard, raking leaves. I waved, and she responded with a fiery glare before throwing the rake to the ground and storming inside her house. Now, Nic Knuckles was an experienced reader of human behavior, but even I was unsure what had happened. But I refused to let that woman ruin my mood. I had suspects I needed to find, interrogations to complete, and a mystery to solve. Nic Knuckles was rolling, baby.

Chapter Ten

Taverns have a certain feel that made me wonder if their architects hated sunlight. Why'd the builders always scrimp on the widows? Did they figure the glowing brewery signage would emit enough light, so patrons could read the *New Yorker* while sipping their morning whisky? How about the stink? Having windows to open once in a while to clear out the smells would've been brilliant. Yeah, it's such a mystery. And I found that Buddy's Tavern was no different than any of the dives Nic Knuckles had spent time in, checking sources, chasing suspects, and trying to forget a woman named Rosie.

"Good afternoon, my kind sir," I said to the barkeep, a milky-complected man with a hairline in full retreat. "Might I have a pint of your finest local brew?"

The man reached underneath the bar and pulled out a sweating brown bottle labeled Old Piss. He popped the cap and delivered the contents into the glass he'd just dried. The golden liquid pushed a foamy white head upward before stopping two inches above the rim. The man had poured a drink before.

"You the snoop," he asked as he slid the glass in front of me.

Maybe only Nic Knuckles felt that way, but why'd barkeeps always look at PIs with such contempt? How come they thought it necessary to call us derogatory names, like a private dick, snoop, gutter rat, meddler, or worse? Sure, we all came across as hard-bitten men and women scarred by life, but beneath the calloused exterior, we had feelings. I swallowed some beer to drown the little sob that rose from my throat.

"I'm looking into the Mindy Bauerman murder case," I said. "Do you know a guy named Buddy Lee Hoot?"

The gentleman placed his hands on the bar and leaned forward. "Yeah, what do you want with him?"

"I'd like to chat with him. Ask him a few questions, you know...*snoop!*"

The eyelids of the man narrowed. "I'm Buddy Lee Hoot. Snoop away."

Wow, that admission surprised me. Buddy looked older than I expected, a lot older. I guessed working all those hours in a speakeasy aged a man fast. Or, it was something else, something more sinister. Perhaps as a sixteen-year-old, he fell into a jealous rage because his girlfriend flirted with some dude. Yeah, maybe he got so angry he chopped her head off. That memory would wrinkle a man's face.

Some folks might say Nic Knuckles was jumping to conclusions. They could be correct, but a great detective sometimes had to trust his gut. And my gut told me I might be onto something with Hoot. Nothing said guilty to me like a jilted ex-boyfriend who'd lost his hair.

"Tell me about the last time you saw Mindy."

"It was at her funeral," he said. "Open casket. I have to tell you, stitching her head back onto her neck was a bad idea. People were puking into the flowers."

"No, no, I mean when she was still alive."

"It was at fifth-period algebra. She asked me if $a2 - b2 = (a - b) (a + b)$, then how could $(a + b)2 = a2 + 2ab + b2$?"

"What'd you tell her?"

Buddy's eyes went dark on me. "You figure it out, wise guy. I'm a bartender, not a mathematician."

A private investigator worth his salt knew when a suspect was about to cave under pressure, and Nic Knuckles was nothing if not salty. I smelled Buddy's vulnerability, so I attacked, pulling conjectures from the air and throwing them fast and furious like darts at a dartboard. "Is it true that fifteen years ago, your last words to Mindy Bauerman were a threat? Did you tell her you'd kill her if she didn't stop flirting with every guy in town? Did you not have a chainsaw in the trunk of your Ford Fairlane, license plate 710-566K?"

Just as I thought he would, Buddy coughed up the answers.

"Nope, nope, and no way would I own a Ford."

Okay, they weren't the answers I wanted, but they *were* answers. I'd better stick with Sandi's insights and put my gut in cold storage.

"I heard that you and Mindy had an unconventional relationship," I said. "You were true blue while she played the field. Is there any truth to that?"

"I'm not ashamed to admit I was waiting for her to finish sowing her wild oats. But I swear, no one was more devoted to Mindy than me."

"I heard that Buzz Rockwell might be a worthy challenger to that title."

"I hate that guy," Buddy said as he slapped the bar. "He loved being considered a suspect during the investigation, that creepy basement-dweller. He didn't have the guts to ask Mindy out, but once she was dead, he was everywhere. It made me mad the way the media hyped Buzz as the demented lover, while ignoring me and my dedication to Mindy."

I finished my glass of beer and swiped the hoppy residue from my lips. "I got one last question, Mr. Hoot. Why did George and Mary Jane Bauerman hate you?"

Buddy's cockiness took flight with that question. He did a one-eighty, going from anger to weepy in a heartbeat.

"Maybe Old Man Bauerman hated my guts," he said in a squeaky little voice. "But Mary Jane and me got along."

"From what I've heard, she considered you a pest."

"That's not true. I was the one person she trusted and confided in."

I felt my smirk tweaking as I tossed a fiver on the bar. "Sure, she did," I said. "Keep the change."

I walked out of Buddy's Tavern, and the **tête-à-tête** with Mindy's old beau had unsettled my mind. Why did Sandi tell me the Bauermans both despised Buddy when he claimed the mother was a big fan? Had Buddy been the doormat boyfriend who turned to murder because he felt stupid for not being able to explain the algebraic equation Mindy threw at him? Was that the last humiliation that triggered a homicidal response? So many questions, and yet, one was more pressing than the others. Why didn't I use the toilet before leaving the tavern? I swear, one beer, and I'm bursting. I have to get that prostate checked out when I get home before I'm the only private eye wearing adult diapers.

Chapter Eleven

I arrived back at Miss Crumble's Cozy Lodge after my Buddy Lee Hoot conversation with two crucial objectives to complete. A quick visit to the bathroom addressed the first, and then I moved into the lodge's small library to use the internet connection and search the world wide web for the Kleinstadt Drifter.

The only clue I had was the guy's first name, Wayne. Finding him would be challenging because drifters lived in the woods or under bridges, not in a house with an address. After more than fifteen years, looking for such an ethereal spirit felt impossible, but Nic Knuckles lived to pursue hopeless causes. I'm built to locate slippery people, the neutrinos of human misery, men and women, boys and girls, cats and dogs living in the shadows.

Unfortunately, today wasn't my day. Facebook gave me zilch, and I tried three other platforms and scored zero hits. What good was social media if all you saw were kittens and fools doing stupid stunts? Finding some vagabond that no one had seen in a decade and a half would be more challenging than I thought. I shut down the computer, thinking I might have better luck later when Miss Crumble served wine and cheese and, hopefully, town gossip.

At five o'clock, I found my way into the parlor for the refreshments previously promoted by Miss Crumble. I sat down on a stuffed chair whose better days were long past. A silver tray with various kinds of cheese rested on a side table; otherwise, there was no sign of a happy hour. I'd only seen one other guest in my four days here, and he'd moved on yesterday. On the positive side, with no competition, I could eat enough cheese that I wouldn't need to buy dinner.

"How's the snooping?" Kate Crumble called out as she suddenly appeared, two empty glasses in one hand and a bottle of wine in the other. "Are you learning anything?"

A seasoned private eye like Nic Knuckles kept his mouth closed when strangers asked about his business. That's what clients paid me to do, keep my trap shut. Sadly, even the people I thought were my friends wanted me to do the same. Nonetheless, how'd a man eat and drink without opening the old pie hole? I had no choice but to talk to her.

"You have an interesting little town here, Miss Crumble."

"Oh yes, we do, Mr. Knuckles," she said, "but, don't be fooled by the small-town charm."

She didn't have to worry. Kleinstadt lacked any appeal that might distract my attention from solving the Bauerman case. The people were cranky, the streets full of litter, and the stray dogs mangy. Or the people were shabby, and the stray dogs cranky, whatever, the roads needed a good sweeping.

"I'm keeping myself busy making introductions," I said. "You know, getting a feel for the town and its citizens."

"Did you talk to that Mary Jane Bauerman? She's a suspicious one."

"Yes, I have."

"And her husband, that George, watch out for him."

"I'll keep that in mind."

"Yes, sir, I wouldn't trust either one as far as I could throw them, and I'm pretty damn strong."

I grabbed a handful of cheese cubes and popped them one at a time into my mouth. "You seem to have a strong feeling about Mindy's parents. What can you tell me about them?" Miss Crumble handed me a goblet brimming with a red wine of uncertain vintage. She pulled up a chair and sat next to me. "Oh, I have a lot to say about that family."

I realized Nic Knuckles wouldn't have a relaxing happy hour, but I might learn a thing or two about the Bauermans. Hopefully, it'd be worth the bout of indigestion since I always suffered an upset stomach if someone hovered over me while I ate. It probably started when I was a newborn, and my mother gave the wet nurse only five minutes to feed me.

"What can you tell me about George and Mary Jane's relationship? They seem like an odd couple."

"Oh boy, do you have that right. I've known Mary Jane and George all my life and you don't know how odd they are." Kate swallowed half her goblet and leaned in. "Where to start?"

I quickly shoveled more cheese cubes into my mouth and mumbled, "The beginning is always a good place."

"Well, the first thing you need to know about George Bauerman is that he's very religious. Even as a boy, he tried to walk in the way of the Lord. I know at one time he thought about joining the clergy, but he had pointy knees that made kneeling painful."

Nic Knuckles hadn't grown up in a religious house, but my mother sent me to Sunday school when I was ten. She said I couldn't understand right and wrong by watching Batman on television. That bible learning didn't go well, and I shut down when I learned that Jesus used words to deal with evildoers rather than fists and feet, and it ended poorly for him.

"Now, Mary Jane was different. She loved to party and ran the streets." Kate scooted her chair closer. "When Mary Jane married George, it stunned everyone in town. Why would such a hell-raising woman like her get hitched to a holy roller like him?"

I stopped in mid-chew to ponder what Miss Crumble had said. The Mary Jane I'd met was docile and had the spunk of a twice-baked potato, and there was no way she was some sexual spitfire unless marriage to George drained her primal energy.

"I have to tell you, Nic, uh, may I call you Nic?"

"Sure," I said, happy to think she felt relaxed enough to get informal with me.

"I have to say, Nic, why they've stayed together this long is the real mystery you should investigate."

I'd only scrutinize the Bauerman marriage if Miss Crumble signed a contract and paid an advance. But I did have an opinion to give her for free. "I imagine in a town like Kleinstadt, the pickings were slim for a young woman. Maybe Mary Jane married him because he was the first one to ask."

"Fiddle-faddle, there were plenty of men her age, and she knew them all."

Like any skilled investigator, Nic Knuckles had gotten good at guessing people's ages. Buddy Lee Hoot threw me off by twenty years, but getting that right wasn't necessary. Unlike someone working a carnival sideshow guessing people's ages. Although I once had a circus job as a kid and got involved with Lulu, who billed herself as the Human Hermit Crab. But I'd rather not talk about that.

"I'm thinking you and Mary Jane might be about the same age, Miss Crumble, am I right?"

The woman wobbled like one of those bobblehead dolls. "Why is that important?"

I wanted to say, "It's important because maybe you had the hots for George Bauerman back in the day. When he married a free-wheeling girl like Mary Jane, you went bat shit crazy and are telling me stories to make her pay for stealing the love of your life."

That's what I wanted to say, but fortunately, I'd learned to moderate my thoughts before letting them out of my mouth. "Did you have any romantic interests in George, considering the limited prospects in this town?"

Boy, did old Nic touch Miss Crumble's third rail.

"That's none of your damn business," she screeched as she rose from her chair. "You pry into my past, and I'll take this cheese knife and slice off your little nose."

I stopped eating, stunned by her aggressive reaction. Obviously, based on her response, Kate had a sensitive history of her own.

"I'm sorry I upset you," I said. "I'll always respect your privacy, I swear." And I spoke the truth because you needed the local gossipmonger on your side when you're poking around a town of tight-lipped citizens. My apology, however, wasn't working. Miss Crumble kept her arms crossed and a pout on her lips. I'd have to employ something from my bag of tricks to get her to come back around.

"I have to wonder," I said aloud. "How'd Mary Jane and George react to their daughter's brutal murder back then? I imagine that must be one juicy story, don't you think?"

Sure enough, I could see Kate starting to sniff the gossip bait as her lips quivered and her eyes dilated.

"I wonder what else I should know about the Bauermans. George and Mary Jane sure acted suspicious when I talked to them, and they seemed to hold some deep, dark secrets. What could those be, huh?"

Whatever resistance Kate had mustered before crumbled with that comment. She dropped back next to me and grabbed my arm. "Well," she said, lowering her voice so much I had to lean into her. "George Bauerman wasn't the grieving father you might think."

I knew it. A gossip had to gossip because it was like breathing air for them.

"The word on the street back then was that Mindy had a sizable life insurance policy on her little head, and soon after that head came off her shoulders, George was driving a new car."

"A new automobile, huh?" I thought about my visit with George and Mary Jane. They were meagerly dressed, and their house looked like a pile of lumber had been blown together. I imagined the family always had money problems, and a life insurance payout would've meant a lot. Yeah, murder for the insurance money. How many times had Nic Knuckles read that script?

Not as many as you'd think. Most of my jobs involved cheating spouses and kidnapped cats.

"I think you're right, Miss Crumble. That does sound suspicious."

The woman smiled and kept her hand resting on my arm. "You can call me Kate."

"Okay, Kate, I'll give George Bauerman a more careful look."

"Don't forget, Mary Jane. She was a horrible mother who raised a horrible child."

"I appreciate your candor," I said. "I'll also give Mary Jane a closer examination."

"Speaking of a closer examination, Nic, I'd like to know more about you since you'll be living here for an extended period."

I swallowed whatever cheese was in my mouth and fumbled for my glass of wine, desperate to wet my whistle. Nic Knuckles asked the questions about people's lives, not the other way around, and I didn't like being on the answering end.

"Not much to say. I'm a big city private eye with a boatload of heartbreak, traversing the universe in pursuit of justice for the little guy."

Kate smiled. "Oh my, I like the sound of that."

That's when things got dicey. Kate unhooked her blouse's top button and waved her hands in front of her exposed cleavage. "My, my, it's warm in here."

I pulled my arm from her grasp. What was she suggesting? It had to be fifty degrees in that parlor, and I could almost see my breath. The woman leaned over, showed more of her womanhood, and whispered. "I noticed that you listed a Mrs. Knuckles as your emergency contact on your room registration. Is that your wife?"

My eyes dropped into my lap, and I mumbled. "That's my mother."

Kate purred. "That's nice. I like a man who's good to his mother."

Yeah, sure, she did. Nic Knuckles had plenty of dealings with ladies who thought they could escape justice by flashing some flesh. Who did Miss Crumble think she was seducing, an Amish schoolboy? I went on the offensive before things got further out of hand.

"I have a question for you, Kate," I said, slowly raising my gaze and locking onto her two pulsating orbs. And I met her eyes. "Back when Mindy was murdered, did a drifter named, Wayne, have a room in this house?"

Kate shrugged. "We had a lot of transient people coming through. I don't recall letting a room to anyone whose occupation was wandering from town to town."

Nuts, identifying Wayne the Drifter, looked to be a steeper climb than I anticipated.

"Going back thirty years ago, did a traveling salesman stay at the lodge?"

Kate stiffened and pulled away from me. "I wouldn't know. My aunt operated this place back then. But sure, I imagine she had a lot of salespeople passing through."

"Well, this salesman might've been an acquaintance of your friend Mary Jane. Does that ring a bell?"

The question may not have rung a bell, but it lit a fuse. Kate rocketed from her chair. "I was *never* a friend of Mary Jane Bauerman, and I surely would not know if she was entertaining one of my aunt's guests." With those words, Kate marched from the parlor.

Wowzer, Kate Crumble had one volatile personality which blew hot and cold, all within the same minute. I had a lot to learn about my landlady, but one important lesson was obvious. I'd better tread lightly with my questions because if I didn't, I'd close off a critical source of information and anger the woman cooking my morning breakfast.

I reached into my pocket, withdrew my trusty notebook, found an unmarked page, and added the name Kate Crumble at the top. My first notation was simple—Miss C gets hotter than a slice of Jalapeno Pepper Jack.

Chapter Twelve

Kleinstadt, Indiana, was Small Town America, albeit on the downside of prosperity. Not that its citizens weren't hardworking. A cynic might drive down Main Street, see the empty storefronts, and mourn a once vibrant downtown. An optimist would see it differently and say, "Look at all those remaining entrepreneurs, those capitalist risk-takers, keeping Kleinstadt commerce alive."

That's what I had uppermost in my mind as I strolled downtown after escaping the carnal choreography of Miss Kate Crumble. I passed by the tattoo parlor, the consignment store, and a nail salon, and I doubted I'd step into any of those enterprises. However, the Speedi Food Mart had an exciting array of culinary offerings, and I anticipated frequent shopping visits.

Crossing the street, I arrived at a brightly lit store called All Things Sharp. A banner hung above the entry, proclaiming a Midnight Madness Sale. Considering the emptiness of the streets at four in the afternoon, there was more madness in the event's timing and ambition than anything.

I stepped through an open door, and a warm salutation greeted me. "Good day," a boisterous man called from behind a large glass display. Even though he was eating what appeared to be a burrito, he continued his greeting. "Welcome to All Things Sharp, where there's never a dull moment."

I couldn't keep a grin from squirming to the surface of my face. The reputed Midwestern jocularity had been absent most of my visit, so hearing some cornpone jibber jabber made me feel welcomed. And let Nic Knuckles tell you that feeling safe was essential when you entered a store with wall-to-wall saws, axes, knives, swords, hatchets, and scythes.

"Are you Buzz Rockwell?" I asked.

"Yes sir, I am. How can I put a full-sized Wayneer's scimitar into your hands today?"

The holidays were too far off for shopping, and my mother only wanted cash for gifts, so I decided to feint interest and see what I might learn from Mr. Rockwell.

"What sorts of axes do you have available?"

Buzz swallowed whatever he'd been chewing and wiped a paper napkin across his lips. "Ah, axes, my favorite instrument of bedlam."

The man waved his hand across the display wall behind him. He pointed at tactical and Viking axes, and his finger danced down the wall at grub, felling, and Hudson Bay axes. He rhapsodized about their weight, handles, balance, and size. The poor man played right into my trap.

"What axe would you use if you wanted to fell a tree in one swing?" I asked.

"How big is the tree?"

I wrapped my open hands around my neck, studied the gap I'd created, and said, "Oh, say about five to six inches wide."

Buzz grinned, reached below the counter, and pulled out a highly polished battle axe.

"This is my baby," he said, holding the weapon up to my face. "If it was sharp enough, and you swung at the right angle with enough force, yeah, no doubt it'd do the job."

I leaned forward, rested my hands on the countertop, and glared at the man. "I guess it could do the same thing to, let's say, the neck of a sixteen-year-old girl."

Buzz's lower lip trembled, and his eyes went cold when the axe suddenly slipped from his fingers. I pulled my hands off the countertop as the weapon crashed through the glass, sending shards and splinters everywhere. I saw Buzz's mouth moving, but all I heard was the sound of my heart pounding blood to my brain. If I hadn't pulled my hands away when I did, I'd be known as Stubs Knuckles. I finally managed to say, "Whoa Daddy, that was close."

Rockwell didn't apologize for the near severing of my hands, and he was no longer in his affable sales mode. "So, you're that private eye snooping around town, huh?"

"Yeah," I said. "I'm Nic Knuckles, and I'm investigating the Mindy Bauerman murder."

Buzz's eyebrows pulled together, and his nose twitched as he stepped back. "I'm sick and tired of people talking about Mindy's murder. Why don't you true crime junkies just leave us alone and take up a new addiction?"

Mr. Rockwell's rude behavior had me wondering. Was the man uncomfortable because a seasoned investigator was finally working on the Bauerman case? Did he fear I'd reveal his deep, unrequited longing for Mindy and gather enough clues to expose him as her killer? Had he let that axe fall on purpose, hoping I'd be too busy mastering a prosthesis to do a thorough investigation? Whatever went on in Rockwell's mind wouldn't deter me.

"I only have a few questions, Mr. Rockwell, and then I'll be on my way."

Buzz lifted the axe out of the shattered display case and carefully returned it underneath. He then folded his arms and flipped his head to one side.

"I'll save you some time, Nic. You can check the video transcripts of my interrogation by the Kleinstadt Sheriff and my testimony during Timmy Hanlon's trial. It's all out there in the public domain. You do that, and you'll get any answer I have to give."

"Thanks for the tip," I said with a smile, but inside, I was seething. Did Buzz Rockwell not know that Nic Knuckles earned a gold star for doing homework throughout his elementary school years? I'd already spent my free evenings watching the videos and reading the written transcripts and knew how Buzz would answer any question I asked. That's why I was there to grill him in person. Mr. Rockwell had always been too perfect in those interrogations, and he gave the exact testimony in every recorded interview with precisely the same mannerism. Any PI with half a brain, and trust me, Nic Knuckle's grey matter took up most of my skull space, would know Buzz had rehearsed his answers. Kenneth Branagh practiced Shakespeare's Henry V less than Buzz did his role of misunderstood neighborhood creep.

"I have a question you've never answered," I said.

Buzz raised his hands. "Stop right there. Yes, I knew Wayne the Drifter, and we bonded over our love of axes and cheap beer. But Wayne and I stopped hanging out days before Mindy was murdered, and no, I had nothing missing from my axe collection."

My stomach dropped to my knees. How did Buzz know those were my next questions? Did my poker face fail me, and he read me like a cheap paperback? Holy Mozzarella, I hoped not because a private eye who couldn't hide his thoughts would have a short career. Hopefully, something else was happening here, like Buzz was a mind reader. Let's see if he anticipated my other questions about Wayne.

I placed the tip of my right index finger on my temple. "What am I thinking now, smart guy?"

"I never knew where Wayne lived or his last name. He'd show up from time to time, we'd drink beer, and then he'd disappear. The dude didn't say much, but since I had no other friends, I never pressed him for his story."

The man had me back on my heels. "How did you do that?"

Buzz bent over the shattered countertop before halting his nose two inches from mine. In words sautéed in the aroma of grilled peppers and onions, he said, "It's a small town, Nic. I knew days ago there was a private dick mucking about, and I'd figured out what you'd be asking me before you finished your wine and cheese at Miss Crumble's lodge."

Wow, the small-town grapevine worked faster than my high-speed Internet connection in Queens. I assume everyone in this burg knew what I was doing and where I was going. Nonetheless, I felt relieved that it was the town's gossip network informing Buzz of my intentions and not my impenetrable investigator persona failing.

"Okay, Mr. Rockwell, I'll admit you're a formidable opponent. Maybe you'll be Moriarty to my Holmes, Valjean to my Javert, or, Bugs Bunny to my Yosemite Sam. Let me tap into that big brain of yours and ask, who do you think killed Mindy Bauerman?"

"First of all, it wasn't me," he said. "I also don't think Wayne had anything to do with it either. I'd scratch from your list Buddy Lee Hoot. Even though

I hate the guy, it's not in his nature. If you're wondering about John Brown or George Bauerman, I think you're wasting your time."

"That pretty much eliminates everyone but Timmy Hanlon," I said.

A twinkle appeared in Buzz's eyes. "Yeah, that's true if you assume that only a man could swing an axe with the proper strength and precision to chop off someone's head."

Buzz probably expected me to be surprised by that comment; if so, he'd be disappointed. When your nana gives you razor blades as a baby toy, you quickly learn that the homicidal mindset isn't exclusive to the male gender.

"You need not worry, Mr. Rockwell," I said. "Nic Knuckles does not discriminate based on gender. I'm looking at everyone in town as a possible killer." Not wanting to have Buzz inside my head any more than he was, I thanked him for the conversation and turned to leave. Before I could walk away, he switched back to the affable salesman shtick. "Nic, before you leave. Can I interest you in a scythe? I have a beauty that's one of a kind."

I told Buzz I thought transporting such a tool on the plane back to the Big Apple would be a problem. He pressed me to make a purchase, lamenting the lack of insurance to cover the shattered countertop, and I suggested he stitch the busted glass together with masking tape.

"My fingers were greasy from that burrito I was eating.," he said. "I didn't do it on purpose."

"I know it was unintentional," I said, despite my doubts. "No harm, no foul."

Buzz's lip curled in an Elvis sneer, and he grumbled, "You show up, making trouble, and don't have the decency to buy something. Thanks for nothing."

"Easy does it, Buzz. Maybe my wallet will loosen up when your attitude becomes more cooperative. Goodbye and good luck with your midnight madness sale."

I stepped out of All Things Sharp and pulled my notebook from my pocket. A lot had gone down during my chat with Buzz, and I needed to record the more salient bits of what I'd learned. Nothing upsets an investigator more than suffering brain lock trying to recall important information, so that was why I took prodigious notes.

On the page I'd designated for Buzz Rockwell, I wrote that this person of interest had an axe that could behead a young girl. He was a beer-drinking buddy with Wayne the Drifter and, as a young man, had a reputed massive crush on Mindy. Buzz also seemed to have an answer for everything, which indicated a cleverness that could hide his culpability. Nonetheless, Rockwell showed he was less bright than he thought. Buzz was baffled when I refused to buy anything from him. Good Lord, the man didn't offer me a discounted price on that one-of-a-kind scythe. What New Yorker with any dignity would pay retail?

Chapter Thirteen

I knew The Next to Last Supper opened at five in the morning for the locals wanting some breakfast before commuting fifty miles to a decent-paying job in a bigger town. They'd silently sip the endless cups of coffee and gobble down whatever the grill cook offered as his special of the day. One early morning regular was Molly Spear. She told me it'd become a habit when she wrote for the newspaper because she never knew when someone might stroll by and drop a rumor into her lap.

Molly would sit in her regular booth for another five hours before Nic Knuckles wandered in.

"You're not an early bird gets the worm kind of guy, are you?" she asked me.

I smiled at her. I thought an ink-stained newshound like Molly would know that private eyes worked the low lives and hustlers, and those folks operated at night. I wonder what else she might've missed by rising with the roosters rather than hanging with the owls. If she had, there might be less mystery associated with the Mindy Bauerman case.

"I had that conversation with Timmy Hanlon," I said. "You were right. It did sound like he was railroaded."

"The Wabash Cannonball couldn't have put him behind bars any faster."

"I'm wondering why Barney Feif was so hellbent on finding him guilty."

Molly lifted her coffee cup to her mouth and slurped. "Sometimes a man will do almost anything to bail out a kid."

Whoa, baby, that comment woke me up faster than the bitter java being poured into my cup by an equally bitter waitress.

"What does that mean?" I asked. "Which kid did Feif help out of trouble?"

Molly hitched her shoulders. "Barney had a soft spot for juvenile delinquents, and that's all I'm sayin'."

Once again, Molly was a woman of her word. That *was* all she gave me that morning, a motive for a man with a scrambled mind, followed by a shrug.

"Yesterday, I also had interesting conversations with Buddy Lee Hoot and Buzz Rockwell."

"I bet that was a laugh," Molly said, "two losers still in love with a girl who couldn't have cared less about either one of them."

"They both came across as high-strung and prone to anger. Why do you think they're so goosey having me asking questions?"

Molly took another sip of coffee. "Men in this town are all touchy and moody, especially when you're digging into their past. Considering Buddy and Buzz were probably every amateur investigator's favorite suspect, you can't expect them to be welcoming."

I asked her to elaborate, and she lifted her shoulders around her neck and said nothing. I saw the same maneuver with my questions about George Bauerman and John Brown, and I swore a turtle spent less time ducking in and out of its shell.

It was apparent that Molly was in no mood to talk, so I excused myself and headed for the door. Before I left, however, I ordered some eggs and toast to go. Miss Crumble hadn't gotten over my inquiry about Mary Jane's relationship with a traveling salesman, and she abused my breakfast that morning. I didn't perform well on an empty stomach and had much to do today. My first stop after I finished eating in my car was the father of the victim, George Bauerman. His story had more holes than my socks, and it was time for Nic Knuckles to do some mending.

Chapter Fourteen

No one answered the door of the Bauerman residence, so I peeked through the windows and saw nothing moving. I was about to leave when a grunting sound, like the rutting of an out-of-shape feral pig, alerted me to activity behind the house.

I surprised Mary Jane as she knelt in her dried-out garden, pulling on surviving weeds. She let loose a scream when I tapped her on the shoulder. "What is wrong with you, sneaking up on me?"

I felt terrible having startled the woman, but an elusive private eye must have the footfalls of a cat. Unfortunately, Nic Knuckles couldn't switch off that finely honed skill for either Mary Jane or the mice in my apartment. My regret escalated when she jumped up and thrust a garden spade at me. "Get away from me, you jerk. If you touch me again, I'll stick this spade so far through your chest your nipples will show up under your shoulder blades."

I stepped back and slowly flapped my hands. "Easy, Mary Jane, there's no need to get nasty. I'm only here to talk to your husband."

I hoped a soft voice and nonthreatening manner would disarm her. The last thing I wanted to do was use my martial arts training to take that spade from her. I'd hate to throw a woman to the ground who, with her hair coated with cheap coloring and a weapon held in a defensive pose, reminded me of my mother.

"My husband isn't here. Now leave me alone."

That was too bad because Nic Knuckles ran a tight ship, and I hated to have my schedule thrown off. I'd improvise and use the time to quiz Mary

Jane. Although she came across as having little to offer when I first met her, maybe with George out of sight, she'd open up.

"How about you and I have a nice chat," I said. "I bet you have some interesting stuff to share." My use of the patent pending Nic Knuckles' warmth and charm worked, and she lowered the spade.

"Okay, what do you want to know?"

"At my first visit, you mentioned other boys who were causing Mindy trouble. Who'd you have in mind?"

The woman chewed on her bottom lip as she appeared to dig for an answer. "Buzz Rockwell lived across the street, and I knew he was stalking her. And John Brown was always pestering Mindy. There might've been some others that I never knew about. I mean, I never heard of Timmy Hanlon until he was arrested."

"It sounds like you're not a hundred percent positive that Hanlon murdered your daughter?"

Mary Jane shuddered and squeaked. "I don't know who did it. Mindy tended to play her admirers against each other, so who knows who finally had enough?"

"Tell me about Buddy Lee Hoot, Mindy's old boyfriend."

A smile swam across Mary Jane's face, and she started chattering like a squirrel. She held the young man in high regard back then and thought he was the best of the eligible young swains in Mindy's school. He had excellent listening skills, she claimed, something few men possessed. I had to give Buddy credit because he'd been correct about Mary Jane's affection for him back in the day.

"How'd your husband feel about Buddy?"

"George never liked any boy who showed an interest in Mindy. He especially disliked Buddy because he was always at our house waiting for Mindy to come home."

I hummed a single note. That was a revealing comment. So, Daddy was possessive, huh, not wanting any beta males sniffing around his little girl. I knew that feeling. No, not that Nic Knuckles ever had responsibility for raising a daughter. But, as a young man calling on girls, I'd receive many a threatening gaze from their obnoxious fathers, uncles, and brothers.

"How'd George react with all these boys pursuing Mindy?"

"He'd get very angry at her, calling her a small-town Jezebel. The more he tried to restrict the boys, the more boys seemed to show up at our door. It drove him mad."

"Did you ever see him raise a hand to Mindy?"

"I never saw it," she said, "but when he was angry, he scared Mindy *and* me."

Maybe Mrs. Bauerman wondered whether George had something to do with his daughter's death like some other town folk. If I got her to validate some of the speculation surrounding her husband, I could wrap this case up within a week.

"Is it true that George drove a new car soon after Mindy's death?"

Mary Jane's mouth dropped open. "Huh?"

"A car he purchased with the insurance money that probably showed up in your checking account soon after Mindy died."

"I don't know," she said. "I knew nothing about life insurance."

I stepped closer, my voice growing more strident. "How else would you explain a working-class man, his family living hand to mouth, suddenly motoring around Kleinstadt in a new automobile?"

Mary Jane shrugged and answered. "Maybe because he owned a used car lot and drove a different vehicle home almost every night."

Nothing irritated a hard-charging investigator like a good answer, and Mary Jane had brought me to a dead stop.

"So, are you telling me there was no new car?"

"We never had a new car, only different used ones."

"Are you sure George didn't take out a life insurance policy on Mindy?"

Mary Jane nodded. "I seriously doubt it. He said the Almighty would keep us safe from disasters, both natural and unnatural."

"I heard rumors that maybe your husband was in trouble with the IRS. Any truth to that?"

Mary Jane stepped back, and her eyes bulged large behind her spectacles. "Who told you that?"

"Let's say a little coffee-sipping bird."

Mary Jane groaned. "Oh, he'll be so angry with me if I tell you."

"Go ahead," I said. "No stoolie ever got harmed working for Nic Knuckles."

The woman lowered her gaze. "For years, he'd donated half of his income to a widow and orphan's charity, and the government wondered why a man with so little money could afford to do that."

The first thought that jumped into my head was that the charity was a tax write-off scam. That thought then leaped from my brain and out of my mouth. "That sounds like a charity tax write-off scam."

Mary Jane smothered that suspicion when she named the three widows and their six children who directly benefited from George's benevolence.

"How'd the IRS resolve the audit, if your husband wasn't a crook?"

"They were so impressed with George's generosity that they awarded him their annual humanitarian prize, a check for one hundred and forty dollars. He hates for people to know."

"That's very interesting, Mrs. Bauerman. I appreciate you clearing up the confusion."

"Now leave me alone. I gotta get this garden ready for winter, or we won't have any vegetables next Summer."

I left Mary Jane with her chickweeds and dandelions and walked to my rental car. Once behind the steering wheel, I pulled out my notebook, turned to the relevant page, and crossed through my previous thoughts on George Bauerman. I had completely misjudged him. The man might come across as gruff, but he had a humble spirit and a generous heart. I wrote a new entry on the page, something more personal. How come my dad couldn't have been like George Bauerman?

Chapter Fifteen

I felt red-faced when I left Mary Jane Bauerman's backyard. I hadn't been that embarrassed about being wrong since I accused my mother of nesting hamsters under her arms when all she needed was a new razor. Poor Mary Jane, I'd stormed into her garden, all up in her face, calling her husband a child-murdering, insurance-scamming, tax-cheating low life. And I'd been terribly wrong.

Why had Sandi Fliminsky's tip about George's troubles with the IRS been so bogus? How did Miss Crumble's claim that George drove a new car purchased from the payout of life insurance be so far off? Why would those two women willingly spread lies about a generous man who appeared to be one step from saintly canonization by the US Government?

If I hoped an answer would fall out of the sky, I'd be waiting a long time. Good luck, and Nic Knuckles never shared much of a relationship, and we weren't on speaking terms. I'd have to grind long and hard to solve this case, and I'd start by revisiting Mindy's so-called best friend, Sandi. She had a lot of explaining to do.

I arrived at Sandi's house, and I guessed my whining about Lady Luck caused her to show me some favor. In the driveway was Miss Fliminsky's truck, and it looked like Sandi had yet to leave for work. Now, I could appear unexpectedly at her door with tough questions that would knock her off her feet.

I snuck onto the porch and pounded the front door, calling her name. Maybe I didn't take her feet from under her, but she looked surprised when she answered. "What do you want?" she said. "I have to get to work."

"I'll make his quick, Miss Fliminsky. You and I need to clear up some confusion."

Sandi, dressed in overalls and work boots, stepped onto the porch and closed the door behind her. "I don't have time for this. I have yards to mow and brambles to hack."

"I bet you're busy," I said and dogged her as she walked toward her truck. "Do your tasks include slandering George Bauerman and feeding me a load of manure so I'd go off on Buddy and Buzz?"

Sandi stopped, looked at me, and shook her head. "You must be the most incompetent investigator walking the planet if Buzz and Buddy fooled you. And, only a nincompoop believes anything good about George. You're an idiot, Nic."

"If you think your name-calling affects me, you're the idiot."

However, inside my head, my kindergarten teacher, Mrs. Cory, accused me of eating a black crayon, and I couldn't raise my tiny voice to tell her my front teeth were missing and that I wasn't a Crayola eater. Yeah, nasty accusations deeply hurt Nic Knuckles, and they always had. Fortunately, having been mocked so often, I knew how to bounce back quickly.

"You're the untruthful one, sister. Your story about George Bauerman and the IRS was so far off I couldn't find it on Google Maps. Contrary to what you told me, Mary Jane adored Buddy."

Sandi scoffed. "If you're fooled by the Bauermans then you'll never solve Mindy's murder. And if you think Buddy and Buzz didn't have their reasons, then you should have your private detective license revoked. I'm telling you. They all had their motives for killing Mindy."

"That's a large number of possible suspects, Miss Fliminsky. But there's one person not on your list who might've had a motive to commit murder, as well. *You.*"

The dismissive expression on Sandi's face morphed into curiosity, and she stopped walking. "What do you mean?"

"You're not a bad-looking woman," I said. "Yet, I've never heard mention about your teenage love life. Was it because the boys you wanted to date, like Buddy and Buzz, all had a crush on your best friend, Mindy?"

Sandi snorted. "Buzz and Buddy were Mindy's playthings. I had no interest in them."

"Maybe so, but is it possible you've pined away for fifteen years, hoping that one of those boys, now a man, would give up their memory of Mindy and pursue your affections? Is that why you've bad-mouthed Buzz and Buddy?"

"They were losers back then, and they still are."

I ignored Sandi's cruel judgment of Buzz and Buddy and continued going at her. "Let me take you back fifteen years when you and Mindy were in high school. If we looked inside the mind of sixteen-year-old Sandi Fliminsky, would we find a girl with a raging resentment of her best friend?"

Sandi tried to move away, but I kept pushing, getting closer and closer until the stink of my breath made her raise her hands to her nose. "Stop it, stop it," she cried, but I didn't relent.

"You were deeply jealous of Mindy because she had one devoted boyfriend, Buddy, and another young man, Buzz, who secretly desired her. John Brown preferred her over all the other dancing girls in town and never gave you a second look. That left you all alone on Prom Night, and the Homecoming Dance, and the Halloween Shindig, and the Sacrificing of the Virgins Festival."

Sandi screamed and balled her hands into white-knuckled fists. "Yes, I was envious of Mindy. Good Lord, did you take a close look at her yearbook picture? She had a face that dropped birds from the sky; she was so homely. Here I was, a pretty girl, and none of the local clowns gave me a chance. And, let me tell you, Mindy didn't hesitate to remind me of that fact. Just because Mindy hurt my feelings at times, doesn't mean I did anything to harm her. I loved her like a sister."

The tears welled in Sandi's eyes, and I felt ashamed for making her recall those painful adolescent times. It may be hard to believe, but I knew what it was like to sit at home on a Saturday night, your hair in curlers and an empty gallon container of chunky chocolate ice cream in your lap. I reached out and patted the woman on the shoulder. "You know, Sandi, I have to tell you that you're still an attractive woman."

"I am?"

"Yeah, and if I had been your schoolmate, I would've asked you on a date, for sure."

Sandi wobbled in response to my kind words, and suddenly, we both were back at those god-awful high school years when insecurity and desire made you act stupid. And stupid, I acted. I took Sandi into my arms, and she sagged. I didn't know if she shivered out of excitement or recoiled from my touch, so I released her.

"That was awkward," she said.

I felt my face grow warm. "Yeah, sorry about that. I hope you don't think that because we hugged, I won't still consider you a possible murderer, you know, business being business."

Sandi laughed and pulled the truck key from her jacket pocket. "It wasn't that great a hug, Nic. Get over yourself."

Sandi and I parted, and it wasn't until I'd driven three blocks from her house that I successfully shoved my old high school insecurities into the back closet of my mind. Now I was pissed. What's wrong with me? I let sentimentality waste a perfect opportunity to learn about Mindy's relationships with Buddy, Buzz, and George. Damn high school trauma. If I hadn't gone soft in the head, I could've pushed Sandi for more details on the mysterious salesman. I also wanted to ask her about the drifter passing through town who went by the name of Wayne.

Sandi could've also answered a question that gnawed at me from day one. Why did almost every man in Kleinstadt have a name that started with the letter B? Good Lord, Buddy, Buzz, Brownie, and Barney. What was up with that?

Chapter Sixteen

T he next stop on my Kleinstadt Truth Tour took me back to the lodge to tangle with Miss Crumble. Figuring Kate was still hot over my questions about a salesman and Mary Jane Bauerman, I looked for something to get me back into her good graces. I spotted a scruffy-looking fellow selling stuff out of a van and thought it was the Kleinstadt equivalent of a pop-up storefront. He could have something a woman like Kate would enjoy. Luckily, there was a box of chocolates, and although the outer wrapping had yellowed with age, I snatched it up.

"Hello, Miss Crumble," I called out as I cautiously stepped into the house. Getting no response, I moved further into the living room, and my private eye instincts kicked into a higher gear. I scanned the area, looking for unexpected shadows or the slight tremor of air molecules. "Come out; come out, wherever you are," I said. "I know you're in here."

Dang, I almost jumped out of my shoes when Kate sprang from behind the drapery, squawking like a demented parrot. "What do you want?" I held out the box of sweets, and she sneered. "What's that for? You can't pay for your room?"

"No, no, no." I pushed the box into her hands and explained I wanted to make amends, admitting I now had more questions about the citizens of Kleinstadt than answers. I turned on the sad eyes and said, "I could really use your help, Kate."

Miss Crumble dismissed me with a side glance, ripped the cellophane from the candy box, and pulled open the lid. Holding a piece of chocolate to her eye like a Diamond District jeweler, she studied it carefully. She examined half a dozen pieces before nodding toward the next room. "Okay, let's sit in the parlor, and we can talk."

And so, we did. We sat side by side chastely on a sofa, and I asked about George Bauerman and why she felt so negatively toward him. What had the man done to her that generated such ranker? Initially, she was evasive, but the chocolates soon worked their magic, and she bottom-lined why she hated the man.

"His saintliness makes me want to puke."

That might sound illogical to most folks, but Nic Knuckles understood. I trusted Goody Two Shoes about as much as I did crooks. Being a moral person was hard for everyone because the Ten Commandments set an awful high standard, and if a person topped that bar, they were up to no good. That attitude explained why I was never a fan of Mother Therese. What was her game anyway?

"I hear you, Kate, but did George do something specifically to you to earn such an intense feeling of hatred?"

Kate popped another chocolate into her mouth and slowly chewed. I felt she'd prefer not to answer my question, so I grabbed her hand when she tried to shove another candy into her mouth. "Come on, Miss Crumble. It doesn't make sense George's decency should trigger such a heated response. Just because the man liked walking around in sackcloth and ashes didn't mean he was evil. What's going on?"

Kate wrestled free from my grip and gobbled down another candy. Fortunately, it was one of those liquor-infused pieces, and soon, her tongue flapped like a hummingbird's wings.

"I was but a young girl, twenty-one years old, when I came to help my aunt run her lodge," she said, her voice as gooey as the candies smeared around her mouth. "I was so naïve back then; it's embarrassing to talk about it."

"Yeah, we're all easy to fool at that age," I said. I thought Kate would feel less silly if I told her about the time twelve-year-old Wanda Wampus convinced fourteen-year-old me that poison ivy would encourage facial hair. I decided not to bring it up because Kate's story sounded complicated, and I wanted to ensure I got all the clues.

"Soon after I arrived in town, I met the only man I ever loved," she said, "and whoever loved me."

Man, was Kleinstadt, German, for Place of Desperate Woman? Did every female in this county carry around a broken heart? The number of romance novels sold in the town must be astronomical.

"Did this man have a name?"

"Tommy, Tommy Lyle."

I pulled the notebook from my pocket and flipped to the page reserved for Kate's commentary. "Was Mr. Lyle a local?" I asked. "Does he still live here in Kleinstadt?"

Kate bit her lower lip. Maybe she did so because she was hesitant to respond, and Tommy Lyle still held some power over her. Or, more likely, she wanted that last taste of chocolate smeared around her mouth. Who knew? A handful of seconds passed before she stopped licking her lips and answered me.

"No, he was a boarder at my aunt's lodge," she said. "He was a traveling salesman."

"Ah-ha," I wanted to yell, but I held my tongue. Hearing Kate confirm Sandi Fliminsky's story about a traveling salesman was the kind of info that excited me. One source was nothing but a rumor, while two sources made it a factoid. Getting a name was a bonus. Hopefully, Kate would give me more dope on the guy, so I could see if he was a suspect worth pursuing.

"How'd you get involved with this Tommy Lyle?"

Miss Kate Crumble slowly shared her story. About thirty years ago, Mr. Lyle showed up one day and immediately flirted with the young and gullible Kate. The man was worldly, having taken orders for his wares from the metropolitans and small towns on either side of the Ohio River. His stories, dark eyes, and perfectly trimmed mustache enthralled the young woman.

"Let me guess," I said. "After a little smoochie-coochie, old Tommy left town."

Kate's eyes flashed. "No, he wasn't that kind of man." The woman rolled away from me, and her bottom lip protruded like a fat chocolate-covered slug.

Dang, why'd I open my big yap and let my low opinion of men of commerce spoil Kate's talkative mood? Hoping to get her back on track, I lifted the candy box and offered her another chocolate, but she shook her head and twisted further away. I held the open box higher so she could sniff the cacao aroma in its most refined form. She sighed and swiftly stuffed some dark brown sweetness into her mouth. That was all she needed to get over her tantrum.

"Tommy was a good man," she said. "He treated me special, and I fell desperately and completely in love with him. He was my sunrise, my afternoon breeze, and my evening dream."

Oh, my Lord, here came another sappy story about unrequited love. Why did women feel compelled to share such sentimentality with me? Did they not think multiple past heartbreaks had tenderized Nic Knuckles' soul? Kate didn't react to my teary eyes and trembling lips because she was too self-absorbed in telling me her woeful tale. "Tommy took me on picnics by the river and introduced me to pleasures I'd never known before."

I quickly composed myself and asked, "What kind of pleasures? Was it the joy of eating a perfectly fried pork chop or the decadence of your tongue gliding over a cool, creamy piece of New York cheesecake?"

Kate didn't say anything, but the sudden coloring of her cheeks suggested it was more likely the pork chops than the cheesecake.

"Why wasn't there a happy ending to this romance?" I asked. "It sounded like the perfect love story."

Kate cast her eyes downward and slowly shook her head. She looked like she was about to break apart and cry. I gently touched her hand. "What happened, Kate? Tell Nic your story."

The woman pulled her hand away and somehow sucked the tears back into her tear ducts. Her face went hard, and her voice cold. "We didn't have a happy ending because someone more experienced in the ways of men stole him away from me."

"Ouch, that must've hurt."

Kate's eyes now shrunk into tiny pools of simmering anger. "Oh, the heartbreak was only a small part of my pain," she said. Her jaw clenched, and a slight tremor shook her body. I waited for her to explode and reveal the awful truth, but she remained coiled. Whatever happened to Kate Crumble thirty years ago seemed too great of a disgrace to share.

As much as Nic Knuckles wanted to respect the woman's privacy, I had a mystery to solve. I didn't have time for her to come around at her own pace. Nonetheless, I'd employ a gentle touch, drawing upon my many hours of court-ordered sensitivity training.

"So, who was the hussy that stole your Tommy?" I asked. "What vixen seduced him away from your loving arms?"

Kate stiffened her body and squeezed an answer through gritted teeth, "Mary Jane Bauerman."

Well, slap my face and call me a taxi. Molly Spear was correct, and that plump, mousey Mary Jane had been the seductress in her youth.

"I'm surprised," I said. "The Mary Jane I know doesn't seem to have the smoldering attributes needed to be a seducer of men."

Kate blew a raspberry. "Maybe not now, but back then, Mary Jane was an unhappy tart married to a man who practiced only one type of sexual intimacy."

I felt an uncomfortable pulsation in my chest, hearing her use the word sex. Now, that might seem surprising since Nic Knuckles was a resident of New York City, where more combinations of sexual undertakings occurred than the human anatomy could accommodate. That notwithstanding, I wouldn't say I liked talking about anything that brought back memories of a woman named Maggie who happened to own an overly protective pet chimpanzee named Chopper.

"I'm confused," I said. "If Mary Jane seduced your dream man, why turn your vengeance on the cuckolded husband?"

Kate lit up like Mt. Vesuvius taking it out on Pompeii. "Because when I exposed Mary Jane's affair to George, he forgave her. That damn fool didn't throw her out, and he didn't punish her. Can you understand my feelings? She stole my man *and* never suffered any consequences."

"Yeah, I got it," I said. "How would've Dostoevsky have handled crime without punishment?"

I wasn't being flippant or clever. My heart did go out to Miss Crumble. She'd lost her first love, didn't get to savor sweet revenge, and had to watch a forgiven scarlet-lettered woman prancing about Kleinstadt for more than thirty years. I felt an obligatory hug coming over me but held back. Miss Crumble had already shown too strong of an interest in my bones, and my embrace of Sandi Fliminsky ended awkwardly. I also worried that cuddling a chocolate-smeared Kate would stain the shirt I'd spent an hour ironing that morning, so I offered kind words instead.

"I'm sorry, Kate, you've been through a lot. Now I understand why you hate George Bauerman."

"Thank you," she said. "I've never been able to get over it."

"Yeah, I imagine it would be hard to forget. But you have to admit, his being a forgiving man doesn't implicate him in the murder of his child."

Kate lifted her face and shot me a look that chilled my spine, pancreas, and left kidney.

"His child, you say? What makes you think Mindy was *his* child?"

My mouth hung wide open like a drawbridge with a frozen gearbox. What could I say? If Kate was correct and Mindy wasn't George's child, then all bets were off. She'd just given George Bauerman the strongest motive for the murder of any of my suspects.

"Miss Crumble, that's a bombshell of an accusation. Do you have proof?"

I didn't know a person could become intoxicated from chocolate, but if Kate had an answer to my question, it'd have to wait. She wobbled and fell off the sofa and onto the floor. Crawling to a wicker wastebasket, she let loose a deep moan and blew a partially digested box of candies into the receptacle. I immediately did what any decent private eye would do in such a situation. I returned to my notebook and started scribbling my latest observation. Never buy discounted candy from a man selling it out of the back of a van.

Chapter Seventeen

Kleinstadt, Indiana, might be called a one-traffic-light town if it had a traffic light. The governing council calculated it was cheaper to post a few stop signs than to burn electricity on a couple of stop lights. It didn't matter much to Nic Knuckles, as I knew Sheriff John Brown eventually would haul me over for violating some community norm. It happened late that afternoon, a few seconds after I'd slipped through the first intersection.

"I know big city folks don't believe in slowing down, let alone coming to a complete stop," the sheriff said as he leaned against the side of my car. "But here in Indiana, stop means stop, no rolling stop, or I'm thinking about stopping stops."

"I hear you, Sheriff. As an advocate for law and order myself, I fully appreciate your concerns. I will do better, I promise you."

My apology and commitment to toe the line didn't persuade the sheriff to show me mercy. He wrote out a ticket that carried a fine of fifty dollars. When I questioned the severity of the penalty, he acknowledged that Kleinstadt had a two-tier fee schedule. Locals paid ten dollars for a moving violation, while out-of-towners passing through suffered far more.

"Soaking strangers to supplement our town's meager resources is the way we roll here in Kleinstadt," he said. "I'm sure you understand, being from New York City."

"I do appreciate the logic of your revenue-generating approach," I said. "What does fifty bucks pay for in this town?"

Sheriff Brown sucked on the tobacco plug planted inside his right cheek and pointed to the crumbling sidewalk across the street. "I think your fifty dollars would repair about two feet of that curbing."

"Will a plaque with my name be attached?"

The sheriff's eyes narrowed into slits, and I assumed he didn't find me clever. "I tell you what, Knuckles. With your attitude, you might have this whole street named for you before you're done here."

As much as I'd love to tell my mom about Nic Knuckles Boulevard running through Kleinstadt, Indiana, I kept a lid on my flippancy. Working with the police in the past, I knew they might help you out with a tip or two if they liked you. Otherwise, they'd make your life miserable. Although I suspected I already knew how Brownie felt about my investigation, I had to ask.

"I have to wonder, Sheriff, is my investigation of the Mindy Bauerman murder case upsetting you?"

The big guy tapped a fingernail on the roof of my car. "I just think you're stirring up people with all your questions. Timmy Hanlon was convicted of the crime by a fair and impartial jury. You snooping around implies we have the wrong man in prison. I find that insulting to my predecessor, Sheriff Feif, and I take offense at that."

"You and old Barney Feif were close, I'm guessing."

Brown lowered his head into the window, and the brim of his hat tipped backward as it pressed against my forehead. "You stay away from Sheriff Feif. You hear me."

"That won't be a problem, considering the man has the mind of a geranium."

Brownie's thick stub of a finger poked me in the cheek. "Leave that man alone, or you'll be wishing a moving violation was all I issued you."

The big guy pulled back and walked away. I knew I should've kept quiet, but Nic Knuckles wasn't easily intimidated. "Hey, Sheriff Brown," I called out. "When you were in high school, did you ever trip the light fantastic with Mindy Bauerman?"

The man stopped, turned around, and grunted. "Trip the what?"

Not surprisingly, Brownie was unfamiliar with Milton, so I brought the cultural references down a notch. "Did you and Mindy ever cut a rug?"

"Why would we vandalize a carpet?"

"No. no, did you ever take Mindy dancing?"

Sheriff Brown's lower lip almost rolled up over his nose. "If you want more trouble, Knuckles, keep asking questions like that one."

As the big hunk in brown and tan trundled away from me, I retrieved my notebook. Turning to Sheriff Brown's profile, I saw my initial note, Brownie not 2 bright. I took my pencil and underlined it twice. I added, but he looked light on his feet.

The thought of John Brown dancing with Mindy got me wondering why he reacted so strongly to my questions about the two of them. Was there something more to it than what I thought? Undoubtedly, Brownie dancing with Miss Bauerman would've involved close physical contact. How did Buddy Lee Hoot feel about that? It'd be far more touching of flesh than anything he had with Mindy. The poor sap must've been crazed with envy. Or, Buzz Rockwell, looking from afar as Brownie spun a sweating Mindy into his arms. He'd have to be insanely jealous. Imagine the moral outrage of George Bauerman when learning about his daughter in the grasp of a hormone-driven John Brown. Oh boy, he'd be livid.

All three men would be outraged at the possible sexual hootenanny between young John and Mindy. Any one of them might've been so full of anger that they'd want to put the big hurt on Brownie. Then again, probably not since it'd require hand-to-hand combat with a kid who probably carried two hundred and thirty pounds of sculptured muscles on a six-foot frame.

If none of those three men could take it out on Brownie, how'd any of them release that built-up masculine fury? They'd have to do something, or the rage would eat away their manhood. Maybe they took it out on someone smaller and weaker who couldn't fight back. Breaking Brownie's heart might've been enough if they couldn't break his arm or leg. Make him cry on Wednesday nights when he could no longer escape gravity with a sixteen-year-old Mindy Bauerman and her happy feet. I'd seen more flimsy excuses for murder.

Chapter Eighteen

The Next to Last Supper had a sign posted over the cashier's stand. It read, "Free Cups of Coffee," in big red lettering. An asterisk drew your eye to the small print, which stated, Toilet Fee - $10. I swore everyone in Kleinstadt had a hustle, and Molly Spear had to be subsidizing the restaurant's toilet fund with her coffee consumption. I found her in her usual booth that midmorning, still sucking down the worst-tasting liquid outside a chemical waste dump.

"Did you have a productive day yesterday, Mr. Knuckles?" she asked.

I answered with a chuckle. "Yeah, I did my share rebuilding the sidewalks of your little town."

"That's good to hear. I almost ripped a tendon walking in here."

Molly slurped a mouthful of coffee and turned on her charm. "So Nic, what did you learn about Kleinstadt, other than we have busted pavement?"

"Much like the broken curbing, too many folks have shattered hearts from unrequited love. Kleinstadt is like the backwash of season four of The Bachelor."

Molly's eyes suddenly took on a smoky appearance. She raised her cup to her mouth. "Yeah, you got that right."

A good private investigator had to watch, think, and observe constantly. Curiosity was our normal operating mode, so looking at Molly, I wondered about *her* story. Was she just a busybody posing as a journalist, or was there more to Molly Spear than met the eye? I'd better not assume she didn't have her share of secrets, only to discover them on my last day in town.

"I heard one tip," I said, "that was so smoldering I thought my ear drums would burst into flames."

Molly looked up from her coffee and stared. "You gonna tell me, or do I have to guess?"

I grinned because it felt good to have the table turned on Molly, where she was squeezing me for the dope, and I let her hang a minute before speaking. "What's the possibility that Mindy's daddy *wasn't* George Bauerman?"

Molly's lips disappeared from her face, leaving an unfriendly slash. "My, my, Nic, you've been sticking your little beak into some pretty juicy places, haven't you?"

"Well, Molly, does that statement have legs to stand on, wings to take flight, or flippers to swim?"

The woman turned her gaze to the contents of her coffee mug. "Talk with Mindy's old beau, Buddy Lee Hoot, because he'd know more about that rumor than me."

"Why would Buddy know the details of Mindy's paternity?"

Molly drained her mug and snapped her fingers at the waitress, signaling for a refill.

"Here's something big city folks don't get about small towns. We don't have the fancy psychiatrists at our beck and call like you all do. Since we can't get our minds retooled with a competent psychotherapist, we find someone who'll listen to our problems *and* keep their mouths shut."

Nic Knuckles knew a thing or two about having a confidant that kept a lid on your shared conversations. I couldn't trust my mother because she used my troubles as firewood stoking a scandalmonger's bonfire. Again, don't get me started.

"Go back and talk to Buddy," Molly said, adding a nod of her head for emphasis. "His close relationship with Mary Jane might illuminate your understanding of Mindy's paternity."

I thanked Molly for our little chat and slipped out of the booth. Once again, she'd given me something to think about, something I probably wouldn't have come up with in a million years. Why would a grown woman spill her guts to a sixteen-year-old boy? Was Buddy a far better listener than anyone else in Mary Jane's life, or was she a devious manipulator preying on a soft-hearted kid? I hoped Molly was correct about Buddy because the more I learned about Mrs. Bauerman's purported relationships with men, the higher up she went on my suspect list.

Chapter Nineteen

I left The Next to Last Supper and walked to Buddy's Tavern to delve further into the nature of his relationship with Mary Jane. I suspected he'd be uncomfortable and even throw me out on my ear. Then again, with so few patrons wandering into his establishment before noon, he might be happy for a paying customer. I hoped so because I needed clarity about Mindy's mother and her weakness for men. I also craved some tavern lunch fare and hoped to get my stomach filled simultaneously.

"Good day, my friendly barkeep," I said as I sat down at the bar. "Might I have a glass of your finest brew and a lunch menu?"

Buddy's evil eye went fuzzy after twenty seconds, and he gave in. A frosty glass of beer soon appeared, with a menu slapped in front of me. "There you go," he said. "There's no deviation from what's on there, and don't ask for substitutions or additions."

I lifted the laminated card to my eyes and scanned the limited offerings. "Mr. Hoot, my kind sir, I'd appreciate you making me that ham and cheese sandwich illustrated on this menu. It looks delicious, and I'm starving."

Buddy pulled a package of cold cuts and a mustard jar from the refrigerator, held it to my face, and snarled. "Is this good enough?" The meat wasn't pastrami from Katz's Delicatessen, but the packaging was at least unopened.

"Thanks, that'd be perfect."

Buddy laid two slices of white bread on a plate and started assembling my sandwich. He acted standoffishly, and I knew I'd never get him talking unless I apologized. "I'm sorry for the aggressive way I treated you the other day," I said. "You were right. I had a long talk with Mary Jane Bauerman, and she confirmed your claim. She thought very highly of you back then."

Buddy hung his head. "I'm sorry too for reacting all emotional. You asking questions about Mindy's murder raised those horrible rumors that I had a hand in it. The thought of having to again deal with the townspeople's dirty looks was upsetting."

"I know how tough it is being the old ex-boyfriend," I said. "Nine times out of ten, in cases like Mindy's murder, you'd be the guy walking out handcuffed with a jacket over your head."

"But it's not fair," Buddy said. "A convicted felon is in prison, and yet, people still wonder if I had something to do with the crime. I'm so tired of dealing with innuendo."

"I'm here to help reduce that load, Buddy, by getting to the truth. What can you tell me about you and George Bauerman?"

Buddy finished making my sandwich and slid the plate at me. His mouth sloped to one side. "On the days he was in a rare good mood, George tolerated me, but he made it clear he hated my guts most other times."

I took a bite from the sandwich and, between chews, asked, "Mary Jane told me you were a wonderful listener. What'd you talk about?"

A reddish tint more vibrant than the tomato slice buried in my sandwich swept across Buddy's face. "We talked about stuff, you know. Mary Jane had issues she needed to share."

"Did you call her Mary Jane? That sounds awful familiar for a kid almost two decades younger than the woman."

Buddy bent over the bar and whispered.

"Not at first. You see, I used to go to the house and wait for Mindy to come home from her extracurricular activities. Mary Jane would sit and talk with me. Initially, it was innocent, you know, how's school, what's your best class, stuff like that."

I nodded and took another bite of my sandwich. What Buddy said sounded like standard parent talk.

"It wasn't long before she started sharing more personal stuff. I mean, once she got going, she bent my ear like it was a piece of origami."

"That must've been uncomfortable."

Buddy leaned closer. "Yes, indeed. One day, she confessed to being weary of wearing rags, while Mr. Bauerman gave his money away to every widow and orphan in town."

I cleared my mouth with a sip of the beer. "Yeah, it's never good that the wretched of your community dressed better than you."

Buddy continued. "That's when she insisted I call her Mary Jane. She told me I had a sensitive soul and was the only person who listened to her. Well, she said, me and a man that once stayed at Miss Crumble's lodge years ago."

That comment would've knocked me to the floor if my butt cheeks hadn't locked hard on the stool. Here was another reference to a mysterious traveler. "Holy parmesan, Buddy, you don't say. Did that guy have a name?"

Buddy's shoulders rose around his neck. "She called him Tommy. That's all I ever heard."

That was a boatload of cheap imports, flooding the US and killing manufacturing jobs. It was also a massive non sequitur that I had to fight off until my thoughts cleared. So, Mrs. Bauerman wanted nice things and was attracted to a salesman who stayed at Miss Crumble's place. Kate spoke the truth and the peddler she longed to have as a young woman *had been* seduced by Mary Jane.

"How'd that make you feel, Buddy, being the confidante of your girlfriend's mother?"

"I think Freud might've written a treatise on the subject, so of course, I felt confused."

I bet he did. The same age as the woman's child, and the kid had his ear chewed off hearing about Mary Jane's empty life. I had to wonder who she blamed for the sorry state of her existence. "Did Mrs., uh, Mary Jane, ever indicate that she wanted to leave George?"

Buddy turned away and absentmindedly started to wipe the top of the bar with a rag.

"Well, did she?"

"I know they didn't get along, but she never told me she wanted to leave him."

"Did this Tommy ever return to town? Did Mary Jane ever sneak away for a lover's rendezvous with the guy?"

I didn't think it possible, but the skin on Buddy's cheeks flushed a darker red. "I can't answer that."

"You can't, or you won't?"

"Mary Jane and I had a pact. I promised never to share her secrets if she'd convince Mindy to date only one boy, me."

I chewed another bite from my sandwich while staring into Buddy's ever-darkening face. Sure, he had to keep a promise, but Mary Jane never marked her end of the bargain. I knew that Mindy was swapping spit with other young men back when she supposedly was Buddy's girl. I hesitated to make that point, not wanting to embarrass Buddy and have him shut down. Of course, the man had given me an answer anyway. If Mary Jane never saw Tommy again, why not say so? As a master observer of human nature, I'd read between his promise and the silence, and I wondered what other secrets Buddy carried in his head.

"Okay," I said. "I'll respect your steadfastness, so answer me this instead. Did Mary Jane ever show resentment toward Mindy?"

Buddy's eyes dimmed. "What do you mean?"

"Was Mary Jane ever jealous of her daughter for being young and vivacious, for having a handsome boyfriend like you, stuff like that?"

"Oh no, never," he fired back. "Why would you think such a thing?"

Why? I wouldn't tell Buddy, but I was assembling a grave accusation. Old, lonely, and affection-starved Mary Jane probably resented her pretty young daughter. Maybe she envied her enough to convince a vulnerable boy that Mindy had played him and Buddy should teach her a painful lesson, something brutally sufficient to get the message across.

Yeah, yeah, that's a horrible accusation. How could Nic Knuckles, a champion of decency, consider that a mother would condone the killing of her daughter? It was easy. Such cruelty happens all the time in nature. The herd gets too crowded, so the mother animal kills and eats its young. I saw it on a National Geographic special called *Gross Animal Things We Don't Talk About*.

But I didn't share those ugly thoughts with Buddy. Instead, I said, "As a private investigator, I have to consider every angle and everybody a suspect, whether it is Mary Jane, you, and even *you and Mary Jane.*"

Buddy's eyes grew larger, and I figured he had to be shaking in his boots. Did he think I'd be thrown off the scent when he introduced a guy named Tommy into the equation? Had Buddy believed I'd give up my premise that the old boyfriend always had the strongest motive simply because he made me a sandwich? Poor old Buddy Lee, sitting at the Bauermans' kitchen table waiting for Mindy while Mary Jane fed into his insecurities. Where was Mindy? she'd be asking. Was his girlfriend too busy flirting with Buzz Rockwell to come home or doing the boogie-woogie with John Brown behind the Sheriff's Department? Did she not care that her mother was driving him toward murderous insanity?

"I have to tell you, Mr. Knuckles," Buddy said. "I don't like the way you're looking at me."

I gazed into the mirror behind the bar and saw what he meant. My complexion had lost all color except for a green flush under my eyes.

"I think that meat you used in the sandwich didn't agree with me," I said, my words slipping out on a burp. "Point me to the toilet, could you? I'm gonna be sick."

Chapter Twenty

I t took me almost twenty-four hours to recover from the food poisoning I suffered at the hands of Buddy Lee Hoot. He swore it wasn't his meat and showed me the package's expiration date. It still had a few days left before going rancid, and the sickening bacteria could've been in the mustard, the bread, the cheese, or a dirty glass holding my beer. Just when I thought I'd unfairly tagged Buddy as a prime suspect, the man did something like that. If he had no reservations about poisoning me, why wouldn't he chop off the head of a cheating girlfriend?

I opened the back cover of my notebook where I'd drawn a risk chart, a practice I'd started years ago. Making your living digging up people's secrets earned you a few enemies, who'd want to knock you off if you got too close to exposing their crimes. If I ever met such an untimely demise, the information in my Suspect Chart could shorten an investigation if they knew who I suspected as the possible killer. I saw it as a professional courtesy to the detective assigned to my murder case.

In the first column of my Kleinstadt Suspect Chart, I had the names Molly Spear, Barney Feif, Kate Crumble, and Sandi Fliminsky. The second column listed folks who seemed innocent but had been mentioned in passing as having some involvement—people like Sheriff Brown and the Bauerman duet. The last roll was those who had probable cause and had attempted to harm me. I added Buddy Lee Hoot as my second entry, noting his skill with poisons. Above him was the name Buzz Rockwell, who tried to cut off my hands with a battle axe. If anyone wanted me dead, it was likely one of those two men, which made my next visit more ironic.

A ten-minute walk from Miss Crumble's lodge had me standing in front of All Things Sharp. While I had my fists, feet, and teeth to defend against attackers, I decided to augment my arsenal with a weapon.

I entered the store to a less than enthusiastic greeting from Buzz until I mentioned my need for protection. His mouth exploded into a big smile, and he eagerly pushed an assortment of monstrous blades in front of me. "Any of these axes will send an attacker scampering with their tails between their legs," he said. "You can't go wrong, my friend."

"Those are all impressive, but I need something smaller, a knife I can carry in my pocket."

The smile on Buzz's face wilted into a frown, and he slowly placed a container of pocket knives on the counter. As he slid the box in front of me, I spotted a hint of a tattoo peeking from his right sleeve, and all I could make out was a stylized letter M.

"Here are some perfectly functional knives for slicing an apple or opening an envelope," Buzz said. "They won't be worth much in a fight, however."

I picked out one with a silver handle, which cost twenty-five dollars. Buzz took my cash and handed me the receipt, which I folded and stuffed in my wallet. Some folks might say, "Nic, why buy a knife from one of your top suspects, a guy who almost removed your front paws by dropping an axe?" I'd answer that I felt obligated to support a local merchant. Even though I could've bought the knife fifty percent cheaper online, we small business folks had to hang together. Yeah, I considered myself an endangered small business. With those big tech companies capturing everyone's data and their expertise in artificial intelligence, they would soon sell cheap investigative services online. However, I had more pressing needs than surviving Big Tech's onslaught against my livelihood.

"Now that I'm a loyal customer, Buzz, I hope you feel obligated to answer some more questions."

The man didn't say no, so I pushed on.

"I want to know more about your friendship with Wayne the Drifter. What made the man tick?"

Buzz returned the box of knives under the counter before answering. "I can't say. We were more acquaintances than close friends."

"Were you in the same class at Kleinstadt High?"

"Naw, he said he'd graduated years before, but I suspected he'd dropped out."

"How old was Wayne?"

"He bought us beer, so either he was twenty-one, or else he had a really good fake ID."

That revelation suggested I give Wayne the Drifter a higher profile in my investigation. If he'd buy beer for a sixteen-year-old, he'd probably be morally reprehensible enough to chop off the head of Mindy Bauerman. Nic Knuckles learned long ago that underage drinking was the gateway drug to all serious crime. I didn't know a murderer on death row who hadn't partaken of a cold brewski as a kid.

"So, you and Wayne were drinking buddies, huh? I bet you had a lot in common, being social outcasts as you were."

"No, we were totally different," Buzz said. "I was a loner who lived in a basement, and Wayne was a mysterious transient with no friends."

I disagreed. Two socially inept young men with buried longings came from the same psychological mold. Who knew what they talked about, Mindy, thwarted love, revenge? I gently nudged Buzz to share more because I knew he had more to say. The loners always did.

"Wayne would show up in town, and I'd find him on my front stoop. We'd hang out, play with my axe collection, and get drunk. Once the beer money ran out, he'd be gone."

"Did Wayne have any other acquaintances in Kleinstadt?"

"I assumed so. He'd talk about doing his laundry at a relative's house."

Now, that was what Nic Knuckles was talking about. So, old Wayne *was* local and liked his underwear freshly laundered. Better than him being one of those skinny little sinister creeps riding the interstate highway system and committing hard-to-solve mayhem. They only got caught decades later when a trace of their DNA showed up at another crime scene, and I didn't have that kind of time.

"Did Wayne say who that relative might've been?"

"Naw, I got the impression that he and his family were not that close."

"Did he have a job?"

Buzz chuckled. "Not likely. The beer money came from my pocket. Wayne never seemed to have any."

"Nothing sucks more than a freeloader, am I right?"

Buzz nodded, but his mind seemed busy digging back in time. "You know, once he did show up flushed with cash. It was the day I last saw him, maybe that Monday or Tuesday of Mindy's murder. He came by with a wad of bills bulging in his back pocket."

"Oh, that must've been uncomfortable," I said, recalling the fierce combat I did with an errant seat spring that popped during a cross-country car chase of the notorious swindling nun, Sister Mary Benevolence. "Did Wayne name the source for that sudden cash infusion?"

Buzz shook his head. "Can't say I recall, but he said it was his ticket out of town."

I pulled out my trusty notebook and found the page dedicated to Wayne the Drifter. I wrote down, a local family – yeah, cheapskate - yeah, stole cash– probably.

"Another question on a different topic, Buzz. Since you spent your youth tracking Mindy, I suspect you observed her comings and goings with the fellas."

Buzz smacked his lips. "I watched her all the time because I had lust in my heart, sure," he said. "But don't make me out to be some weird neighbor kid hiding in the bushes."

I, and the rest of humanity, defined weird neighbor kids differently than Buzz, but I'd let him have his delusion. "In those months before Mindy's murder, can you remember the names of the boys who hung around her?"

"She spent time with Buddy, of course. Everyone knew John Brown took her out on Wednesday nights to go dancing. I don't know; you could probably take a look at our old high school yearbook and compile a list of boys who talked her up. Mindy tended to make goo-goo eyes at any man wearing pants."

That comment caused my esophagus to twitch. Something didn't sound right. "I'm curious, Buzz. If Mindy looked at every fella sporting pants, why did she ignore you?"

A tiny hitch pulled under Buzz's right cheek. "I was into wearing kilts at the time."

I smacked my forehead. Holy Camembert, did that kid have one iota of common sense in his head back then? What was he thinking? "Okay, Buzz, moving on. Did you know if Wayne and Mindy ever spent time together?"

Buzz clenched his teeth with that question, and I waited until he unclenched them to follow up. "Well, did you?"

"Yeah," he said, covering his mouth with his hand. "That time he showed up with all that cash, the bastard told me he'd be skipping our scheduled beer and axe mixer. I found out later that he took Mindy to some expensive restaurant to eat lobster."

"How'd that make you feel?"

"I was mad as hell. When we hung out, he made me pay for the beer, and we'd eat *my* taco chips. He finally got some cash, and suddenly, I wasn't good enough for him."

My mind chugged for a minute, processing the idea of young Buzz being treated poorly by his only friend. It reminded Nic Knuckles of when I caught my girl Lucy Long Legs with my friend, Ernst, in a trailer north of Poughkeepsie, singing old minstrels. A man, especially one who couldn't carry a tune, never got over that kind of betrayal.

"Did your friendship with Wayne end that night?" I asked. "What with him being cheap, and then blowing a big payday on Mindy, the girl of your dreams?"

Buzz snapped a reply. "I never saw him again, so yeah, I guess that was the end of it."

"How soon after Wayne's disappearance did Mindy get murdered?"

Rockwell stared off into space. Maybe his mind went back to October 2005 to calculate the days between hearing about Wayne and Mindy dining on shellfish and Mindy never using her mouth to eat again. Yes, that's precisely what he did.

"Two days," he said. "I saw Mindy sneaking out of her house Wednesday night to hook up with Wayne, and she was killed that Friday night."

"That's good to know, my friend, thanks a bundle."

Contrary to Buzz saying he knew little about Wayne, he gave me some good stuff. I whipped out my notebook and jotted down the new information. I now had my first solid data point for the criminal timeline. Wayne had a pile of cash by Tuesday, a date with Mindy on Wednesday, and then he disappeared.

I added an asterisk to my sentence about Wayne vanishing. Just because Buzz never saw him didn't mean the man drifted out of town immediately after his date with Mindy. For all I knew, Wayne might've been lurking in the woods, a sharp implement in his hands, seething over something Mindy did. Maybe he dropped a bundle for dinner, and she left him hot and bothered with nothing more than a good night peck on the cheek.

"There's something bothering me about you that I need cleared up, Buzz," I said. "The court and investigative records and transcripts were very thorough except for one topic. They never addressed the intensity of your one-sided love for Mindy?"

Buzz stuttered, and his eyelids fluttered. "My crush on her wasn't that intense. Molly Spear thought it made for juicier copy, so she was the one pushing it in the newspapers."

"I don't know, Buzz. I have another reliable source telling me you had a serious case of lovesickness back in the day."

"Don't try and make me out to be some sex-crazed freak stalking her. Sheriff Feif quickly determined I was just a lonely neighbor kid, living across the street from a cute girl."

"What about the time when you were seven and got stuck crawling through the Bauerman doggie door?"

"That never happened. Hanlon's defense lawyer did everything he could to paint me as some pervert. It was never anything more than innocent longing on my part."

I reached over and grabbed Buzz's right arm, the one sporting the hint of a tattoo I'd spotted earlier. I pushed the shirt sleeve up beyond his elbow.

"Oh yeah," I said, pointing at the tattoo on his flesh. "If your longing for

Mindy was so innocent, whose name is that?"

Buzz turned his arm into my line of sight. "It says, Mom."

And so, it did. Man, that was uncomfortable.

"I guess you're not so smart after all, Mr. Big City Investigator." Buzz pulled away from me. "Now take your purchase and leave my store."

Nic Knuckles may get stumped, but I'm never baffled for long. My brain cranked and spun and dug deep into the cognitive functional sector. Sandi had been confident of Buzz's crush on Mindy and swore it bordered on pathological. Buddy hated the guy because he claimed Buzz enjoyed being labeled Mindy's sick secret admirer during the trial. What was I missing?

"Wait, wait," I said. "The left hand is closest to the heart." I grabbed Buzz's left arm, and he pulled back, trying to wiggle away. I smiled and held his arm fast before slowly sliding up the shirt sleeve, exposing his forearm. There it was, inscribed in his flesh, a large red heart encompassing the words, *Forever Mindy Bauermon.*

"You know Buzz, you misspelled her last name."

Buzz jerked his arm away from me. "Yeah, I know, but I was fourteen when I got it, and the only tat artist who'd do it was a newbie. I didn't want to ruin his self-confidence by pointing out his error, so I let it pass."

"Wow, that *was* nice of you."

Buzz pulled down his shirt sleeve to his wrist. "I knew even back then that you couldn't make it in life unless people show a little kindness from time to time."

The man's last line made so much sense it repeated in my head. No one made it in life without receiving occasional kindness, empathy, or understanding. Nic Knuckles sure understood. How many times had a stranger given me the benefit of the doubt? Unfortunately, so few they could be counted on one hand.

"You've given me much to think about, Mr. Rockwell."

Buzz looked away as he mindlessly shuffled some inventory on a shelf. His kindness toward the young tattoo artist indicated a good heart, and I may reconsider my opinion of him. I could understand his longing for a woman from afar. The farther my longings were, the better for all involved.

But that didn't mean I liked being alone. You could put the most self-assured man on a deserted island, and he'd soon be talking to volleyballs. That's a documented fact.

"All those years ago, Buzz, did Mindy ever give you the time of day?"

The man shook his head. "Naw, never even a look of disgust."

"That must've hurt," I said. "Day after day of seeing her across the street, in school, walking with Buddy, or flirting with some other boy."

"Yeah, it ate away my heart like an acid on meatloaf."

I reached out my right hand and squeezed his shoulder. "How'd you take it, man? How'd you deal with that relentless disappointment?"

Buzz dropped his head, too ashamed to look me in the face. "I'd retreat to my basement bedroom with my sharpening stones and work my axes to a perfect edge. Oh yeah, I'd eat a whole package of jalapeno-infused taco chips."

A chill slipped up my spine at the thought of young Buzz Rockwell, seething with resentment, in a cold basement bedroom with one bare bulb casting a yellow light over him and his axe collection. I had to wonder. Had there been a limit to what kindhearted Buzz could take? What if on that October day in 2005, when Mindy was walking through Stickerbacker's Woods, Buzz ran out of jalapeno-infused taco chips? Did he find solace with plain potato chips, or did the young man with a trampled heart give in to his rage?

"I have to tell you, Buzz. I don't know how you took it all those years."

"It was tough, but I got good at mastering my feelings."

"You sure you never acted out against Mindy, you know, maybe pranked her by dipping her braids into an inkwell?"

"What are you talking about?" Buzz asked. "What's an inkwell?"

"Ah ha, here is what I mean. I think your mind compartmentalized your feelings toward Mindy. There was the good Buzz, who kept everything inside and only has memories of the basement, the axes, and the taco chips. What if there was another Buzz, an evil Buzz who acted on your rage? Maybe that's why you don't recall dipping her braids into an inkwell. Maybe that's why you won't remember something obscener, like chopping off Mindy's head."

The eyebrows on Buzz's face collapsed upon themselves into one giant wooly worm.

"Do you think I'm some kind of Dr. Jekyll who doesn't remember the crimes committed by Mr. Hyde? Are you nuts?"

Being called nuts was insulting to most folks, but as any creative investigator knew, nutty ideas sometimes led to brilliant solutions. I folded my arms and gave Buzz a cold, hard stare. When I finished laying out my insight, let's see who'd be calling who nuts.

"Let's say we *are* dealing with a Dr. Jekyll and Mr. Hyde situation here. You're the good doctor. A kind and patient man who internalized his anger. But what if, after an extra-strong whiff of the axe cleaning fluid, your mind set free the Mr. Hyde buried in your heart?"

Buzz's reaction threw me off. He laughed so hard he bent at his waist.

"Why do you think that's so hilarious?" I asked. "I'm accusing you of having a multiple-personality disorder with a homicidal overlay."

In between wheezes, Buzz answered. "If you'd read everything that had been written on the Mindy Bauerman case, you'd seen my interviews with multiple criminal forensic psychiatrists."

Yikes, Buzz had me there. I'd skimmed that part of the report, and I guessed my horrible experience when I was eight with a shrink named Dr. Von Noodle, and his electroshock teddy bear scared me off from reading in detail.

"I had my mind scrubbed by one of the most eminent head doctors in the world," Buzz said, "and she found no sign of mental illness. Yes, I was classified as profoundly quirky, but I was deemed harmless."

A good investigator had to be quick on their feet, and I was, countering Buzz's point and stuffing his laughter like sour cream in a hot baked potato. "Perhaps those psychiatrists were correct, and you didn't have a Mr. Hyde lurking inside you. What if there was someone in your life who already had the criminal impulses? What if your Mr. Hyde was another person altogether, who went by the name of Wayne?"

Sometimes Nic Knuckles got carried away with his nutty ideas, and people erupted in anger. That's what Buzz did, screaming at me. "That's it. Get out of my store, or I'll take your cheap little pocket knife and cut out your tongue."

Nic Knuckles liked the idea that his newly purchased knife was sharp enough to cut out someone's tongue, but I didn't want it to be mine. I ran from the store, and only after I stopped a block away to catch my wind did I pull out my notebook. I jotted down everything important Buzz had shared with me. He'd been a cornucopia of information about his past, Mindy's dating life, and his relationship with Wayne. Unfortunately, our interaction generated even more questions, like how much was Wayne's fat cash haul, and why'd Sandi Fliminsky never say anything about Mindy's hot date with the drifter? Indeed, I suspected Mindy would've talked about it with her best friend before falling asleep that night.

I turned to the back inside cover of my notebook and added another name to my likely suspect column. Flushing out the background on Wayne the Drifter gave me reasons to make him one of my three prime suspects, bumping him ahead of Buzz Rockwell but behind Buddy Lee Hoot. While I'd never met him, I figured any man who enjoyed picking out a live lobster from a tank and watching it dropped in boiling water might kill someone without thinking twice.

Chapter Twenty-One

I closed my trusty notebook after recording the highlights of my Buzz Rockwell interrogation. He'd given me some juicy leads that I was anxious to bite into. Hustling to my car, I dropped into the driver's seat and fired up the engine. My next visit would be with Sandi Fliminsky to find out why she never dished about Mindy's hot date with Wayne. Considering he was at least five years older and loaded with cash, how could she not know about Mindy's crackling bit of news? Something wasn't right about that omission, and I was determined to find out the problem.

I made it down the street about a block when the sirens of a law enforcement vehicle screeched in my ears. Looking into the rearview mirror, I saw that big lug, John Brown, inside the gold and tan cruiser of the Kleinstadt Sheriff's Department. I turned off my car's engine, figuring it'd be a lengthy detainment.

"How you doing this fine afternoon, Sheriff Brown?" I said after rolling down the car window. "Can I assume you've stopped to wish me a good day?"

Brownie got right to the point. "I saw you coming out of Buzz Rockwell's establishment. You know he's had a problem with shoplifters."

"That's not good," I said. "I imagine his monthly sales are slimmer than someone selling kale salad at a Donut Festival."

Sheriff Brown tilted his head menacingly and snarled. "Step out of the car, Knuckles, and spread 'em," I complied, and Brownie roughly patted me down, stopping when I felt him pull from my coat pocket my recent purchase.

"Why do you have a weapon on you?" he asked.

I didn't want to make his day by admitting I'd purchased the knife for protection, so I gave him an answer with some truth. "I'm trying to pump cash into the local economy, so I spent a little money at Rockwell's place. Is that a crime?"

"It is if you don't have a receipt."

"In my wallet, Sheriff. It's in between my Hair Booster membership and my proctologist's loyalty card."

I was irritated that Brownie didn't bother to look because I wanted the pleasure of shutting up the obnoxious town sheriff. He handed me the knife and growled. "Get in your car, drive back to Miss Crumble's lodge, pack your belongings, and get the next flight to New York."

As tempting as it was to return to the Big Apple, I had a job, and I couldn't let the sheriff think he intimidated me. Nic Knuckles learned as a child that if you didn't confront a bully, your nana took your lunch money for the rest of your life. I slid my tuchus into the car and started the engine, but before I put the transmission into drive, I came at Brownie with a question.

"Did you know Mindy went on a date with a stranger named Wayne a few days before she was murdered? Did Barney Feif ever check that out?"

Sheriff Brown blew half the chew from his mouth onto the side of my car. "I keep telling you, Knuckles, that case is closed. Timmy Hanlon is serving a life sentence for the crime, and no amount of your troublemaking will change any of that."

I wanted to suggest the sheriff not underestimate Nic Knuckle's trouble-making skills but figured I'd only provoke him. Why encourage Brownie to make my life more miserable? A different approach was needed, so I appealed to his sense of professionalism.

"You know, Sheriff, the sooner you help me, the quicker I'd finish my investigation and leave town. Let's work together for a change, huh? What do you say, big fella?"

John Brown pushed out his dip-stained bottom lip. "I have no interest in working with you on anything."

"Ahhhh geez, John, that hurts my feelings." Brownie pointed his stubby finger at my face. "More than your feelings will hurt if you keep sticking that nose into the Bauerman case."

I didn't want to throw gas on a smoldering fire, but I had to counter the sheriff's aggressive response with one of my own, or he'd eat me alive.

"Speaking of hurt feelings, John, how angry were you with Mindy, when she skipped your last Wednesday night dance date?"

"Shut up, Knuckles."

"You must have been coo-coo with rage when you learned she'd gone out with a waster named Wayne?"

Thank God the door window quickly closed, or else the sheriff's hand would've pulled me out of the car by my throat. He screamed. "I'm telling you, Knuckles, get your ass out of Kleinstadt before something bad happens."

"Thank you, Sheriff Brown," I said. "You have a nice day serving and protecting."

I pulled away, and in the rearview mirror, I swore I saw heat waves coming off Brownie's head. I'd never seen him so angry, and I wondered why. His over-the-top reaction to my questions about Mindy made me think protecting Barney Feif was secondary to keeping his long-ago relationship with Mindy under wraps. The man was hiding something.

Once I got out of the sight of Sheriff Brown, I pulled to a stop and grabbed my notebook. Too many thoughts were competing for the limited memory space in my brain, and I wanted to write down all my concerns before they drifted off. My first scribbling was a question. If Brownie wished to use his fists on me because I asked sensitive questions about Mindy, did a younger John Brown have even less restraint? How did he behave when Mindy stood him up? Did he sulk, yell, threaten harm, or worse? What kind of man was I dealing with here?

Any good investigator knows that an angry man with a secret is dangerous. As much as I hated to think it, I might have to move John Brown into my prime suspect's column, joining Buddy, Buzz, and Wayne. However, I still had too many questions about the man to feel comfortable doing so. I'd have to consult the town gossip, Kate Crumble, to fill in the missing pieces. But first, I'd visit Sandi Fliminsky and get the details about Mindy's date with Wayne the Drifter. How she'd forgotten to tell me about the event was curious. That night might be crucial to determining who, what, and why Mindy Bauerman met an early demise.

Chapter Twenty-Two

I strolled up the walkway to Sandi Fliminsky's house, admiring the flower beds in front of the porch, now overflowing with recently planted bright red, yellow, and orange flowers. You'd think she'd be sick of plants and trees after working all day fixing other people's landscapes. I guessed the woman loved what she did for a living, and I could relate since there was nothing better for me than solving crimes and administering justice.

Hopping onto the porch, I rapped my knuckles against the front door. I noted the swing hanging from the ceiling and empty pots off in a corner. A circular lay at my feet, so I picked it up. The Speedi Food Mart ad hyping prunes on sale grabbed my attention. A bucket for ten bucks, huh? I might have to stop by and pick some up. A private investigator had to be quick and not risk being bogged down by constipation. I grimaced, thinking about when I was left in the dust chasing the Mongolian art thief, Picasso McGillicutty.

Pounding again on the door, I shouted, "Hello, Sandi, it's me, Nic Knuckles."

I swore I heard a television broadcast, so I stepped over to the front window and peeked between the blinds. The living room was dark, and the television in the corner was off.

I left the porch and walked around to the rear of the house to see if Sandi was there. Her truck was in the driveway, so I figured she must've been home. I moved to the back door, hammering on it and calling out Sandi's name. Again, I failed to raise a response, and I wondered if she could have ridden to the work site with one of her employees. A friend might've picked her up for a long lunch, or the woman could've gone for a walk. While there were many reasons why Sandi might not be home, something felt wrong. I couldn't explain it, but my supernatural sixth sense was tingling.

I returned to my car, and before I crawled in, I saw the red-headed older gal who lived across the street. She was hiding behind a tree, giving me a snarky look. "Excuse me, madam," I called out. "Do you know if Miss Fliminsky's home?"

"If she was home, she'd answer the door, numbnuts."

Spending one week in Kleinstadt and experiencing the general unfriendliness of the populace, the neighbor lady's hostility didn't bother me anymore. I'd been thrown for a loop if she'd acted friendly.

"You have a nice day," I said. The woman's face screwed itself into such a knot that you'd thought I'd told her to take a flying leap off the Verrazzano-Narrows. She cried, "Don't tell me what to do, you pervert."

I grumbled and got into my car, thinking what a wasted trip it had been. All I got out of it was a tender fist from pounding doors and a nasty comment about my character from a crazy neighbor. I started the engine and shifted into drive, and at that instant, I felt an electrical current fire up and down my spine. My supernatural sixth sense alerted me to a stalker closely following my movements. I jerked my head back toward Sandi's house, my eyeballs rolling across the exterior, expecting to see someone in the windows. Nope, I saw nothing, no one looking at me, no shadows moving across the glass, absolutely nothing. Damn, why did I have such a useless supernatural sixth sense?

Chapter Twenty-Three

It was late in the afternoon when I found Kate Crumble in a rocker on the lodge's porch, tugging the ear of a black and white cat she called Rudy. Both animals seemed docile, but I was wary, knowing the nature of each species. Nic Knuckles didn't want to exit the conversation with bloody scratches on my face after setting off one or both.

I parked my big behind on the porch railing facing the woman. "I need some information about your sheriff," I said. "The man implies he'll use his superior size to get me out of town, and I want to know how seriously I should take his threats."

"It depends on how uncomfortable you make Sheriff Brown feel."

"No doubt, but do you have any insight as to why he's taking my investigation so personally?"

Kate smiled and turned her gaze down at the cat. "You have to understand how important the old sheriff, Barney Feif, was to John."

"I'm listening."

Kate took in a deep breath and slowly spun the story. Brownie grew up on a farm outside of town. His parents, Mike and Jean, were ordinary, hardworking farm folks who scraped together a decent living until Mr. Brown suffered the consequences of getting between a randy bull and a receptive heifer. Soon after the funeral, Jean gave up the farm and moved the family into Kleinstadt. It was a hand-to-mouth existence for the woman and her ten-year-old son.

"So, I assume young John lacked a proper role model and got into trouble," I said, hoping to move Kate's monologue along. "He probably got picked up by Feif for shoplifting, and the old sheriff saw something good in the troubled lad. Feif then turned him around, you know, groomed him into the law-abiding citizen we all see today."

Kate giggled. "Nice thinking, Nic, but John's story is far more complicated." She rubbed the side of the cat's face, and the animal purred loud enough to be heard from across the porch. While the kitty was happy, I wasn't. Good Lord, Kate's meandering Hoosier style of storytelling would eat up the rest of my day. If Nic Knuckles was in imminent danger at the hands of the sheriff, I wanted to know sooner rather than later. I might have to return to All Things Sharp and upgrade my personal protection.

"Is there more to this tale?" I asked. "Or do I have to feed you another box of chocolates?"

Kate's smile stretched wide as her cheeks flushed. Miss Crumble wasn't interested in rehashing *that* afternoon. Remembering how she ended up with her head in the wastebasket made me want to forget it, as well. I only hoped her sober lips would reveal as much as her drunken cocoa-covered ones.

"Yes, yes, there's more," she said, holding the cat up and cooing. "Rudy, tell Mr. Knuckles to keep his shorts on."

I shot back, "My shorts aren't going anywhere."

Kate smiled at the cat and winked. "We'll see about that, won't we, Rudy?"

The rational part of my brain reminded me that we were outside in broad daylight, and the woman wouldn't dare make a move. Nonetheless, my animal brain calculated how far off the ground I sat and whether a backflip would aid my escape or break my neck. Fortunately, neither scenario played out as Kate returned to the topic.

"Okay, back to John Brown and Barney Feif," she said. "You know how with any group of children, there's the one who's naturally decent, while the other kids are messy and full of trouble?"

Of course, I knew what she meant, but I didn't feel like talking about my siblings, those hateful little cretins. I just nodded.

"Well, John was the good one, and he always had a strong sense of right and wrong."

"So, you saying Feif didn't turn Brownie toward the light? That he already bathed in it."

"Yes, you got it. The old sheriff and John first connected when the boy tried to issue a citizen's arrest of Feif for illegally parking his cruiser."

"Sounds like even as a kid, Brownie could be pretty obnoxious over any perceived flaunting of the rules."

"Yes, and at first, Feif found him to be a pest. But he soon grew impressed with the kid's deep-seated integrity, and he took the fatherless boy under his wing."

"That's a sweet story," I said, my response thickly sarcastic. Nic Knuckles had few emotional triggers, and hearing about men behaving as good fathers was one. The only thing my old man took under his wing was fast women and slow ponies. Fortunately, Kate resumed talking and pulled my attention from the cesspool of my paternity.

"When John hit high school, Feif made him an unpaid intern. He had a uniform custom fitted for him and let him go on ride-alongs, you know, the whole nine yards."

"The *whole* nine yards," I asked as my voice climbed to its highest octave. "Even letting him be part of the Mindy Bauerman murder investigation?"

"Yeah, the first real-life law enforcement experience he got was Mindy's murder."

"That's a lot for a kid to handle," I said. "He had to be affected in some way."

Kate shrugged and shared how Feif was reportedly impressed with the young man's cold-pressed nerves. "It was John who found Mindy's corpse in Stickerbacker's Woods. Feif said the adults in the search party doubled over puking their manhood, while John stoically recorded the physical evidence."

That impressed me, but not in a good way. The only people I knew who wouldn't be bothered seeing decapitated corpses were sociopaths like Sawbones Jones, the demented oral surgeon, or Smokey Joe, the Diabolical Furnace Repairman. The more I heard about the cold-blooded nature of young John Brown, the higher up he rose on my prime suspect list.

Kate continued spilling. "John went to the police academy after finishing

95

high school. Unlike most young people who left Kleinstadt, he returned home. Feif hired him on as a deputy and when the old sheriff retired, John was elected to replace him. No one has run against him since."

I didn't particularly appreciate hearing that, either. In my years interacting with law enforcement, I'd learned that a sheriff with a secure job tended to interpret the law as they saw fit. Nic Knuckles, however, was dedicated to that lady in the nightgown. The one with the bandana tied over her eyes, holding the scales high above her head. Maybe Brownie and I were both for law and order, but he preferred order, while I took the law side.

"What can you tell me about John and Mindy Bauerman?" I asked. "Other than him finding her corpse?"

Kate pulled on Rudy's ears. "I think they were in the same high school class."

"Did you ever hear of a romantic relationship between the two?"

"Why would I hear something like that? I was busy running the lodge."

I threw out a half-baked reason for why she might know about it. "I've learned that the town's grapevine is quite adept at sharing the local news. As one of the community's communications leaders, I just thought you might've picked up on it."

Kate's chalky complexion slipped into a darker, unfriendly-looking hue. "I can't believe you'd ask me something like that, knowing my romantic heartbreak. Why would I care about a couple of teenagers while still grieving over my lost love?"

"Sorry, Kate," I said. "I forgot we all grieve differently." What I was thinking, however, wasn't as discreet. Good Lord, woman, I wanted to shout; you got dumped by a traveling salesman fifteen years before the Bauerman murder. How long did you need to get over it? Nic Knuckles was like a rubber ball regarding his busted romances. After my heart got stomped, I'd bounce back into the dating scene within a week. I guessed developing resilience was the bright side of being frequently cheated on by my girlfriends.

Figuring Kate was shutting down, I slipped off the railing and slowly moved toward the front door. "I'll leave you and your kitty alone to entertain each other, and thanks for the background on John Brown."

Miss Crumble and Rudy's eyes followed me as I moved away. I wasn't sure which of them might pounce first, so I jumped and ran into the lodge. Once back in my room, I kicked off my shoes and fell atop the bed. Updating the inside cover of my notebook, Sheriff John Brown climbed a few places on my suspect ranking, and while I once thought Brownie was too slow and rigid to be dangerous, now I believed differently. The man might be like a crocodile with a tiny, reptilian brain, but it didn't mean it couldn't chew an arm off or, in Mindy's case, a head. After all, young Brownie did find Mindy's body. Maybe he knew where to look?

Chapter Twenty-Four

After a good night's sleep and a full measure of Miss Crumble's gravy and biscuit breakfast, I needed some morning exercise. Fortunately, my first interview of the day was walkable from the lodge. The Kleinstadt's Auto Emporium stood on the corner of two quiet streets, and I wondered how the proprietor sold any vehicles in such an isolated location. No customers competed with me for attention, and I quickly entered the red-roof shed that constituted a sales office. Sitting behind a gray metal desk was the owner, George Bauerman.

"Good day, George. Do you have a minute?"

Typically, when Nic Knuckles strolled into a room and asked, in a gravelly voice, if the other person had a minute, arched eyebrows over quizzical eyes greeted him. Not with George that morning. Unlike my first meeting with him, the man smiled and pushed a meaty hand toward me. "Sure, Mr. Knuckles, what can I do for you?"

My surprise lasted but a second when I realized what was going on. It was the old used car salesman's fake grin and hardy handshake routine. What was wrong with that guy? Did he think Nic Knuckles had never bought a previously owned automobile? Did he not know I've purchased an old Ford Pinto, a used AMC Pacer, and three finicky British sports cars? No matter how hard he pitched, I *would not* leave that lot in one of his finely curated automobiles.

"I'd like to ask you some questions about your daughter," I said. "You good with that?"

George nodded his bald head. "Shoot."

"What sort of relationship did you have with Mindy?"

"Typical for that age, I guess. I grunted at her, and she huffed and slammed doors."

"As I've talked to people, it's clear to me that Mindy attracted the boys like flies on an August roadkill. How'd you feel about that?"

George's smile morphed into a thin line and vibrated at the corners. "I didn't care for the boys she attracted."

"I've met her old boyfriend, Buddy Lee Hoot. I don't know what he was like as a kid, but he seems harmless."

The jowls on Bauerman's face vibrated ever so slightly as if he were a seismometer picking up an earthquake deep inside the planet. "You're correct that you don't know what he was like as a kid."

"I heard that he and your wife were close. Was there any truth to that?"

George went quiet, and the trembling moved from his face to his shoulders. What seemed like a minute passed, and then he spoke. "He made a pest of himself, hanging around my house and eating my food. Mary Jane found him annoying. She didn't like him."

I pulled out my notebook and pencil and scribbled that comment, noting it contradicted what Mary Jane and Buddy, both told me. If his wife's affection for Buddy fooled old George, let's see if he was also clueless about Buzz Rockwell's interest in his daughter.

"I understand the boy that lived across the street had the hots for Mindy. The kid named Buzz."

George's cheeks swelled, and he blinked several times before he answered. "I wouldn't know."

My scratching on the notepaper was the only sound in the room as I recorded George's physical reaction when claiming ignorance of Buzz coveting his daughter. I finished writing and asked another question that I was certain would start George oscillating.

"Did Mindy like to dance?"

Bauerman slowly rotated his head before growling. "Yes, she did."

"Did she ever go out dancing on Wednesday nights with a young man named John Brown?"

The window of the sales shed rattled as George sucked in enough air to inflate a dirigible. He slowly exhaled. "That would've been impossible. I gave Mary Jane and Mindy explicit instructions to stay inside the house on nights I was away."

A lot was going on underneath George Bauerman's snout. As far as I knew, Mindy and John were tapping their heels every Wednesday night for the last three months of her life.

"Where were you that you couldn't guard the hen house, as I'm sure they like to say here in Indiana?"

"I was out doing the Lord's work. I led a twelve-hour prayer service at my church on Wednesday and Friday nights. We prayed from sundown to sun up."

"Does the name, Wayne, as in Wayne the Drifter, ring a bell?"

"If he didn't attend my church, I never heard of him."

George seemed to have all the answers to my questions about the boys in Mindy's life, so I mixed it up. Let's see how he'd respond to a sensitive personal question straight out of the left field. "One more question for you: did you ever do business with a salesman named Tommy Lyle?"

At first, I thought Bauerman's body had been taken hold by some demon because his eyes flashed and his nostrils flared. I braced for a revelatory blowout, a blazing scream, a colossal release of pent-up rage. How else could he react to my subtle yet pointed attack on his masculinity and Mindy's paternity?

"Can I interest you in a convertible, Mr. Knuckles," George blurted out, the sweat sliming his forehead, "I have a beauty on the lot that has less than fifty thousand miles on it."

I sucked on my teeth and shook my head. "I don't think so."

"I'll include the undercoating."

I stood in awe of the man's self-restraint. His desperation to contain his emotions *and* sell me a car was a marvel. "No, George, I prefer riding the subway when I'm home."

George countered. "I think I can reduce the asking price by a thousand dollars, if you take it today."

CHAPTER TWENTY-FOUR

"That's tempting, and I'll think about it, but not now."

I turned and walked out of the sales shed, and the rush of air from a door slamming swept over me. George's answers to my questions pumped up my suspicion of him. He claimed his daughter didn't go dancing with John Brown when everyone in town knew she did, and George swore ignorance of Buzz Rockwell's widely known crush on Mindy. And how could he say Buddy was a no-good bum when the poor boy put up with Mary Jane's blathering?

Toeing the line the Almighty put down was a heavy burden for any person, and I wondered if such high standards broke George Bauerman. When your daughter ran the streets, and your wife wanted Manolo Blahnik on her feet, maybe you could no longer look the other way before you reacted. As I witnessed only minutes before, you push a tightly coiled man like George too hard, and he'd get dangerously emotional. Apply more pressure, and he might lose all restraint and kill someone. At a minimum, he'd sell them a used car at a great price.

After leaving Kleinstadt's Auto Emporium, I walked over to Buddy's Tavern to start my second interview of the day. I discovered the opening time wasn't until eleven o'clock, but when I looked through the small window on the front door, I found Buddy inside. I pounded on the door and yelled at him to open up.

"I'm closed," he shouted back.

"All I need is a minute of your time."

Buddy pulled open the door and stuck out his face. He complained that his patrons wondered why Nic Knuckles was always in his tavern, asking questions about an old murder case. People gave him looks of suspicion like they did fifteen years ago, and he told me to stay out of his bar.

"I'm sorry, Buddy, but I just need a few minutes."

"Go away, Knuckles."

I reminded Buddy of my near-death experience eating lunch at his joint and how I didn't report him to the County Health Department. He chewed the inside of his mouth before conceding that he owed me a favor in return.

"I don't want to feed the town's gossip machinery," he said. "Meet me at my apartment tomorrow morning, about nine."

I agreed and stepped away as Buddy slammed shut the door and reset the deadbolt. I had no problem compromising, but I had the rest of the day with no one to interview. With so much free time, I'd most likely get harassed by Sheriff Brown, cornered by Kate Crumble, or buy too many high-caloric, packaged snacks from the Speedi Food Mart. Luckily, after wandering two blocks down the street, I saw the County Court House, a limestone-fronted structure built in the neo-Greek classic design. My attention moved to the cornerstone and its date: 1888. I had to think such an old building housed a motherlode of governmental and legal records. As a believer that a good investigator always needed more background on a community, I approached the first woman behind a desk who exuded authority.

"Hello there," I said. "Any chance I can kill the day digging through your local government regulations and records?"

Her eyes narrowed, and she leaned toward me. "Oh, you're that weaselly private eye who's snooping around town."

Knowing that the bit players in a murder investigation often provide the most important tip, I turned on my charm. "Yes, I'm Nic Knuckles, and it's a pleasure to meet you."

The woman smiled and introduced herself as Grace, a rock-solid midwestern name if there ever was one. "Why would you want to sit in a dank basement and page through moldy records?" she asked.

"I'm a seeker of the hidden clues, the misplaced tip, the lost evidence that might help solve a fifteen-year-old murder."

The woman rolled her eyes and jerked a thumb at the door behind her. "Okay, Nic Knuckles, knock yourself out."

Chapter Twenty-Five

I arrived that next morning at Buddy's apartment at the agreed-upon time of nine o'clock. Finding his domicile was easy because it was up the side stairs of the tavern. Poor man, living in a small town wasn't enough—he kept his world even tinier by residing above where he worked.

My previous day spent in the mustiness of the County Court House basement was less fruitful than I had hoped. I'd discovered some exciting trivia, however. The community's animal control regulations made dressing up pigs on Sunday illegal. Did it mean swine wore clothes the other six days of the week? I'd be looking for piggies in pantsuits to decide, but I had an important meeting at the moment with Buddy.

"Good morning, sunshine," I said after a disheveled Buddy opened the door. I pushed past him, cheerily announcing, "I brought some coffee and doughnuts that the Speedi Food Mart had on sale."

Buddy took the coffee and poured in creamer, and I charged ahead with my questioning as he stirred the muddy mix. "During that last year with Mindy, were you aware she went out dancing with John Brown?"

Buddy drew in a deep breath. "Not at first. She told me she needed alone time on Wednesday nights to study for a geography exam."

"When did you suspect she was pulling your leg?"

"When she gave a class report holding a globe sideways and insisting Antarctica was called the East Pole. After that, I doubted she was doing extra bookwork."

"How'd you find out it was John Brown?"

"I waited outside her house the following Wednesday night. About eight o'clock, her bedroom light went off; the window went up, and out climbed Mindy."

Buddy told me how he followed his girlfriend to the street corner where a red convertible waited. The girl hopped inside the car and gave the driver a big smooch.

"And the driver was John Brown, I'm guessing," I said.

"Yeah, Kleinstadt's future sheriff."

"Did you tell Mr. and Mrs. Bauerman about what you saw?"

Buddy snorted. "I knew George would go ballistic if he found out, and as much as I'd enjoy watching that, I didn't want Mindy to get in trouble."

"What about the chatterbox, Mary Jane?"

"Actually, I did tell her, and I immediately regretted saying anything."

Buddy paused, bit into a donut, took one chew, and spat it onto his open hand. "You might get better information from me if you spent a little more on the pastries."

I apologized to him for the poor quality incentive. I knew those donuts would taste terrible when I picked them out, but I couldn't pass up a six-for-a-dollar promotion.

"How'd Mary Jane react to the news her daughter was out dancing the night away?"

"Not very well," Buddy said. "The next week, she threw out Mindy's best party shoes to keep her from going out. They fought in front of me, and I heard mean things said by both."

Buddy sipped from his coffee cup, and his eyes watered. "Good Lord, that's the worst coffee I've ever tasted."

He should try a cup offered at The Next to Last Supper if he thought the Speedi Food Mart brew tasted horrible. But I wasn't there to share tips on caffeinated breakfast drinks. "What was said between Mindy and her mother that sounded so terrible?"

"Oh, the usual stuff mothers say to their daughters when they're fighting. I hate you, you're a tramp, and I wish you'd never been born."

"Ouch. How'd Mindy respond?"

"Mindy shut her mother up when she said she didn't need those crappy old shoes. She said she'd get fancy ones from someone who loved her."

"Whoa, how'd Mary Jane handle that comeback?"

Buddy hunched over. "Her face got all fiery red, and she told me to leave the house. I heard nothing else other than the front door slamming behind me."

I shuddered, envisioning what might've gone on behind closed doors between the two women. When my angry mother entered my bedroom with a belt in her hand, I wanted the door wide open. I learned the hard way as a teenager that the bedroom window was too small to use as an escape.

"Did Mindy ever tell you what happened?"

"Yeah, that night she called and said she hated her parents and wanted to run away."

"Did she ask you to go with her?" I wished I could've pulled back that question when I saw Buddy's mouth quivering. "No, she never suggested I run away with her."

Ah gee, poor Buddy. Mindy never gave him a chance to ruin his life by hitting the road with her as a teenage runaway.

"How about her father? Did he learn about Mindy's threat to get new shoes from some stranger?"

Buddy shook his head. "I doubt it. Mindy and her mother were both pretty scared of George."

"That's interesting," I said. "George told me he and Mindy had a fairly typical father-daughter relationship."

"I don't know what his definition of a typical relationship is, but once Mindy acted uppity with him, and he told her that if she ever misbehaved again, he'd cut her, cut her bad."

"Cut her as in, cut her off from her allowance, or cut her out of the loop, or cut her off at the pass?"

Buddy raised his palms toward the ceiling. "I assumed something harsher."

"Like maybe chopping off her head?"

Buddy's eyes widened. "I don't know, but whatever he meant, Mindy was terrified of him."

So, Mindy was scared her dad might cut her up, huh? If Buddy knew about the threats, that could be another reason George hated him. First, his wife confided her unhappiness, and then his daughter shared her fears. George must've felt that if anyone in town knew the Bauerman family secrets, it'd be Buddy Lee Hoot.

"Do you feel John Brown would have bought Mindy those shoes? He did have an incentive."

Buddy shook his head. "John had trouble putting his shoes on the correct feet. I doubted he knew where to buy fancy women's footwear."

"Mindy said it was someone who loved her, right?"

"Yeah."

"Was it you?"

The man's face flushed so hot I half expected the coffee in his hand to start boiling. He looked away and mumbled. "I wouldn't know where to get fancy shoes either."

Buddy was so uncomfortable that he mindlessly took a bite from the tasteless dried donut and washed it down with the bitter coffee. I'd better move to another question before he made himself sick.

"Can you recall when Mindy got those new shoes?" I asked.

"I'm sure it was the week of her murder."

"That's awfully specific for something that happened fifteen years ago."

Buddy's focus drifted into his coffee cup. "Yeah, I'm positive. The last time I saw Mindy was when she walked out of Algebra class and she was wearing dirty sneakers. When I saw her in the casket at her funeral, a shiny new pair of fancy shoes were on her feet."

I closed up my notebook and thanked Buddy for his answers. I offered to take the refreshments I'd brought and dump them, but he shook me off. He thought the coffee might be strong enough to clear the clog in his shower drain.

I climbed down the stairs from Buddy's apartment, feeling good about the visit. I'd gotten all but one of my questions answered, and that one I'd purposely held back. Knowing how much Buddy hated Buzz Rockwell, I couldn't suggest Buzz was the other young man who could've bought Mindy new shoes. The guy had built an impressive axe collection at the time, so he knew how things were bought and sold. What if Mindy, unbeknownst to anyone, played upon poor Buzz's infatuation and got him to purchase a new pair of shoes for her?

Maybe Buzz Rockwell was more than an axe geek hiding in the bushes. I wouldn't rule that out. Not with so many questions still unanswered.

Chapter Twenty-Six

I left Buddy Lee Hoot more determined than ever to visit Sandi Fliminsky. I had grown desperate to learn the details of Mindy's dinner date with Wayne the Drifter, and Sandi remained my best possible source. I needed her phone number so I could call and avoid wasting another trip if she wasn't going to be home. The fact that Kleinstadt still needed to get in step with the digital telecommunication revolution proved to be a blessing. Miss Crumble had an old-fashioned paper phone book, and I located the Fliminsky number. I gave the woman a buzz and got an answering machine. The darn thing beeped off after two seconds, making it hard to complete a message. Sandi didn't want people leaving her voicemail either by design or incompetence.

Not that such an inconvenience would stop Nic Knuckles from letting her know I needed to see her. It took me a dozen calls and a dozen one-word messages, but I communicated with her. Sandi. Nic. Knuckles. Must. See. You. About. Mindy. And. Wayne's. Dinner. Date.

Noon rolled around, and I still had yet to get a returned call from Miss Fliminsky. With my patience shot, I hopped in my car and drove by Sandi's house, finding her yellow pick-up truck in the drive. It seemed highly unlikely the woman would've been out again without her vehicle.

I drove around the corner and parked at the end of the block so Sandi wouldn't see me coming. With the skills of a phantom, I edged my way between the houses and fences. My extensive training in the art of stealth paid off as I approached undetected within twenty feet of Sandi's front door. Then the red-headed older woman across the street stormed from her house, screeching, "What are you doing over there? I want to talk to you, you pervert!"

Being exposed, I moved quickly, leaping from the bushes and onto the porch of Sandi's house. With my face planted against the front window, I saw a shadow move from the sofa into the hallway. Unlike last time, I didn't need to rely on my supernatural sixth sense to pick up a presence in the house. The television was on, and I recognized one of my favorite soap operas flickering across the screen. I loved watching The Rich and Hedonistic.

I yelled as loudly as I could. "I know you're in there, Sandi. I need to talk to you."

I hammered on the door and intended to keep it up until Sandi came out. Unfortunately, the old neighbor gal, her hair a tangled tumbleweed of scarlet, crossed the street and shouted, "I'm calling the sheriff, you pervert, and you'll experience some old-fashioned Kleinstadt justice."

She had that right. If John Brown treated me harshly for rolling through a stop sign, he'd thump me into pulp for forcing my way through Sandi's front door. I didn't have to contend with a fight versus flight impulse because I already had enough get-the-hell-out-of-there inside me. I sprung from the porch, ran to my car, fired up the engine, and sped away. I'd gone about a mile without hearing sirens, so my heartbeat slowed, allowing me to think about what had happened. Number one was the obvious question of why Sandi refused to see me. Did Mindy's dinner date with Wayne the Drifter prompt such a fearful reaction that she'd hide from me?

"What the heck's going on with her," I asked myself. "I don't know," I answered. "Well, what are you going to do about it? I don't know. Get off my case, and let me think."

When Nic Knuckles berated himself, it was a sign I was exhausted. I figured I'd done enough sleuthing for the morning and deserved some time off. I'd recharge my batteries by returning to Miss Crumble's Lodge, talking her into making me a late lunch and turning on her television. We could sit nicely, hands on our sandwiches, watching the second hour of afternoon soap operas. That'd make me feel better. I loved those programs because their storylines about cheating lovers, suspicious deaths, and inexplicable comas were more believable than what I dealt with in my work. Kleinstadt, was no exception.

Chapter Twenty-Seven

Watching soap operas with Kate Crumble had gone nicely at first. She made me a sandwich, and we settled in our chairs to watch the episode, where sultry Charlene and the schemer, Douglas, finally got together. Unfortunately, yet not unexpectedly, my landlady ruined the experience when she announced she wanted to roleplay what we saw on TV. She'd be the irresistible temptress while I played the hapless swain. I slipped away from the lodge during a commercial break, my half-eaten lunch in hand.

I found myself walking down Main Street, struggling with the last of my sandwich. Kate toasted the bread to the point where it crumbled, smearing mayo and pickles on every finger. At least it didn't involve gastrointestinal blowback like Buddy's sandwiches, but it still left me dreaming of New York City. Now, that's where they knew how to build a sandwich. A juicy vision danced in my head of a stacked Rueben overflowing with corned beef, Swiss cheese, sauerkraut, and Russian dressing between slices of rye bread. That delicious image evaporated when a blue-green Cadillac Deville pulled alongside me.

"How'd you like to own this beauty, Mr. Knuckles?" That voice belonged to George Bauerman, calling out from the darkness of the car interior. "Wouldn't you rather tool back to New York in a swell automobile than fly in a germ-infested airplane?"

I rocked back on my heels. What the heck was Bauerman doing approaching me?

"Hello there, George," I said, sputtering like a two-cylinder gas mower running on fumes. "Yeah, you're right. That car *is* nice looking."

The man pushed open the passenger side door. "Hop in, and let's take a ride."

A little voice in my head suggested I refuse the offer, so I held up my hands. "My lunch was a sloppy mess, and I'd hate to stain the upholstery."

"No problem, Mr. Knuckles. The plastic seat covering is the same material used to protect workers cleaning up Chernobyl after that reactor explosion."

That little voice inside my skull again started talking, only more frantically. Don't get in, Nic, it said; something's wrong. Unfortunately, that little voice sounded exactly like an old girlfriend who brayed like a jackass. She was such a screed that I'd automatically reject any advice she gave me, regardless of how much sense it made. I dropped into the Caddie's front seat and stretched my legs. My living room was smaller.

"Wow, this is nice."

"I'll take us out on some isolated country roads," George said. "That way I can demonstrate this monster's horsepower. You'll be impressed when your head snaps back as I accelerate."

Was I worried that jumping into a murder suspect's car and driving off into the remote countryside was a deadly mistake? He had an anger issue and hinted at snapping my neck, didn't he? Did Nic Knuckles blunder? I wouldn't think so unless, an hour from now, I'm the proud owner of a blue-green Cadillac Deville. Then I'd regret ever climbing into that car with George Bauerman.

"I want to apologize," George said as he floored the gas pedal and threw me back in my seat. "I think we got off on the wrong foot."

"Wrong foot, it was more like the wrong feet. It seemed whenever I asked you a question, you got all tight-lipped and agitated."

"Yeah, I'm sorry about stiff-arming you," he said. "You have to understand, reopening the investigation of Mindy's death triggers Mary Jane's depression. You know how mothers are, right?"

Of course, Nic Knuckles knew a thing or two about mothers and their melancholy. Even though my mother had promised to dance on my grave more than once, I knew she'd be sad if something fatal happened to me.

Her grief would be even greater after learning I'd removed her as my life insurance beneficiary.

"I'm sorry I'm creating problems for your wife. That's the nature of the private eye business, unfortunately. We're archaeologists of the criminal mind, and sometimes innocent people get buried in the rubble."

Bauerman kept his eyes straight ahead on the road as Kleinstadt disappeared from view, and corn and bean fields took over the landscape. Considering the man had just shown me some sensitivity, I decided to build upon it and get some insight from him about my other suspects.

"I'm sure you found it difficult reliving Mindy's brutal assault by a cleaver-wielding teenager, as well. I'd guess a father, the man responsible for protecting his daughter, never gets over that kind of loss."

"Actually, I hadn't thought about her much until you showed up," he said.

Holy Provolone, that was a disturbing revelation climbing out of Bauerman's mouth. I couldn't believe what I had heard. Just when I thought he was human, he admitted his daughter's gruesome death hadn't bothered him for years.

"I have to tell you, George, that makes you sound hardhearted."

Bauerman shrugged. "It's been fifteen years. I figured she probably burnt off whatever sins she took to purgatory and is now with our heavenly Lord. Life is for the living, after all, and you need to move on."

I turned my gaze toward the passing cornfield and tried to swallow a knot of anxiety stuck in my throat. I thought the man finally revealed a speck of caring, and then he said something like that. What could I do with a callous man other than elevate him higher on my suspect ranking?

"Having you ask questions about Mindy's murder did do one thing, however," George said. "You made me think about the trial."

"Go on, I'm listening."

"I always thought Sheriff Feif and the prosecutor moved awfully fast getting Timmy Hanlon charged and convicted."

I rose in my seat, and my ears tweaked to my left to catch every syllable formed by George's lips. That was why he picked me up: he had a bombshell he wanted to detonate in my lap. The tenor of George's voice softened as he continued. "I thought there were others with more powerful motives to kill Mindy than Timmy Hanlon, yet I didn't say anything."

"That's a heck of a burden, my friend. Why'd you keep your opinions to yourself?"

"I didn't want Mary Jane to suffer through a long trial. When she gets upset, she tends to wander off, looking for someone to comfort her."

With him racing down a country road at seventy miles an hour, I buried the impulse to ask if a traveling salesperson would've been one such refuge. I decided it'd be more fruitful to encourage him to continue talking.

"It sounds like you were being a thoughtful husband. It must not have been easy to hold back, being the righteous man as you were."

George dropped his shoulders, and his mouth sagged at the corners. "I appreciate you saying that. Most people think I'm an unfeeling chucklehead who only wants to save their souls or sell them a used car."

"I hear you, brother," I said. "Most people think I'm a ruggedly handsome, but misunderstood fighter for justice, who only wants to put them in jail."

If someone was riding in the backseat and witnessed that exchange, they might've thought old Nic Knuckles was a softie for not calling out George's insensitivity. But they'd be wrong. It was an old trick used by investigators since Cain killed Abel. Make the perp feel human, and they'd eventually trust you with their inner feelings. I felt a self-congratulatory grin spread across my face when Bauerman heaved a sigh and continued confessing. "Nonetheless, the thought of the wrong man serving a life sentence has eaten at me for years."

"That'll do it. Guilt weighs nothing, but if you don't address it, it has the heft of a wet sack of cement."

"Yes, sir," George said. "The Lord's punishment is lightened when a man confesses his sins. Otherwise, he's damned for eternity."

I didn't know how to respond, so I mumbled, "Yeah, that's what I meant."

George's foot on the car's accelerator never let up as the fields zipped by, and I felt a bead of sweaty anxiety trickle down my back. What was going on here? Did George want to help me prove Timmy Hanlon's innocence to ease his remorse? What if it was something else, like him trying to divert my attention toward another person? How much of this suspicious behavior had to do with him failing to make his monthly sales quota? I had to move this conversation along and get some answers before we ended up in Ohio.

"I have to tell you, George. I'm not convinced that Hanlon did the crime either, but I'm having trouble culling the long list of locals I do suspect."

I swayed to my left as Bauerman took the car into a sharp turn. We were soon enveloped in dust as the pavement gave way to gravel. Even with impaired vision, I could see enough to know that there wasn't a farmhouse for miles. The second trickle of sweat raced down my back.

"Maybe I can help you," George said. "What are you thinking?"

"High on my list is that boy who lived across the street, you know, Buzz Rockwell, the axe fanatic."

George sniffed. "Buzz wouldn't do something like that."

That comment caught me up short. George told me back at the sales shed that he didn't know about young Buzz's interests. "How would you know what the kid would or wouldn't do?" I asked. "You claimed you had no knowledge of Buzz, other than he was the neighborhood loner."

George hiked his shoulders. "I'm sorry, but I didn't want to embarrass Buzz. You see, I once caught him peeping in Mindy's bedroom window. Instead of a righteous anger, I felt a calling from the Almighty, and decided to mentor the boy."

Well, isn't that a tasty piece of news? So, Daddy Bauerman and Buzz the Axe Wheeling Peeping Tom were tight back in the day. Why'd Buzz never volunteer that information?

"How'd your mentoring of Buzz work out?"

George smiled and thumped his chest. "I got him on the straight and narrow very quickly and eventually helped him start his business. As you might know, he's operating one of the town's few prospering enterprises."

Upon hearing about George's rescue mission, most people would've admired him, but Nic Knuckles wasn't most people. I'm a guy who'd seen how the strong manipulated the weak, and I wondered why Buzz never mentioned George's role in his life. I wanted to pull out my notebook and record what I was thinking, but I'm prone to motion sickness, so I'd have remembered everything.

"It sounds like the rehabilitated Buzz would've been a boy you'd want to have dated Mindy."

"I preferred Mindy date no one. She was too young and gullible, and those boys with their filthy desires only wanted one thing from her."

"Yeah, boys at that age only think about sex, don't they?"

George reared back, looking at me like I was too stupid to breathe. "Are you crazy? They wanted me to sell them a car *at cost*. Boys at that age only cared about the wheels they rode around in, not how a working man had to make a living."

Nic Knuckles couldn't relate to Kleinstadt boys and their car obsessions. When I was sixteen, my wheels were on one of the Q buses leaving Queens.

"Another contender for the murderer is young John Brown," I said. "He seemed to have had a volatile temper and a close relationship with Mindy."

I planted the palms of my hands onto the dashboard as George slammed the brakes, bringing the car to a complete stop at the intersection of soybeans and feed corn. He turned to me; the skin around his eyes pulled so tight his eyeball could've popped out. "Don't be stupid, Knuckles. John Brown had nothing to do with Mindy."

"Is that so? Don't you think that young John taking Mindy out every Wednesday night to dance was an interesting point of consideration?"

George started vibrating just like he did earlier at the car lot. The third bead of sweat joined the other two pooled in my shorts, and I gripped the edge of the car seat, ready to escape from the car if George blew.

"That never happened. Mary Jane locked Mindy in her bedroom when I was at my Wednesday night prayer service. You speak as the viper did to Eve—with lies."

Since we weren't barreling along a country road at seventy miles an hour, I went to the next interrogation level. "I have multiple sources saying John took Mindy out on Wednesday nights."

"That's a lie!"

I twisted in my seat and looked directly at George, sensing I was close to making him reveal secrets he didn't want to share.

"Is it possible that since John Brown already owned a red convertible, that your fear he'd wanted a discounted car was no longer valid?"

Bauerman growled, and spit bubbles formed in the corners of his mouth.

"Were you afraid that John had other intentions, and Mindy's virtue might be in jeopardy if you allowed him to date her?"

Sometimes, Nic Knuckles goes too far. Maybe the mere mention of Mindy's chastity being at risk reminded George of his wife's early tendencies to stray. Whatever I said lit his fuse, and the man's eyes flashed metaphorical daggers. "Get out of my vehicle, you sick degenerate!"

"No, not now, George; if you don't think it's John Brown, Buzz Rockwell, or Timmy Hanlon, then you gotta tell me who you think did kill Mindy?"

The man's breathing slowed, and his knuckles loosened their grip on the steering wheel. His lips formed numerals, and when he hit ten, he slowly bared his teeth like a snarling pit bull. "It's Buddy Lee Hoot."

I didn't think George liked my reaction. I laughed, slapped my knee, and howled. "Oh, come on. Are you saying Buddy killed Mindy? You have to be joking."

Bauerman pounded the steering wheel. "Are you blind? She treated him like a doormat throughout their years in school. He had every reason to go nuts over her mistreatment."

I didn't care how forcefully he made his accusation; George hadn't convinced me. All he'd done since I met him was besmirch Buddy's reputation. Sure, it might've been annoying having a teenage boy clear your refrigerator, but the kid did listen to his wife's whining. How could he claim that sad sack Buddy had the motive, let alone the energy, to behead Mindy?

"I find that hard to believe," I said. "Give me something more substantive to chew on." And that was what the man did. He gave me a big hunk of roasted speculation that made me gag.

"The primary reason I know Buddy killed my daughter was because he was height impaired."

"Huh?"

"He was short,"

"What's wrong being short," I asked as I pushed myself taller.

George's eyes slid to the side. "Well, you know."

"No, I didn't know."

All I learned about being short came from a blind date with a woman named Shelia. She must've stood five foot ten, and then, throwing in those four-inch heels, she towered over me. But she didn't seem to care, so I didn't either. That good night kiss, however, ruined it. She closed her eyes and puckered, so I did the same and went in for the smooch. Dang, I reached up but still planted my lips on her throat.

"You see, Mindy had a good two inches on Buddy," George said. "People laughed at them when they walked together. I'm sure Buddy resented Mindy for being taller. He had to because his deficiencies were right there in his face every time, he looked up at her."

I didn't know why George thought Buddy's height would've driven him to murder. Usually, a man committed such a heinous crime because of rage or envy or had a screw loose, not because they had to look up at their paramour.

"Sorry, man, I don't see how Buddy being shorter than Mindy made him a cold-blooded killer."

Bauerman shouted at me. "Can't you see the obvious? Buddy suffered from a severe case of the Napoleonic Complex. Any psychiatrist would tell you he'd sooner or later flip out. I mean, look what Bonaparte did to Europe and Egypt."

"If so, why chop off her head? That seems so extreme, even for a guy who could never look his girlfriend in the eye. I mean, if you wanted to level things out, you'd chop off her feet."

George made an animal noise, like the cross between a hyena and a hissing cockroach. "I've had enough of you, Knuckles," he said, using his big hands to open the car door and push me out.

I jumped to my feet as Bauerman accelerated, the spinning tires spitting gravel into my face. I shouted at the ever-shrinking vehicle, pulling away. "Come back, George. I want to know your thoughts on Wayne the Drifter."

Bauerman didn't care to answer that question, and he most definitely gave up on closing a sale because he never slowed down. The dust cloud from the departing vehicle settled, and I realized I was out in the middle of nowhere. As a native New Yorker, my first impulse was to look for MTA signage, hoping a subway station wasn't too far away. It took me a few seconds to realize I'd have to walk back to town. That prospect put me in a foul mood. My tushie already hurt from Bauerman shoving me out of the car and onto the ground. My face stung from the road shrapnel his tires sent my way. And by the time I returned to Miss Crumble's lodge, my feet would be red and blistered.

I felt hot emotion bubbling up from deep inside as my situation reminded me of all the times as a kid when I'd been shoved to the playground or slapped around by bullies. Desperate for a bit of sympathy, my memory searched for that one instant when my mom wiped my tears and told me all would be okay. I came up empty.

Chapter Twenty-Eight

I spent the morning soaking in a hot bathtub filled with Epsom salts, trying to ease my bodily trauma. My truncated road trip the day before with George Bauerman gave me blistered feet, aching calves, screaming hamstrings, and stiffness from my buttock up to my shoulders. I hadn't been that physically beaten since I walked in on two raccoons raiding my garbage can.

As I marinated my body, my mind kept going over my conversation with Bauerman. What if my skepticism of the man's theory about Buddy Lee Hoot was unwarranted? Maybe I was fooled by Buddy's passive appearance, and he could let his shortness get the best of him. I knew from experience that the thwarted love interest tended to be the murderer, but I still couldn't picture Buddy chopping off a head when he barely managed to cut a sandwich in half.

Thirty minutes later, with my flesh the texture of a plucked chicken, I grasped the side of the tub and pushed myself out, feeling triumphant. A half-hour of seriously ruminating led to a brilliant scheme that'd settle where Buddy Lee Hoot stood on my prime suspect ranking once and for all. All I needed to make it work was for the Speedi Food Mart to carry western wear and the help of an axe-loving businessman.

That afternoon, I put my plan into action by calling Buzz Rockwell. I told him I wanted to ask him a few more questions, but he turned me down. Knowing he liked beer, I suggested we talk over a few cold ones. He hummed and hawed until I committed to picking up the tab for us. He arrived at Buddy's Tavern two minutes after I sat at a table.

As we waited for the waitress, Buzz gave a TED Talk on the efficiency of a Bowie Knife for shaving the hair off of a man's head. It was more interesting than I'd ever imagined, but after fifteen minutes, the waitress still had yet to take our order. Considering there weren't but two other customers, I felt irritated and called the woman over.

"Is there a problem taking our drink order?" The waitress stopped chewing her gum and flipped her head toward the man working behind the bar. "Buddy doesn't like seeing Buzz Rockwell in here."

I pushed away from the table and stood but had to grab the back of my chair as I staggered forward. The gaze of both Buzz and the waitress slipped from my face to the floor.

"What the hell you got on your feet?" Buzz asked.

"Oh, they're my new cowboy boots."

The waitress cupped her mouth and chuckled. "That's gotta be a two-inch heel, Tex. Can you handle that?"

She had it right. The Chinese knockoff sold at the Speedi Food Mart added two inches to my height. What made me wobble, however, was the inch lift I inserted inside. I steadied myself, stumbled over to the bar, and confronted Buddy. "Two brews, Shorty," I said. "And hold the attitude."

Buddy's mouth pulled at the corners, and he mumbled. "Don't believe anything Buzz Rockwell tells you."

"What are you afraid of, Buddy? That he'll tell some *tall* tales."

Buddy grunted and turned away, reaching into a cooler for two bottles of beer. "And while you're at it," I said, "can we have some salted nuts?"

Some people would avoid making such a request regardless of their intense craving for a tasty snack. Why get in the crossfire of Buddy's animosity toward Buzz? Who knew how he'd desecrate those nuts if he thought Buzz would pop one in his mouth? My hunger for Mr. Peanut's offspring was more powerful than my fear of food tampering, and I arrived back at the table with two beers and a bowl brimming with salted goobers.

"Here you go, Buzz," I said. "But before you stuff your mouth, I recently learned from George Bauerman that you were more than neighbors. Was that true?"

Buzz halted the beer bottle an inch from his mouth. "Uh, yeah. I guess so."

"Why don't you tell me a little more about your relationship with Mindy's dad?"

Rockwell sighed, took a swallow of beer, and gave me an answer. "Mr. Bauerman helped me out when I was a troubled teenager. It was back after my dad had died, and my mom was struggling with her jellybean addiction."

"Jellybeans, was that the local colloquialism for amphetamines?"

"No, jellybeans were, you know, candy you ate on Easter. She worked as a confectionary sales rep and had access to tons of jellybeans. She'd gotten hooked, bad, her teeth were rotting, and she lay around all day in a stupor. Nasty stuff, that processed sugar, let me tell you."

"And how'd that lead to you being friends with George?"

Buzz stared down at his hands. "I got into a bit of trouble, and George helped me out."

I wouldn't tell Buzz I knew his so-called trouble was him peeping under the window shade of Mindy's bedroom. I'd let him talk and see if his story clicked with what I'd heard from George.

"He treated me kindly and became like a mentor, you might say."

"How'd that work out for you?"

"George was very understanding, until he wasn't."

I dipped my head closer to Buzz, hoping he'd clarify that comment. He threw a handful of nuts into his mouth, chewed them into pulp, and swallowed. After a long draw from his beer bottle, he ended the suspense.

"I let it slip that I saw Mindy going into the Swing and Swoon Dance Hall one Wednesday night, and he went off on me."

Ah, so George did know about Mindy and Brownie dancing. I swore that that man would win the International Liar's Olympics gold medal.

"So, he wanted to kill the messenger, huh?"

"Yeah, he was angry, yelling and screaming at me."

Buzz dumped some nuts into his right hand, but I grabbed his wrist before he could lift it to his mouth. At the rate he ate, I'd be there all day. "Finish your story, Buzz."

"George didn't like Mindy hanging out with guys he didn't approve of."

CHAPTER TWENTY-EIGHT

"Guys like John Brown?" I asked.

"Yeah."

"Guys like Buddy Lee Hoot?"

"Uh-huh."

"Guys like Buzz Rockwell?"

Buzz shrugged and dropped his head further. "George said I was the son he never had, and I should treat Mindy as the sister I never had."

"How'd you feel about that role?"

Buzz raised his eyes and snapped off a reply. "I didn't like it. My feelings toward Mindy weren't brotherly."

I shifted in my seat. The mere mention of sister and brotherly affection brought back uncomfortable memories of a childhood filled with slamming doors, crying women, and canned spaghetti on Thursday nights. I buried those horrors and turned my attention back to Mr. Rockwell because I still had to see my Buddy Lee Hoot plan to completion.

"Did Mindy ever talk to you, you know, ask you for a favor?" I said, wondering if I could get him to admit to buying Mindy those last pairs of new shoes. "Surely, you would've done anything she asked."

Buzz answered with a resounding no and quickly stuffed his mouth with nuts. I couldn't understand why the boy never pursued Mindy more aggressively. Sure, I knew what it was like to have a girl show you the palm of her hand when you approached her, but I never gave up.

"You're telling me over all those years, you and Mindy never shared a word?"

"Nope, I never said anything to her, and she never spoke to me."

I leaned closer to Buzz and whispered. "Then explain why Buddy Lee Hoot believes you were trying to seduce Mindy. What gave him that idea?"

"It was Molly Spear's fault," Buzz said, wiping nut crumbs off his face. "During the trial, she painted me as the crazed basement-dwelling lover. I might have been a bit crazy, but I never spoke to Mindy, so how'd I get spurned?"

"Why'd Buddy hate you for that? It wasn't your fault."

Buzz slowly rolled his head. "I don't know. People believed I had the truest passion for Mindy, while Buddy gave off the heat of a cold meadow muffin in winter."

"I tell you what, Buzz. Let's go talk to Buddy and work this out. Neither of you has such a huge circle of friends that you can afford to hold grudges."

If someone overheard the conversation, they'd think Nic Knuckles was more than a dogged investigator and that he was also a humanitarian interested in harmony among people. They'd only be half right. My purpose was to get Buzz, who looked to be six feet tall, standing near Buddy. Add me towering in my boots and lift, and the bartender would feel like a child in a forest of Redwoods, and I could test George Bauerman's theory that Buddy was inspired to kill because he was height impaired.

Buzz and I got to our feet, and I reached for Buzz's shoulder to steady myself. We hobbled to the bar, and I called Buddy over. He came and cranked his head up to look at Buzz and me. "What do you want?"

"I want to talk about your assumption that Mr. Rockwell, aka Stretch, tried to seduce your girl," I said. "He claimed he didn't. He thinks you took a *small* misunderstanding, a *half pint* of an issue, a *shrimp* of a problem, and made it bigger than it really was."

"I don't think so."

"Buddy," I said, "you have to admit that Mindy's needs *dwarfed* your own. How could you air your grievances when hers always seemed gigantic while yours were so *puny?*"

Buddy twisted his mouth as if trying to form new words to capture his anger but fell back on the old, reliable ones. "What in the hell are you saying?"

Before I could push any more of Buddy's hot buttons, Buzz spoke. "I think what Knuckles is trying to say is that Mindy wasn't nice to you. I watched from afar, and I saw it all. She could be pretty cruel."

Buddy dipped his shoulders. "Yeah, she was a challenge."

"I admired how you managed to keep your sanity," Buzz said. "I was too intimidated to even try what you did back in high school. Believe it or not, you were my hero."

The color on Buddy's face pinked up, and he hitched his shoulders. "Being

Mindy's boyfriend was like going to war, sometimes. I hadn't hit my full share of puberty yet, so we were the same size, which explained why I avoided making her mad."

Buzz recalled witnessing fights between Mary Jane and her daughter and agreed Mindy could be scary. The two men laughed about how she'd mix it up with anyone who set her off. They decided they both were afraid of Mindy back then.

"I guess another thing we shared," Buddy said, "was living with the rumors that we had a hand in her murder."

"You're right," Buzz said. "There are still town folks who won't step in my store."

Buddy sighed. "Must be the same people who won't give me any business."

I felt like I was at a Chamber of Commerce meeting of disgruntled business people moaning about ineffectual branding and lousy sales. It felt like the two might go on for another hour whining about being powerless, so I interrupted. "How about we toast Mindy," I said. "A gal too hot for the boys of Kleinstadt to handle."

We clinked our bottles, and as I tilted my head to swallow the last of my suds, I lost my balance and fell backward, landing hard on my rear. Buddy came around from behind the bar, and he and Buzz lifted me to my feet. I wobbled and grabbed both men to keep from ending back on the floor.

"Get out of those ridiculous boots before you break your neck," Buddy said. The two men pushed me into a chair and pulled off the boots. With my feet now free of those cheap imports, my mind could focus on what I'd just accomplished. Me and Buzz standing over Buddy as I let loose relentless taunting, failed to elicit any response, let alone an angry one. I incorporated every trigger I could think of for upsetting a short man, and Buddy rolled with them all. The man was unaffected by his size and proved that George Bauerman's theory was nonsense.

"You know, fellas," I said. "This has been my best day in Indiana, and I want to celebrate. I'm buying a round for the house."

Buddy and Buzz cheered, and soon, the premium beer was flowing, and the patrons and staff were enjoying a midday Oktoberfest. The best part for me was concluding that Buddy had nothing to do with Mindy's murder, and neither had Buzz. I moved Wayne ahead of Brownie as my number one suspect and added George as number three. Small progress shrinking my suspect list, for sure, but with a few more long soaks in the bathtub, maybe I'd be inspired with the one idea that'll break this case wide open.

Chapter Twenty-Nine

I returned to Miss Crumble's lodge after Buzz, Buddy, and I emptied the second bowl of salted nuts and a few more bottles of Buddy's favorite pale ale. I stumbled back in my stocking feet, a combination of alcohol and leftover muscular soreness making me unsteady. I climbed the staircase on my hands and knees up to my room and into bed. I was wasted.

Serious true crime fans might wonder, since famous private investigators consume large quantities of alcohol without slipping off for some afternoon shuteye, was Nic Knuckles embarrassed? No, what did I care? I marched to my own tune, and today, it was a nappy time lullaby.

I woke sometime later in the shaded darkness of my room, thinking about where things stood with the Mindy Bauerman murder case. My Buddy Lee Hoot plan worked better than expected, revealing both Buddy and Buzz as two hapless admirers of a girl that neither had the skill to handle, and they now realized it. That revelation also allowed me to remove both men from my suspect list. However, because of his desire to smear Buddy, I had to elevate George Bauerman into the upper echelon along with Wayne and John Brown.

The man I wanted to focus on next was the most dangerous. As the local law, Sheriff Brown dictated the definition of the reasonable use of force. He also had the brutish physical strength to dish it out. Before confronting him, I needed a fuller understanding of what made that guy tick. It had to be more than his affection for Barney Feif and a girl who liked to dance.

It took me another hour to clear my head before I left my room to search for my favorite town gossip. I found her making bread in the kitchen, in her usual cranky mood.

"What do you want now?" Kate asked. "Can't you see I'm busy?"

I apologized and promised I had only one question, knowing there'd be plenty more. In the Basics of Private Investigation class I took when starting my career, that technique was called conversational foreplay. You began slowly with one question and got the person talking about the mundane, like the weather or their out-of-control eczema. Then, you escalated your query until you had them singing like a canary. I never knew how a bird song moved an investigation along, but that's what they taught me. Wouldn't a parrot be a better bird than a canary? Sometimes, those classroom teachers were long on theory and short on real-world experience.

"You did a great job helping me understand John Brown's strong feelings toward Barney Feif," I said to Kate. "But why does John get all squirrelly when I asked him about his past relationship with Mindy Bauerman? I mean, as far as I can tell, they were just two crazy teenagers going at it hot and heavy."

Kate stopped kneading the dough but didn't look up at me. I swore I heard the gears in her head whirling before she finally spoke. "I'm not sure I'd know why." I saw a tightening around her mouth that suggested she wasn't forthcoming. "As I told you, I think they were school chums at old Kleinstadt High."

"That's an easy guess," I said. "But did you know they were socializing right up until Mindy died?"

Kate turned her head and mumbled. "You said one question."

"Ah, come on, Kate, you knew there'd be more when you let me sit down. Answer the question. You knew Brownie and Mindy were dance partners, didn't you?"

"You don't say?"

Good Lord, why did the mention of John and Mindy going dancing make *everyone* act squirrelly? Why was normally talkative Kate Crumble shutting down and shutting down fast?

"Sandi Fliminsky told me that Mindy snuck out at night to go dancing with Brown. Buzz Rockwell confirmed it, and although George Bauerman denied it ever happened, I now know he lied to me."

"You don't say."

"I have to tell you, Kate, I don't know why you know nothing about John Brown and his dancing days with Mindy when everyone else did."

Kate's face went soft as the dough she was mauling. "Why do you assume I know everything that goes on in this town?"

I bent over the table and forced her to look at me. "Don't make me find a new rumormonger, Kate. I'm getting close to breaking this case, and you don't want to be left out when it all goes down, do you?"

It was like watching a glacier calving a giant iceberg. Kate groaned, and her resolve splintered and came crashing down. "Okay, here's the story," she said, sliding into a chair across from me. "As a teenager, John spent his free evenings at the local dance hall, The Swing and Swoon. The place had a live band playing on Wednesday nights, and apparently, there wasn't a girl in Kleinstadt that could keep up with him on the dance floor."

Nic Knuckles knew something about the allure of dancing. I scuffed up a few pairs of shoes in my youth. Usually, they were on the feet of my dance partner, but I still loved to boogie.

"John was frustrated not having a good partner until *that* girl showed up."

I pulled my notebook from my back pocket with one hand and my trusty pencil with the other. "Go on, Kate, let it pop."

"She was this kid who walked in with rye whisky on her breath, and as much as John probably wanted to arrest her for underage drinking, that girl could hoof it." Kate confirmed what I already knew. The youngster was Mindy Bauerman. "And John was totally and completely smitten after their first dance."

Oh my, so young Brownie did have the hots for little Mindy. I *knew* he had more of an interest in the Bauerman murder than protecting the reputation of Barney Feif.

"Did Mindy feel the same way?"

Kate's mouth turned down, and she returned to massaging the dough. "John and Mindy sparked like a frayed extension cord plugged into a high-voltage wall socket. Whatever sense of right and wrong John held dear went out the window that night."

"How'd you know all that teenage drama, Kate? It wasn't like you were sneaking a smoke in the girl's restroom at old Kleinstadt High."

Kate stopped working the dough and looked at me. "Remember I told you about John's father getting killed and his mother selling the farm? Well, Jean and her son moved into town without a place to stay. My aunt took them in for a while, and I got to know Jean. We grew close, kind of like two sisters. You know what I mean?"

Did Nic Knuckles know what she meant? Hell, yes, I knew what she meant. My three sisters were close, close like a pack of snarly jackals. Don't get me started on sisters.

"After they eventually moved from the lodge, I still kept in touch," Kate said. "When Jean fell into a silo of chicken feathers and suffocated, I felt an obligation to keep an eye on her teenage son. When I heard about what was going on, I knew Jean would've been horrified knowing her boy was involved with a tramp like that Bauerman girl."

I dismissed Kate's commentary on Mindy's character, figuring that her hatred of Mary Jane and George tainted her feelings toward their child. But I was still curious why the rest of the town seemed interested in the relationship between two teenagers.

"Tell me why'd two kids who liked to swing to the beat at a dance hall made the local grapevine? Why'd anyone care?"

Kate laughed. "Are you serious? Can you imagine how those young girls hanging out at The Swing and Swoon felt? Some zit-faced teenager barely old enough to drive comes in and steals the most eligible boy in town, just because she had loose joints and a sense of rhythm?"

"Good point," I said. "I'd imagine some of those girls might've been angry enough to slander Mindy, am I right?"

The corner of Kate's mouth tucked high under her right cheek. "Oh, you're right, Nic. There might've been one or two of them who'd do something more than trash talk her."

"What are you suggesting?"

Kate dumped a handful of flour on the bread dough and mashed it together.

"I'm suggesting maybe you going after John Brown because he and Mindy liked to dance, is fruitless. I've known John almost all of his life, and I've never heard of him physically hurting anyone."

I found that statement difficult to believe, what with the bruises I'd gotten from Brownie's pat downs and finger jabs. It was my turn to reply, "You don't say."

"I'm serious, Nic. The girls in this town were terribly jealous of Mindy. I'd look carefully at all of them, especially Mindy's best friend, Sandi Fliminsky."

Kate's suggestion wasn't something I hadn't considered. After the boyfriend, a dead girl's best friend was always my favorite choice as the killer.

"If you think digging deeper into Miss Fliminsky's story will pay off, then I will."

"Oh, I do, Nic. I just want to help you solve your case."

"I know you do." I felt my mouth pucker, as it often did when I lied. A private eye learned early on that freely offered information usually had a selfish motive behind it. I never trusted someone who said they wanted to help me, which is why my therapist couldn't get anywhere with me on my mother issues.

Kate bared her teeth and arched her back. "Since I helped you, Nic, could you do something for me?"

"Uh, what'd you have in mind?"

Kate rolled her head and groaned. "My shoulders and neck are sore from working this bread dough. A deep massage from those manly hands of yours would help me tremendously."

Oh man, oh man, how'd Nic Knuckles let himself get pulled into such an uncomfortable situation? As a man of honor, I had to reciprocate Kate's generous information sharing. But putting my paws on her body would violate my professional code of ethics. I put away my notebook and pencil and proposed an alternative approach. "How about I flour up my hands and work the dough while you sit and relax?"

Kate wasn't happy with my suggested way of alleviating her muscular stiffness, but I refused to budge. Thank God I didn't. As I squeezed and pressed the bread dough, Kate closed her eyes and softly groaned. Each time I slapped the glutenous mass, her moaning grew louder. Whatever fits the woman was working up were too fearsome to ignore, and I hopped from my chair and was in my room behind a locked door before Kate opened her eyes.

After washing the flour from my hands, I retrieved my notebook and recorded what Kate shared before attempting her carnal ambush. Her history with John Brown seemed more encompassing than she'd hinted at earlier, and I wanted to know what happened to teenage Brownie after his mother died. Who took him in? Was it Feif, or did Kate provide the teenager home at the lodge? Did Kate's belief that a woman might've had a hand in killing Mindy have any merit? Did she want to help me solve this case, or was she feeling guilty about charging me high season rates during the off-season?

So many questions to ask Miss Crumble, yet to secure answers, I had to find a repellant to stymie her romantic desires. I was in a strange territory with Kate. Usually, by now, any woman I attracted had discovered enough of my flaws that she'd be on the next train out of the city. Something wasn't right with Kate, but I couldn't put my finger on it, and I wouldn't say I liked that feeling.

Chapter Thirty

I stood in line the following day at the Speedi Food Mart with a six-pack of toilet paper. The tissue provided at Miss Crumble's Cozy Lodge was coarse and thin, and that's all I wanted to say about it. My head turned as the door swung open, and in walked Molly Spear. I felt like a grade-schooler seeing my teacher outside the classroom. "What are you doing here," I asked.

"Grabbing a cup of java," she said, "before I head over to The Next to Last Supper."

"Can't you wait five minutes to get free coffee at the diner?"

Molly shook her head. "Two years ago, their coffee maker broke, and they didn't have any for days. It was hell for me, so I never walk around without a cup in hand."

Molly pushed aside an older man who stood at the coffee dispenser. His angry expression did nothing to slow her down as she snatched the most oversized cup available and filled it with steaming black liquid.

"Can I join you at the diner?" I asked. "I have some questions I'd like answered."

"I'll see you there," she called out as she pushed her way to the counter and threw a crinkled bill at the checker. "I'll save you a seat."

Fifteen minutes later, I carried my toilet paper into The Next to Last Supper and found Molly. She must've consumed her Speedi Food Mart brew walking over because a mug of the house coffee sat in front of her.

"What can I do for you, Nic?"

"I'm afraid I might be suffering from law enforcement bias," I said. "You

133

know, assuming that no police would ever be involved in a crime."

"The old Blue Blindness."

I sat back as the waitress dropped a menu and snapped at me. "You gonna take up space or order something?"

"I'll take the Mountain Man Pancake Special," I said after a glance at the offerings.

The waitress snatched the menu and walked away. I don't know why she acted so cranky with me, and I wondered if she somehow knew about my fling with a waitress named Mabel that ended poorly. It didn't make sense, but I imagined a vast underground network of diner waitresses communicating about men who broke their hearts or left lousy tips.

I returned my attention to Molly. "I've learned that Sheriff John Brown, as a young man, spent more than a few hours dancing with Mindy Bauerman."

Molly nodded.

"I also learned he was an intern with the Kleinstadt Sheriff's Department back when Mindy died."

"Yeah, that's true," Molly replied. "That boy was made to do police work."

"The man is absolutely tightlipped about the Hanlon investigation," I said, "and takes great offense if I challenge the old sheriff's work."

"John Brown and Barney Feif were definitely close." Molly two-handed her mug to her mouth and gulped. "Yes, they were."

I reached into my coat pocket and pulled out my notebook. I quickly found the page with my Molly Spear scribblings. "At our second meeting, when I asked why Barney Feif was so determined to find Timmy Hanlon guilty, you said, and I quote, 'Sometimes a man will do almost anything to bail out a kid.'"

The corners of Molly's eyes, already the texture of a prune, crinkled further. She took my notebook and laid it on the table. "You didn't get that right, Nic. The precise quote should be, "Sometimes *a father* will do almost anything to bail out a kid."

"What does that mean?"

Molly smiled and raised the mug to her mouth. There she went again, sharing only bits and pieces of information and leaving me hanging, but I wouldn't let her get away with it this time.

"I don't understand, Molly. Is there more to John Brown's story than him being orphaned as a teenager and taken under the tutelage of Barney Feif?"

Molly's eyes twinkled like a chipped quarter-caret diamond ring in a pawn shop window.

"Here's some Kleinstadt history for you to consider," she said. "Back in 1989, a local farmer named Mike Brown and his wife, Jean, came home with a baby boy. Now poor Jean was as barren as a Kansas wheat field during the Dust Bowl, so folks knew she'd picked up the child from one of those homes for wayward girls."

I reached for my pencil, but Molly slapped my hand. "None of what I'm saying is going to be written down. I don't want people getting hurt."

Okay, Nic Knuckles could do it that way. My mind was like a steel trap, chomping down on a fact and never letting go of it. Unfortunately, once that trap snapped closed, nothing new could get caught. I'd focus on Molly's coffee-stained teeth and hope to retain everything she said.

"That baby was named John, as in, our John Brown, and that's why I don't want you to write it down. I don't know if the Sheriff knows of his origin."

I felt a flush of hot relief. How much more aggressively would Sheriff Brown treat me if I inadvertently called him Brownie the Bastard Boy?

"About ten years later, Mike Brown was killed in a farming accident, and newly widowed Jean was in over her head trying to raise a rambunctious youngster."

I heard a mournful sigh come from my mouth. Did Nic Knuckles know something about being a rambunctious youngster raised by a single mom? No, no, I didn't. I was a teenager when my father disappeared, and I wasn't rambunctious. However, as a kid, I did suffer from a misdiagnosed case of ant in his pants syndrome.

"I knew that Molly, Jean, and John moved into town and Kate Crumble's aunt took them in for a while. But who raised John after his mother died?"

Molly took another swig of her coffee and answered. "Before she married Mike Brown, the mother went by the name of Jean Feif."

I expelled a long ah. "So, the connection between Feif and Brown was

135

more than a mentor helping out a teenager. Barney was his uncle. Now I understand why Brownie gets so irritated with me. I'm threatening the reputation of his beloved relative."

Molly nodded. "Yup, Uncle Barney became *the man* in John Brown's life after his parents passed onto the great cornfield in the sky."

I wondered why Kate Crumble had never shared any of this with me. Indeed, if she was like a sister to Jean Brown, she knew about her kinship with the old sheriff.

Molly scanned the room and leaned across the table. She cupped her mouth and whispered. "Now here's something that very few people know about the Feif Brown family tree."

A plate of pancakes a foot high suddenly fell between Molly and me. "Here's your breakfast," the waitress said. "Do you want regular or flavored maple syrup?"

"Regular syrup, please," I said as I eyed the towering stack of pancakes, "and lots of it."

Ten minutes later, my stomach was so full it pressed hard against the table's edge. The fuzzy vision of me forking syrupy pancakes into my mouth slowly faded as Molly's voice broke through the sugar-induced fog in my head.

"Do you understand the importance of what I just said?" she asked.

"Yeah, yeah, I got it."

I looked down at my empty plate and wondered how I could've quickly consumed such a massive pile of hotcakes drowned in buttery syrup. My loss of control was frightening, but boy, they were delicious.

"Thanks for the info," I mumbled and pushed myself out of the booth. "You've given me something to think about."

Molly stopped me from leaving by grabbing my arm. "Here, take your notebook," she said. "You're going to need that."

I thanked her and tried to step away, but she held onto me. "Is there anything else?" I asked.

"Treat what I told you carefully. If I'm right, you'll break the Mindy Bauerman case. If I'm wrong, then a lot of innocent people will get hurt."

"Okay, okay, I'm nothing but careful."

I again tried to leave, but Molly's grip held me in place. "Is there something else, Molly?"

"Yeah, Nic, there is one more thing. I'm not paying for your breakfast. Give me ten dollars, you freeloader."

Chapter Thirty-One

The muddy Wabash River ran through the middle of the rural county that claimed Kleinstadt as its third-largest community. I'd arrived at a deeply wooded area about two miles up the river that morning. The mature willows, the swirling brown river, and the rabid overgrowth made for a perfect spot if you wanted privacy. If you needed to hide a corpse, it was an excellent place for that as well. It would be a while before anyone would discover the bones.

People might wonder why I'd even think that way. What was wrong with me that I couldn't appreciate nature's beauty without thinking of mayhem and death? Unfortunately, every place looked like a crime scene when you're Nic Knuckles and spent your waking hours investigating evil. That explained why I never enjoyed Disneyland. Who knew the number of bodies hidden in that so-called magic castle?

I wasn't standing there along the river planning to bury anything. Instead, I hoped to unearth something. Hearing the snapping of twigs, I turned and looked behind me. Sandi Fliminsky waved as she walked toward me, her work boots stomping the undergrowth.

"Hello, Sandi," I said. "I didn't know if you'd show up."

The woman called last night and claimed she'd been busy and just now gotten my message. When I mentioned seeing someone hiding in the house when I called on her, she admitted being there. She blamed her reluctance to answer the door on the neighbor woman, the red-headed she-devil, as she called her. Sandi feared the woman would spread rumors if a world-famous private eye kept showing up at the house. I doubted the veracity of her excuse but didn't argue. I was desperate to hear about Mindy's date with Wayne the Drifter, and I agreed to meet Sandi wherever she wanted. She picked the most comfortable place for her, among the trees and grasping vines of the woods down by the Wabash River.

Being a big city guy in a forest always made me nervous, what with the animals, trolls, and fairies creeping about, ready to do something unnatural to you. The sooner we paved over Mother Nature, the safer I'd feel. Sandi pointed at a large boulder as she approached me. "Let's talk over there," she said. "We can sit as I answer your questions."

That proposition made me feel uncomfortable. No, Sandi's offer of a case-busting insight didn't bother me, but sitting on that big rock did. My tush was still very tender from getting shoved out of Bauerman's car and falling at Buddy's Tavern. I sucked in a breath and gently eased against the granite boulder.

"Okay, Sandi, now listen up. I had another source confirming Mindy's dinner date with Wayne the Drifter. I now believe that was a critical event that could shed light on the who and why of Mindy's murder. You have to quit stalling and tell me what you know about that evening."

"Sorry to break the bad news, but I don't know anything about it."

My head snapped back, and I heard a growl of disbelief rise out of my mouth. "I can't believe Mindy broke her longstanding dance date with John Brown to sup with a mysterious big spender and didn't dish with you. Come on, who do you think you're talking with?"

Sandi shrugged. "I don't know, maybe a big dummy who knows nothing about teenage girls."

Ack, she had me there. "You mean to say your best friend didn't tell you anything about her date with Wayne?"

"All she said was that the lobster was chewy, and Wayne got really mad at her. That's all she told me. She promised to share everything on Friday night, after the football game, and as you know, that was the night she was murdered."

My body sagged. "But when you called me, you said you had an important bit of information, a promising clue, you said."

"I do have something important to share with you. Hang on to your shorts."

First, it was Kate, and now Sandi told me to keep my shorts in place. Was that a Hoosier expression, or did those women have a fascination with men's underwear? Another mystery I'd have to put aside until I solved the Bauerman case. Right now, my disappointment with Sandi turned to anger.

"All your so-called help has been innuendo that proved to be inaccurate at best, or completely wrong. You claimed Mindy's parents hated her boyfriend, and I've learned that Mary Jane was very fond of him. You shared little about Mindy's relationship with John Brown, and I'm learning some smoldering details. I'm sorry I'm impatient, but you've been anything but forthcoming."

Sandi's eyes moistened, and she looked away. "I'm sorry, that was a very traumatic time when Mindy died, and I blocked out a lot of stuff because it was painful. Only after your first interview did things start dribbling from my memory. Please understand I wasn't purposely evasive."

Nic Knuckles knew what it was like to have a leaky memory that revealed long-buried incidents in dribs and drabs. I'm still assembling a recollection of the week I spent at a nudist camp in the Catskills. Somehow, a watermelon and a cactus came to mind, but that's all I knew.

"Okay, whatever's coming back to you better be good because I don't appreciate being dragged out into the woods with dang leaf mold and swarming insects."

Sandi planted her hands on her waist. "Okay, Mr. Knuckles, you want to know it all, well buckle your seat belt."

I pulled out my notebook and pencil and braced myself against the boulder. "Let it pop, Sandi."

I was glad I'd locked my knees because Sandi unloaded so much information that I could hardly keep my balance while furiously writing it down. George wasn't the only Bauerman who didn't like Mary Jane's relationship with Buddy, and Mindy also found it embarrassing. The young girl demanded her mother stop spending time with Buddy, but Mary Jane refused. She supposedly told Mindy if she treated Buddy like a boyfriend instead of a cocker spaniel, Mary Jane wouldn't have to entertain him.

"Did Mindy change her ways?"

"Absolutely not. It was Thursday, the day before she was murdered, that Mindy lied to Buddy, telling him she'd be late because she had to clap the chalk dust from the school's erasers. Poor dumb Buddy never noticed that chalk and blackboards went out of use ten years before."

"Why'd she lie to him?" I asked.

"Because she was meeting someone in Stickerbacker's Woods, that's why."

Ah, the old cheating girlfriend scenario. Nic Knuckles knew that subplot well. I couldn't count the number of unfaithful spouses and lovers I'd exposed in my career. Infidelity made me a lot of money over the years, but it also broke my heart more than a few times.

"Did you know who Mindy was meeting?"

"No, she wouldn't say, other than swearing that after she did, her mom wouldn't keep her from having fun."

I shook my head. "Something doesn't feel right to me, Sandi. First, Mindy shares nothing about her date with Wayne, and then she won't give you the inside dope on her fight with momma or who she's meeting in the woods. I thought you were her best friend."

Sandi shoved her hands into the pockets of her jacket. "Mindy liked to keep me guessing, you know, play mind games."

"Why'd you put up with it?"

"I couldn't help it. I was sixteen and desperate for Mindy's approval."

I added a sidebar to my Sandi Fliminsky page. Mindy appeared to have had a cruel streak a mile wide, and not only did she treat Buddy shabbily, but Sandi as well.

"I don't suppose you have any guesses who Mindy secretly met in the woods, do you?"

Sandi pushed her hands deeper into the jacket pockets as she looked at the ground.

"Well, do you?" I asked, "Or, are you again wasting my time?"

Sandi's eyes widened, and she repeatedly swallowed gulps of air. "I have a memory of that afternoon, but I can't trust myself enough to describe it accurately."

"Why don't you tell me the whole story, and I'll tack on a big asterisk to whatever you say, so I'll know you weren't a hundred percent sure."

With a nod of her head, Sandi gave up the details. "It was that Thursday when Mindy lied to Buddy about clapping erasers. After school let out, I walked out with her, because I was bursting with anticipation, waiting to hear all about her fight with her mom and the date the night before with Wayne. But she blew me off, claiming she had an important meeting and we'd talk later. When I asked who she was seeing, she said it was a secret. I was so mad at her. I was her best friend, right? How could she treat me so horribly?"

"Yes, Sandi, Mindy violated the best friend code. What'd you do?"

"I was tired of being treated so poorly, so I followed Mindy to Sticker-backer's Woods, determined to catch her and her mystery man."

I held my breath. The woman might finally be the firsthand eyewitness who could confirm a Tommy Lyle meeting with Mindy. "Go on. What happened next?"

A pink streak flushed Sandi's neck as she shrunk further into her jacket. She mumbled her response. "I'm ashamed to admit this, but I was pretty stoned at the time."

Oh, great, a drugged-out teenager. Was Sandi ever going to give me something I could trust?

"What were you high on, 2.3 beer, two-dollar wine, weed, horse, smack, acid, crank, Maui Wowie, greenies, reds, or dippy dots?"

The pink tint moved up Sandi's neck and covered her face. "I'd rather not say, but at the time, I saw winged mushrooms fluttering around my head."

I couldn't guess the chemical composition of Sandi's hallucinations, but I knew it made everything she reported suspect. I'd learned the worthlessness of a mind-addled by chemical supplements long ago. Yes, sir, I'd never forget that night in Hoboken, New Jersey, when I stumbled upon a one-eyed drug dealer with a Mexican Chihuahua named Needles.

"Okay, Sandi, I understand you were under the influence, but go on and tell me what you think you saw in Stickerbacker's Woods?"

"I may have been whacked out, but I'm sure I saw Wayne the Drifter."

My notebook slipped from my hands as I stumbled sideways, stunned in disbelief. "When we first met, you claimed being unaware of a drifter passing through town. Now you're telling me that you *did* know him."

"I'm sorry, but like I said, I was messed up back then."

I took a calming breath, afraid my frustration might confuse Sandi even more. One of us had to keep a clear head. "What was Wayne doing?" I asked. "Tell me what you saw."

"He was hunched down in the tall grass, staring at something further into the trees."

"Could you make out what he was looking at?"

"No, but I swear I heard a man's voice calling out Mindy's name."

Maybe it wasn't the high-quality proof I needed, but I finally had Mindy and Wayne simultaneously in Stickerbacker's Woods.

"Could you make out what the man was saying?"

Sandi shook her head. "He wasn't saying anything. He was singing."

"Can you remember what song he sang?"

"I swear it was 'Daddy's Little Girl'," Sandi said. "But then I saw a wallaby wearing a top hat hopping from the trees where Mindy was hidden, so maybe that was who was singing."

I felt my head drop. Oh my God, what a waste of time. Doper Sandi's recollections were worthless. Wallabies have kicked and punched people, but they didn't sing. No darn marsupial serenaded Mindy Bauerman, no matter what Sandi Fliminsky wanted to believe.

"Forget about the wallaby. What about Wayne? Did he look threatening?"

"No, not really. He wore blue jeans, a grey hoodie, and a machete hung off his belt."

"Did you say a machete?"

Sandi nodded. "Yeah, it was a big silver one."

"I never saw anything in all the investigative notes about a machete wheeling man. Did you tell the sheriff what you saw?"

I again almost slipped off the boulder when she said she didn't think it was relevant.

"Are you saying you saw a vagabond, stalking your best friend with a machete, and you never told the sheriff?"

"I thought maybe he was working for the Park Department clearing brush, you know, as a way to rid the woods of wild wallaby."

I slapped my forehead. "Yeah, that's one way to see it, Sandi, but come on, what were you thinking."

"Okay, I was wrong," Sandi said. "My brain was messed up by drugs, and now I realize that Wayne, as a shadowy transient with a lethal weapon, was more of a menace than I thought at the time. That's why I called you."

Sandi had nothing else to add other than she went home that afternoon and never saw Wayne or heard from Mindy again. Thanks, a lot of good that does now. Wayne disappeared fifteen years ago, Mindy's long dead, and poor Timmy Hanlon lost a decade and a half of his freedom. I decided I'd better keep the lines of communication open with Sandi, so I bottled up my anger.

"I realize that was hard for you, exposing your moral weaknesses as a youth," I said. "If something else emerges from the murkiness of your memory, please let me know."

I thanked Sandi and sent her on her way. Returning to my notebook, I tried to make sense of what I heard. I had a stranger singing to Mindy, flying mushrooms, and a wallaby in a top hat. Sandi's observation of Wayne with a machete rested on more solid ground, but even that was sketchy. If Sandi's recall was accurate and she could put Wayne and Mindy in the woods on Thursday, it would counter Buzz Rockwell's testimony that Wayne left town several days before Mindy's death. I felt disgusted, however, knowing that my best evidence rested on the fifteen-year-old recollections of a former hophead. Had Sandi, again, wasted my time?

I shoved my notebook into my jacket and tried to calm myself by looking at the trees with their yellowing leaves, listening to the soothing rush of the river's flow, and feeling the cool, crisp autumn air on my skin. Above my head, I could see a cloudless, bright blue sky through the upper branches of the trees, and I felt my heart rate slowing. I may have had the wrong perspective on the outdoors, and it was a place of wonder and retrospection.

It would do my spirit good to commune more often with nature. That possibility immediately took flight when a noise startled me. It was shrill and loud and nothing I'd ever heard in any borough of New York City. I high-stepped it through the bramble, desperate to escape the trees, vines, wild animals, and wallabies. Nic Knuckles didn't care if my primitive ancestors lived in the jungles and savannahs. I needed to be standing on asphalt to feel safe.

Chapter Thirty-Two

I came upon Buzz Rockwell as he turned the key to lock up his store. His greeting was friendly but outside his usual, how can I sell you an axe way, which was nice. I did, however, want to chat about his inventory.

"Back when you were a teenager," I said as we walked from his store. "Did you have a machete in your collection of lethal cutleries?"

"Yeah, I had a few."

"Did Wayne ever ask to borrow one?"

Buzz stopped walking, and his eyebrows dipped deep on his forehead. "Yeah, funny you should ask. Once, he told me he had a temporary job hacking overgrown shrubbery. Some elderly woman wanted her property cleared, and he asked to borrow one of my machetes."

"Did he return it to you after he'd finished the job?"

Buzz shook his head. "He claimed it flew from his hand while he was chopping a bush, and he couldn't find it in the undergrowth."

I didn't need to ask how Buzz felt because the rising heat from his face indicated he was about to let me know. "I knew that was a damn lie. That machete was a two-hundred-dollar Jamaican Sugarcane Wacker Extraordinaire with a special, slip-proof grip, and no way did that blade slip out of his hand."

"That must have made you mad, maybe angrier than Wayne skipping your regular beer and taco chip night. You know, that evening, he left you hanging while he took Mindy Bauerman out to dinner."

Rockwell clenched his jaw and stared at me. Then, the ends of his mouth dipped, and his face drooped. Whatever anger he stoked, it seemed to disappear in an instant. "Yeah, I was upset he treated Mindy to dinner," he said as he wiped his hand across a tearing right eye. "And that machete was only one of three in the world, and he lost it. Man, the two things I loved the most, and Wayne ruined them both for me."

I felt terrible reminding Buzz of Wayne's mistreatment. A long-lost machete and a girl who never knew he existed still brought him to tears. Nonetheless, I had a job, and since it was suppertime, I'd better push for answers before I grew faint from hunger. "Buzz, did you ever introduce Wayne to George Bauerman?"

"I don't think so," he said. "Why would you ask?"

"I'm trying to see if I've missed any connections Wayne might've had with other people. The man's threatening nature and ability to disappear might've been a skill set that others in the community would've been willing to pay good money to employ."

"Oh, I don't know about that. I can't see Mr. Bauerman involved with Wayne."

"Why not? If I were a desperate George Bauerman and had a rebellious daughter running the streets, I'd hire someone with enough menace to talk sense to her."

Buzz's face lit up like a kid on Christmas morning after a freight car dumped a load of toys at his door. "You know, that could explain Wayne's wad of money around the same time it all happened."

I smiled. Buzz was doing a great job of confirming my theory, and I'd keep working with him and see what else he'd reveal. "Do you think George would've been that desperate and Wayne that devious?"

"I think George might get that frantic," Buzz said. "Mindy was a handful back then. Living across the street from her, I saw her get into terrible fights with her mother."

"Mary Jane couldn't handle her either, huh?"

Buzz slowly rotated his head as if recalling something horrifying, like a high-speed collision between a gasoline tanker and a bus full of kittens. "Oh, my Lord, Mindy, and her mother got into horrible screaming matches over Mindy's behavior. You could hear them all the way across the street."

I asked if Wayne had any connection with Mary Jane, and Buzz said he didn't think so. He did admit that Wayne knew who she was. "We'd sit outside on the stoop whenever Mary Jane and Mindy brawled. It was the most entertaining show in Kleinstadt. While I never saw Wayne talking to Mary Jane, he knew her circumstances."

"Instead of George procuring Wayne, was it possible that Wayne, recognizing an opportunity, offered his services to a mother who needed her daughter intimidated?"

Buzz bounced his head and answered. "I hadn't thought of that, but yeah. There were times where George had to peel Mary Jane's hands off of Mindy's throat." He chuckled. "That Mindy could be a terror. She even drove her best friend crazy."

"You mean Sandi Fliminsky?"

Buzz laughed. "The week of the murder, I saw Mindy and Sandi rolling in the dirt outside of school, fighting over something. Mindy tangled with anyone if you made her mad."

I pulled out my notebook and pencil. I had to get this down before my mind drifted off, thinking about what I might eat for dinner. Buzz confirmed my thinking that George could've hired Wayne to do his dirty work. He also made it plausible that Mary Jane used the delinquent drifter. And whoa and behold, he said enough to make me think Sandi Fliminsky could've been Wayne's employer.

At that moment, Nic Knuckles felt good about the Mindy Bauerman investigation. I had a potential stone-cold perpetrator in Wayne, the possible weapon used to commit the crime, and co-conspirators galore. I owed Buzz Rockwell a big thank you.

"You know Buzz, I'm getting hungry. Want to join me someplace that served a decent burger and enjoy a little downtime?"

"Me, you're asking me?"

The hitch in Buzz's voice gave him away. The man tried to mask it, but I knew he was stunned that I wanted to socialize without prodding him about the Mindy Bauerman murder case. Even though he was a relatively successful businessman in his thirties, Buzz Rockwell would always be sixteen years old and a basement-dwelling loner.

"Of course, I'd like to hang out with you," I said. "I've been wanting to learn how they turn a hunk of steel into an axe. Does the raw metal come out of the ground in a lump, and they polish it until it looks right?"

Buzz chuckled and patted me on the shoulder. "Well, actually, it's an amazing process," he said. "I know of a truck stop that serves a good burger about ten miles from here, and we can talk axes there if you want."

"Great, Buzz. That sounds perfect. Let's do it."

People might think an uncompromising private eye like Nic Knuckles couldn't be sentimental. How could I care about people with all the horrible criminal behaviors I saw in my job? It was true my outer shell was as hardboiled as the next investigative professional. Still, I had a tender heart toward the loners, the misfits, and the sad sacks rejected by the hoity-toity of society. The folks living on the edges of normalcy with their strange obsessions that filled the emptiness in their life, whether it was axes, running a bar, consuming coffee, or solving crime. Those oddballs, those misfits, were my brothers and sisters, and I'd gladly share a meal with them.

And if I could get Buzz to pay for my burger, even better.

Chapter Thirty-Three

The green paint on the walls of the visitor's room was peeling, and I assumed prison décor wasn't high on the concerns of the Indiana Department of Corrections. The smell of the place could've also used some attention, although I didn't know how you'd remove the scent of desperation from the air. I hoped my visit would be worth the long drive from Kleinstadt because being here depressed me. The place reminded me too much of my childhood bedroom.

A corrections officer pulled open the steel-reinforced door, and Timmy Hanlon shuffled into the room.

"Great to see you, Mr. Knuckles," he said. He dropped into the chair across from me, showing off his yellowed toothy grin. "Thanks for coming."

"I got your message. You mentioned you had some useful information that might help me clear you."

"Yeah, I do."

"And how'd you come about that information?"

Timmy tapped the side of his head. "When you're locked up all day and night, you have time to think."

"I bet you do. So, talk to me."

Timmy started yapping about a night in 2005 when he had his first paid comedy gig at a bowling alley. An older dude, as he called him, kept heckling. Being that was Timmy's first professional performance, if you could call getting paid in free shoe rentals professional, the performer was pissed.

"I confronted him afterwards out in the parking lot," Timmy said. "He dared me to punch him. He said he had a machete that could," Timmy sliced his hand through the air, "remove my head with one swing."

My sphincter twitched hearing that, but I kept my face locked onto unimpressed mode. I was talking to a convicted murderer who hoped to get out of prison with this new testimony, and I had to be cautious. After all, Nic Knuckles hadn't fallen off the turnip truck yesterday. However, I once hitchhiked atop a pickup filled with beehives. That was the day I learned to pronounce anaphylactic with lips swollen the size of a bicycle inner tube.

"Did the guy have a name?"

"I didn't know him," Timmy said and then winked in his oily way. "But I heard someone call out, 'Don't get in a fight, Wayne.'"

My heart did a little pitapat with that answer. There we go again, my drifting friend Wayne, a machete in hand, this time threatening to behead a struggling young comedian.

"Any chance you knew the fella who stopped the fight?"

"No, I didn't look at him," Timmy said. "You know, when an angry dude stands a few feet away with a machete, you stay focused on him."

"Yeah, I imagine that's true." I also wondered why Timmy didn't recall that incident before now. Why was he stringing me along? I had my answer when I remembered what his father once said. "My boy wasn't the brightest knife in the drawer."

"But Wayne did say something weird to the other dude."

My ears perked up. I liked weird because weird usually gave Nic Knuckles more insight into a crime than boring, straightforward usual. "What was that, Timmy?"

"Wayne yelled at the dude, 'You ain't a sheriff, so get off my ass.'"

I repeated what Timmy said, and he confirmed I had heard him correctly. After recording the comment in my notebook, I asked, "Is there anything else you want to share while I'm here?"

Hanlon waved his hands and stood. "Yeah, yeah, listen to this." He moved from foot to foot and balled up his left hand as if holding a microphone. "Hey, it's great to be back here at the Jailhouse Comedy Club. Did you ever wonder why prisons have bars on the windows? Wouldn't it make more sense to make the windows too small to crawl out? I suppose that might not work if you were an octopus. But hey, why would an octopus be in prison anyway...for armed robbery?"

Timmy's mouth froze into a gaping grin. "Get it, an octopus *in jail for armed* robbery?"

I could tell he expected a reaction, a giggle, at a minimum, but I couldn't deliver. The guard at the door didn't help either when he shouted, "You suck, Hanlon."

Timmy's body drooped as if his muscles had turned to jelly. He explained that his material was observational comedy similar to Jerry Seinfeld or Chris Rock, and he'd moved beyond knock-knock jokes to more nuanced material. Since I came from New York, he thought I'd have the sophisticated sense of humor necessary to appreciate him.

"Sorry, man, I didn't get it," I said. That's not to say that Nic Knuckles lacked a funny bone because I'd sat in more than a few New York City comedy clubs hearing great joke masters. I always thought Hemlock, the Clown, was far more amusing than any of his contemporaries. Too bad for American audiences, his comedic act had been ended by an electrical short in a faulty microphone. Oh man, I can still smell the odor of a burning rubber nose.

"You can't let one bad crowd ruin your dreams," I said. "Keep working at it, Timmy."

My words of support didn't improve Hanlon's mood, so I made him an offer that might brighten his day. "Is there anything I can do for you when I get back to town? Can I take a message to your folks or stop by the bowling alley and see if they have your celebrity photo on the wall?"

Timmy mulled my offer for a few seconds. "Yeah, actually, I could use your help doing one thing."

"Sure, my funny friend, tell Nic Knuckles what you need."

Hanlon expressed frustration with the Indiana penal system's unwillingness to let him send gifts. He asked if I could have flowers delivered to someone he owed his life. "It's her birthday, and it'd make both her and me happy."

I agreed, and he used my pencil to scribble an address and message on a sheet in my notebook. "I'll pay you when I get out," he said.

I couldn't envision any future cash deposits going into my savings account from Timmy Hanlon. The odds of his exoneration were slim, and his chances of making a living as a comedian were zero. But how could I make it an issue when a guy wanted to send his mother flowers for her birthday?

"Don't worry about reimbursing me. Your tip about a machete wheeling heckler covered the cost of any flowers."

I signaled the guard that he could retrieve the convict. "Let me know if anything else comes to mind," I said to Timmy as he shuffled away. "I'm still sorry I didn't find your joke funny."

Timmy looked over his shoulder and shrugged. "I just need to find the right audience. But thanks for having those flowers sent for me. She'll appreciate getting them."

"Sure, it'll be nice to make someone happy."

"Yellow roses," he said as the guard pulled him away. "She loves yellow roses."

Chapter Thirty-Four

I got back into Kleinstadt about four o'clock that afternoon. I felt exhausted from the long drive through the Indiana countryside but wanted to keep my promise to Hanlon and get those dozen yellow roses to his mother before her birthday passed.

Kleinstadt's last florist made a fortune when the Mindy Bauerman funeral exhausted her inventory. Sadly, with murder so rare in town, she struggled for a decade afterward before giving up and finding a more reliable source of income selling NFTs on the Internet.

The enterprising owner of the Speedi Food Mart sensed an opportunity and added floral bouquets and delivery services to their offerings. I found the flower display between the sweating wieners rolling inside a small oven and the soda dispenser. I gave a young woman Timmy's message for the card and the delivery address and was out of there in fifteen minutes.

I returned to Miss Crumble's Cozy Lodge, where I wanted to close out my long day with yet another conversation with its proprietor. Driving back from visiting Hanlon, my mind organized the various leads and tips I'd gathered into plausible theories. I ended up with a Swiss cheese of a case, and Kate left me with more holes than anyone else. I swore that she never said all she knew, no matter what she told me.

"Hello, Miss Crumble," I called out as I stepped inside the parlor. "Are you here?" The now familiar caw of Kate came from the back of the house. "I'm in the kitchen."

My heart kicked up a few strokes as I recalled my last time dealing with Kate in her kitchen. I didn't stick around then to see how her loaves of bread turned out, but I had to admit the toast at the next morning's breakfast was tastier. Hopefully, she was involved in something that wouldn't get her all hotly touchy-feely. I walked into the kitchen and tossed out my usual greeting. "Hello, Kate, can I ask you a few questions?"

The woman looked up from a pile of bills and pointed to an empty chair. "Sit. What's on that little mind of yours, Mr. Knuckles?"

"I prefer to stand," I said, wanting to be on my feet if she made an aggressive move. "I have a few follow-up questions from when we last talked."

A smile formed and danced across Kate's face. "Yes, I remember we made some beautiful gluten, didn't we?"

I ignored her and continued with my question. "When your friend, Jean Brown, died, her son, John, couldn't have been older than eleven, am I right?"

Kate clasped her hands together and leaned on her elbows. "Yes, he'd celebrated his birthday two months after his mother passed. Even with a clown, it was a very sad party, as I recall."

"So, who took the boy in after his mother died?"

"A relative, an uncle."

I lifted my notebook from my coat pocket and soon found the notes I wanted to review. As I suspected, Kate's answer had all the depth of tissue paper. I wondered how long before she'd tell me that uncle was Barney Feif.

"You once said that Jean had nowhere to stay after her husband's death. You said your aunt took in the widow and her son for a spell. Why didn't they live with that uncle?"

Kate sat back in her chair and expounded on the circumstances surrounding Jean Brown's local relative, a brother. After Jean's husband died, the uncle could not take in her and John because the man's wife and son had a history with Jean and John, and cohabitating was out of the question.

"It wasn't until Jean died from that fall into the chicken feather silo, did the man's wife relented and allowed him to take his nephew in."

Nic Knuckles knew something about the perils of blending families. My mother's second husband brought into our home his two teenage daughters. They were nice enough, other than being possessed by demons. Addressing them as Lucifer and Beelzebub wasn't a problem, but their sulfuric breath was eventually too much. We fought all the time until they packed up and left.

"In that same conversation," I said, "you mentioned how John was a naturally rule-following kid. Was the reason Jean's sister-in-law didn't want to take in John because his cousin was on the other end of the moral spectrum?"

Kate nodded as she studied an invoice. "That's pretty much right."

"Did this cousin have a name?"

Kate laid the invoice down and looked at me. "He was much older than John, and all I ever heard was that this kid was bad to the bone."

"All the way to the bone, you say?"

Kate nodded and returned to her bills.

Nic Knuckles didn't claim to know much about the human body, but I suspected you'd need bones saturated with evil to murder someone. I had to be sure what Kate meant.

"Was he the stealing a dollar from his mother's purse bad, or a diabolical genius planning to destroy the world with mutated virus he'd created in his basement lab?"

Kate rolled her bottom lip. "All I know is that he greatly embarrassed the family, so no one talked about him."

"Do you think Brownie is afraid my investigation might expose his wastrel relative?"

Kate slanted an eyebrow. "Nice guess, Sherlock."

Calling somebody Sherlock was an insult, implying they'd stated the obvious. Kate's rudeness didn't bother me, however. Calling an investigator that name was the highest compliment you could get, and all PIs were honored with any Sherlock Holmes comparisons.

"I think you know by now, Nic, everyone in Kleinstadt has secrets they don't want exposed."

I felt a grin etching my face. Kate walked into that one. "It seemed to me that you have one of those secrets, and John Brown is a big part of it."

"I don't get what you mean."

"Sure, you do. It's obvious that you have feelings for John."

The woman pushed aside the pile of paper in front of her. "I think you're guessing there, Nic."

"I don't think I am," I whispered. "Tell me about it, Kate. Is there more of a connection between you and Brownie than being his guardian angel?"

Kate wrinkled her brow and turned away from me. "Like I told you, after Jean passed, I kept an eye on her son from afar. I owed it to her. Don't make it more than it was."

So, the volatile Kate Crumble was an old softie with a heart of gold. I understood her affection for little John Brown because caring for the young and innocent was natural for humans. Like her, I never married nor had a child with which to bond. I did watch my neighbor's cats, Nip and Tuck, so I knew how a lonely person could transfer their stunted parental instincts to someone else's kid.

"You have a good heart, Kate, but I feel you're holding back on what you know about John Brown."

The woman blew out a frustrated sigh. "Good Lord, what do you want me to tell you?"

"I want you to tell me why you never mentioned that Brown's uncle was Barney Feif."

Kate looked up, and a grin slowly moved across her face. "Oh my, it looks like Nic has been doing some good investigative work."

The expression of amazement on Kate's face made me smile. It was nice to feel the power equation between Kate and me shift slightly in my favor. If she thought I had other ways of learning what was going on in Kleinstadt, she might be more revealing. Or, more careful.

"Thanks for the conversation, Miss Crumble," I said. "I'll leave you to your business-threatening debt. Good day."

"Good day to you, Mr. Knuckles."

I turned and took two steps before stopping and throwing one last question at Kate. "What are the odds that Brownie's bad seed of a cousin and Barney Feif's son was named Wayne?"

Kate continued to focus on the papers held in her hands. "I wouldn't know, a billion to one, maybe?"

I didn't care if she was my landlady and made my breakfast, and I wouldn't let her think she'd pulled one over on Nic Knuckles. "You know, Kate, I like those odds."

I left the kitchen and went up to my room. My mind was unsettled, not because the pile of bills on Kate's table suggested she was close to bankruptcy and I'd be out on the street. What bothered me was Kate's continued duplicity regarding John Brown. If she was so close to his mother, she'd heard the name of the evil kid living under the Feif roof. Why didn't she share that with me? I was dealing with more than a simple Indiana landlady with raging sexual desires. Kate Crumble was a master manipulator hellbent on protecting herself and local law enforcement, but why?

I pulled out my notebook and turned to the John Brown entry. No matter how much Kate encouraged me otherwise, I couldn't remove Brownie from my suspect list. His ranking may not be at the top, but if straitlaced by the book, young John quickly ignored Mindy's underage drinking; he could also bend the rules for other people. How much did his loyalty to Barney Feif play into things? Would it be strong enough for him to ignore his troublemaking cousin? And why'd Kate play it so coy with me about her relationship with that family?

I closed the notebook and decided to call it a day. Yeah, I'd get a good night's sleep and rise early in the morning, skip breakfast, and arrive at The Next to Last Supper soon after the doors opened. I'd risk my stomach lining drinking some of their coffee while squeezing an old newshound about a sheriff's teenage intern and a wandering bad boy with a stolen machete. I'd also like to hear what Molly thought of Kate Crumble.

Chapter Thirty-Five

Anxious to learn more about John Brown and Wayne the Drifter, I was up and hustling to The Next to Last Supper early in the morning. My previous day's discussion with Kate Crumble about bad-to-the-bone relatives had me believing that Brownie might be protecting one of my longstanding primary suspects. No matter how I turned this case over in my mind, a restless young delinquent named Wayne seemed to be at its center. Hopefully, Molly could validate my thinking. I couldn't trust Kate to be objective, not with her affection for the local sheriff blinding her.

Stepping through the door of The Next to Last Supper raised the memory of my last visit. I recalled being extremely hungry when I placed an order for pancakes, but after that, I sleepwalked through town with sticky fingers. I realized now that the excessive amount of maple syrup I used to drown those flapjacks induced some type of walking coma. I vaguely remembered Molly telling me to be careful with the information she'd given me. But what was it? Hopefully, Molly had a better recollection.

I surveyed the dining room and spotted people in booths, but none of them was Molly. As a veteran investigator, Nic Knuckles had developed a sense that buzzed whenever something didn't seem right, and it was roaring in my head like an infuriated bumblebee. I hated that noise. Nonetheless, it motivated me to stiffen my backbone, and I approached that nasty waitress who seemed to be constantly working.

"What do you want?"

"I don't see Molly Spear in her usual booth. Do you know why?"

The waitress crossed her arms, well-muscled from decades of hefting trays loaded with diner grub. "Yeah, I know why."

"Why?"

"You don't see her because she ain't there, dumbass."

Whoa, that was an uncalled-for critique of my intelligence. Who did that gal think she was disrespecting, some Girl Scout on a field trip to a diner? Nic Knuckles lived in New York City, where the waitresses would knock you to the floor and steal your wallet over a feeble tip.

"Listen, missy, I've used the toilets in this joint," I said. "Tell me where Molly is, or I'll have the county food and beverage commission close you down for violating Code 825, section 15A, paragraph three."

I knew those hours spent in the basement of the County Courthouse a week ago, reading the Kleinstadt business and restaurant operation codes, would pay off. I just didn't know when.

"What's it going to be, you giving me an answer, or you not working for a month while the owner installs proper plumbing?"

The snarl on the waitress' face went spongy. "Molly collapsed early this morning, and they rushed her to St. Vitus, the only hospital within fifty miles that served humans."

I was out the door and into my rental car before realizing I didn't order a carryout breakfast. I swung by the Speedi Food Mart and grabbed a breakfast burrito before hitting the highway to the hospital. Nic Knuckles didn't think clearly on an empty stomach, and I had a dreadful feeling that this hospital visit would require my full attention.

An hour later, I pulled into the parking lot of St. Vitus Hospital with remnants of my breakfast burrito dotting my shirt. It only took a minute before I found the head nurse running the emergency station, and I asked about Molly.

"Your friend is dying," she said. "I wouldn't make any plans for Sunday brunch with her."

Holy Roquefort, the angel of mercy, didn't pull her punches. "What's killing her?"

"The Black Death."

"What? You telling me that she's dying from the bubonic plague?"

"No, no, that's what we in the medical profession call a terminal coffee habit. Her blood pressure was off the charts, and she blew an aneurysm. She's a goner."

I cursed. My best source did in by caffeine, and she was dying all alone. I couldn't let that happen, and I swore Molly wouldn't leave this earthly coil without someone holding her hand and asking her one more question. I climbed the stairs to the third-floor Intensive Care unit and crept into a dark room. I found Molly connected to a beeping machine that relentlessly updated the status of her bodily functions. I'm no doctor, but it never looked good for the patient when a monitor had the rhythm of a funeral dirge.

"Molly, Molly, can you hear me?"

The woman raised her finger. I slipped closer and spoke into her ear.

"Molly, it's Nic. Can we talk?"

She lifted her chin.

"The last time we met, you wanted to tell me some juicy gossip about John Brown. Do you remember what you told me?"

The woman motioned me to move closer to her mouth. Her halitosis made my eyes water, but I pushed on. I had to know what she had shared with me that morning. For all I knew, it might be the missing clue to identifying Mindy Bauerman's actual killer.

"It's…."

I grabbed her arm and shook her. "It's who, Molly, tell me."

"In the book."

Molly shuddered and belched, and the monitor screamed. She was gone, as in deader than a doornail. The only person in Kleinstadt willing to help me solve my case had died. And just like she'd done every time we'd met, her last tantalizing clue was annoyingly vague.

Recalling a documentary I'd seen on the dying, I looked toward the ceiling and shouted. "Molly, before you head toward the light, what did you mean about the book?"

Suddenly, a flickering buzzing light bathed the room, and I froze. Had Molly reached across the great divide to signal me? Did she want to offer one final clue before passing into eternity?

I sensed that the source of the blinking light was behind me. Had, by some miracle, Molly returned to provide me with one last tip? What a trooper. As I turned around, my gut tensed in anticipation of seeing the ghost of Kleinstadt's former newspaperwoman.

Nope, I discovered Molly Spear wasn't there in any form. All I saw was the bathroom fluorescent bulb sputtering and flickering. Cheap illumination had fooled me. Nonetheless, I had to admit that a sense of relief swept over me. I found ghosts scary, and I'd rather not deal with them, regardless of how many clues a spook might have for me.

I left the hospital in a sad mood. Although I had known Molly for two weeks, she was probably the only person in Kleinstadt that wanted to help me. Sure, she was crusty and curt and smelled like dirty socks, but I felt she and I were alike. Molly was a fellow seeker of truth and revealer of secrets, and now she'd be forever gone from my life.

I pulled out my notebook and decided to go to my Molly Spear entry and shade the outer edges in black, and I'd draw a skull drinking a cup of coffee on the last page. That would be an appropriate tribute to my friend. I turned to that section and was surprised to see some handwriting I didn't recognize. Who'd gotten hold of my notebook and scribbled in it? Then it hit me. Molly's last words were about a book; sure enough, she meant my notebook. I remembered I left it on the table before I went semiconscious while diving into my syrupy pancake pile. What she wrote was typical of Molly because it left me curious and confused. It read *Kleinstadt Klarion, 1998, issue 27, page two.*

Chapter Thirty-Six

T he cremation of Molly Spear hadn't gone well. Apparently, coffee-infused body tissue was almost a fire retardant. They had to cook her longer than a Memphis BBQ joint smoking a rack of ribs. I swore that the more time I spent in Kleinstadt, the strangest things I learned. It wasn't until two days after she'd died that Molly's cremains cooled enough to be sprinkled in front of The Next to Last Supper. I knew doing so would violate the local health code, but that bitter old waitress, who always snapped at me, was so heartbroken that I said nothing. Let John Brown arrest the miscreants in his town because I had a murder to solve.

I wasn't the only one thinking about the job I had to do. My cellphone sizzled with an urgent-sounding ring, and I quickly answered it. "Nic Knuckles, how can I help you?"

"You can help me by bringing me up to date on your investigation. You promised me a resolution in three weeks, and your time is almost up."

I recognized the gruff-sounding voice. "Oh, hello, Mister Client."

Yeah, it was my mysterious benefactor calling, the guy with the bucks and the curiosity. He wanted to know the status of my investigation, so I told him, knowing he wouldn't be happy.

"Just when I eliminate one suspect, another one pops up. I feel like I have at least three people with stronger motives to commit murder than Timmy Hanlon."

I'd been right about Mister Client not being happy with my update. I heard a few profanities and what sounded like him kicking a wall.

"Sorry, sir," I said. "But Kleinstadt is a snake pit of people with conflicting emotions and intentions. It seemed like everyone I talked with had a history with Mindy Bauerman."

The man grumbled. "Okay, keep working at it. It's been fifteen years since someone murdered that little girl, and I can wait another week. The important thing is that you spend every waking hour ensuring Mindy gets the justice she deserves."

"To be transparent, sir, I did spend an hour today not thinking about the case. One of the town's recently deceased citizens was cremated, and I attended the dispersal of her ashes."

Mister Client asked for a name, and after I informed him that it was Molly Spear, he said, "I'm not paying you to mourn that old gossip. Stay focused on the job." He harrumphed like a backfiring motorcycle and hung up.

The call left me feeling low and disrespected. I would've appreciated it if Mister Client had said something like, "Good work, Nic" or "Atta boy, champ." Was a little encouragement too much to ask?

At least the call made it clear to me that Mister Client had once lived in Kleinstadt and had enough contact with Molly Spear to hate her. Did she expose some misconduct from Mister Client's past? Maybe it was something during the Bauerman murder trial when Molly wrote an enormous quantity of copy. Yeah, that made sense. I imagined Molly's reporting was hot with speculation and rumor back then, making some folks angry. Buddy and Buzz held hard feelings toward her, but I knew the sound of their voices, and neither could pass as my caller.

I hummed, wondering if I'd met Mister Client while making my rounds. I didn't think it was John Brown since he spoke with a threatening baritone, and George Bauerman growled as much as enunciated his words. Barney Feif babbled in a near falsetto, and Timmy Hanlon would've had to make a collect call. His father, Pa, spoke with such a distinctive accent that I'd have recognized it.

The only male person of interest left was Wayne the Drifter. I never heard his voice, but the man would now be close to forty years old. What if, after leaving town, he'd settled into respectable adulthood and made enough money to finance my investigation? He'd be one person eager to decide once and for all who killed Mindy. Maybe old Wayne wanted to clear his reputation before returning home and visiting his dad and cousin. Perhaps I'm not just solving a murder but laying the groundwork for a family reunion.

I swore, the more time I spent in Kleinstadt, the stranger the Bauerman case got.

Chapter Thirty-Seven

My tushie pressed hard on the wooden chair in Kleinstadt's Auto Emporium sales shack. The proprietor, George Bauerman, sat across from me, wearing a cold stone look of restrained hatred. I didn't feel threatened because I knew the look after decades of cornering rats. Well, actual rats had a snarling, sharp tooth expression that scared the be-jeepers out of me, and I'd quickly back away. But as far as human vermin, Nic Knuckles didn't run.

"I appreciate you giving me time to answer some questions," I said, although I had to push open the door to get in. "I won't be long."

"You bet you won't be long, Knuckles. I'm tired of you wasting my time with your misguided investigation."

I suspected the source of George's ire was more my unwillingness to buy one of his used cars than my follow-up questions. Not that I didn't appreciate his needs as a small business desperate to make a sale, but the man didn't know how traumatic driving in New York City could be for me. The flashbacks of being stuck in a swarm of VW Super Beetles driving off the upper level of the Verrazzano still terrorized me, and I couldn't afford to spend that much time in therapy.

"I tested your short man theory on Buddy, and it fell apart when my relentless baiting failed to get any reaction. I also learned that Buddy was the same size as Mindy, back when they were sixteen, not two inches shorter like you claimed. Once again, George, you've lied."

George's lips squirmed, and his eyes shifted back and forth. "I keep telling you, Buddy is a murderer. You have to make him pay."

166

"Come on, George, what's your game? Why the hate for Buddy?"

The man clasped his hands and looked away as if praying on my question. He sighed and looked up. "He killed something dear to me."

I sucked in a lungful of irritation. Bauerman was standing on my last nerve with his unhinged jibber jabber. "I'm leaving if you don't stop with the nonsense, and any chance of selling me one of your cars will walk out that door at the same time."

George reached out and grabbed at me. "Okay, okay, don't go," he said. "Maybe Buddy didn't kill Mindy, but he murdered my marriage."

Whoa, Mrs. Robinson, what was the man suggesting?

"Do you care to elaborate?"

George hunched over his desk, looking into his hands. "When Buddy was a teenager, he hung around my house, I mean, like *all* the time. He'd empty the refrigerator, lay about on my sofa, and watch my television. Every time I turned around, the darn kid was there."

"Isn't that what teenagers do? It seems normal to me."

"Yeah, that part you'd expect, if his supposed girlfriend was there. But she wasn't. Mindy would be at school, in the library, or at a football game, and Buddy would be at my house, listening to my wife's blathering on and on about how unhappy she was with me."

How curious. Even as a teenager, Buddy had preternatural skills at appearing to be interested in what other people were saying. I had no doubt that the lad's destiny was to be a bartender.

"You telling me, you'd ruin Buddy Lee Hoot because he once gave your wife the attention you wouldn't?"

George covered his head with his arms and sniffled. "I couldn't help it. Mary Jane whined about not having new clothes, or jewelry, or a nice house. She sucked all the joy out of being a principled pauper."

So, George was happy walking around in sackcloth while his wife craved Versace. In my mind, however, that explanation of why he hated Buddy was too simple, and I came back on him hard.

"Maybe Buddy's willingness to listen to Mary Jane raised painful memories from your past. Perhaps knowing your wife had someone who listened, reminded you of another man she once found to have an empathetic ear."

George's mouth skated sideways and pinched shut his right eye. "You don't know what you're talking about."

I jumped up and threw my index finger into his face. "And that memory of the young, sexually vibrant Mary Jane canoodling with a traveling salesman roared back to life whenever you saw Buddy at your house, listening sympathetically to your wife. Fifteen years later, the mere thought of Buddy being friends with Mary Jane still sets you off."

George rose out of his seat, and fiery hives spotted his face. "Stop speaking such filth about me."

"Yes, George, you thought you had the strength to forgive your wife's infidelity, but it was always in the background, tormenting you."

The man turned and snatched a set of car keys hanging from a hook and threw them at me. "Here, take that 2012 Honda Civic for a test drive. You'll love it."

"No, George, I'm not done with you. There was also one other person in your life to remind you of Mary Jane's unfaithfulness, wasn't there?"

The man folded in half and mewed like a kitten. "Don't say it. Please don't say it."

Usually, Nic Knuckles would back off in such a situation. I wasn't a cruel man by nature, having suffered more than a few of my own humiliations. But George had climbed up my suspect ranking with each lie and fumbling attempt to sell me a used car. I also remembered him kicking me out on that country road and my painful five-mile hike back into Kleinstadt. Even a mensch like Nic Knuckles had my limits.

"Yes, there was Mindy," I said. "Little Mindy with the eyes and mouth and fingernails of neither you, nor your wife. Mindy, with the devil-may-care attitude of a younger Mary Jane and a passion for dancing."

George let loose with a wail that shook the windows. I ignored him and fearlessly drove toward my grand closing statement. "I don't know which of Jesus's holy guys wrote this, but I believe the quotation goes something like this. If the right hand is nasty, cut it off, for it does you no good, and better that thing goes into the garbage than for your whole body to rot, and you end up in hell."

George looked at me with eyes red and wet from crying. "It's Matthew, but you're close enough," he said. "And yes, I did struggle every day trying not to see Mindy as the walking, talking byproduct of Mary Jane's sinful behavior, but I had nothing to do with her murder."

"Maybe not, George, maybe not. All your crying, praying, and lying won't stop me from keeping you on my prime suspect list, however."

I stepped out of the shack, leaving George sobbing at his desk. My visit had been rough on him but fruitful for me. The man admitted that he hated Buddy because Mary Jane once found succor with him. His revelation that Mindy's mere existence greatly troubled him was even more critical. The big enchilada, in my mind, and pushing George to the top of my suspect list, was in my right hand. It was the key to that 2012 Honda Civic. George must've felt I was closing in on him to let me test drive a car without him riding along.

The automobile had an attractive dark blue exterior and was surprisingly spacious inside. Impressed with how comfortable I felt, I wondered if a car that size might work in the city. It'd be nice to come and go whenever I pleased rather than wait for the next bus. Was I being bought off, if my prime suspect gave me a great deal on a car?

I slipped the key into the ignition and turned it. Instead of the engine roaring to life, I heard the starter clicking, indicating a dead battery. Maybe it was the ghost of Molly Spear or the patron of private eyes, Saint Cephalopoda, intervening, but whoever, I was going nowhere. Sorry, George, I didn't care if it was a sweet ride; the spirits wouldn't let Nic Knuckles falter in his convictions by purchasing a car from a man who may have had a hand in his daughter's murder.

Chapter Thirty-Eight

I found her again, butt up, pulling weeds. Even though I whistled and hooted so I wouldn't startle her, Mary Jane Bauerman jumped like a frog on a trampoline when I entered the backyard. The woman had either the worst hearing or a bad case of the jitters, and maybe it was both.

She snarled her greeting. "What do you want?"

"Easy, Mary Jane, easy," I said. "I only need a few answers, and you'll be back to your gardening. Now lower that spade."

The woman's frown didn't soften, and she refused to let loose her gardening tool, so I kept ten feet between us just in case she lunged. There's a thin purple scar riding across Nic Knuckles' chest that I acquired years ago. The lesson learned that day was the importance of distance between you and an angry suspect with a weapon. I was undercover at the Little Pee Wee Preschool at 73rd Avenue and 188th in Queens. Her name was Penny, and she had an outsized temper at four years of age. Yeah, she came at me with scissors when I interrupted her naptime. She had to have been eating paste or something to act so crazy.

"I'm trying to get a handle on one of the boys who had the hots for your daughter," I said. "As her mom and a former Jezebel yourself, I'm guessing you were clued in with what was going on."

Mary Jane narrowed her eyes as if focusing her vision would penetrate my head and read my mind. I'd save her the effort by getting on with my questions.

"What'd you think about your daughter going out dancing with John Brown?"

"I wasn't happy about it," she said. "George forbade her going out on Wednesday nights and left me with the hassle of trying to enforce his rule."

"I heard that wasn't an easy task."

Mary Jane opened her mouth wide and pointed to a space where a molar had once been. "Tell me about it."

I didn't waste time reminding Mary Jane of her claim at our first meeting that she and Mindy never shared a crossword. One thing I'd learned about the folks of Kleinstadt was most first impressions needed to be corrected.

"George said his concern about the boys in Mindy's life was they'd expect a discounted price on one of his used cars. Was that your worry as well?"

For the first time since I met her, a half-moon of a smile formed on Mary Jane's face. "Was that what he told you?"

"I'm getting the feeling you disagree."

Mary Jane snickered. "It probably wasn't them getting a break on a car, but what they'd do in the backseat of that car that concerned him."

I agreed with Mary Jane. When I was a teenager, my girlfriend Tina suggested we move into the back of my car. I went along after she hinted at some romantic ju-jitsu. I don't know how she did it, but I ended up alone and locked in the trunk.

"Did you have any concern about Mindy and John getting physical?"

Mary Jane sighed. "No, I didn't take it seriously until Kate Crumble raised the issue."

I felt my jaw drop and bounce against my chest. Holy Cheddar, what did she say? "Wait, wait, wait, Mary Jane, did you say it was Kate Crumble?"

"Yeah, the bitter old spinster that runs the lodge over on Main Street."

"I have to tell you, I'm surprised to hear Miss Crumble would've contacted you about anything."

Mrs. Bauerman laughed. "Me too. It was the first time in more than sixteen years that we were within spitting distance of each other."

"What did she say to you?"

"She spun some bull about how she'd promised John's dead mother she'd look out for her son. She wanted me to stop Mindy from going out dancing with him. She claimed my child was a bad influence."

"How'd you react to that?"

"I called her a busybody and told her to mind her own business. My kid could do whatever she wanted with whoever she wanted to do it with."

"So, you never tried to stop Mindy from going out with John Brown?"

"Oh, I did. I even threw her dancing shoes away, but I did it to keep peace in my house, not because that crone Crumble asked me to, that's for sure. I hated that woman. Now, leave me alone. I have to put this garden to bed."

I didn't care if Mary Jane wanted to get back to digging weeds because I still had more poking. "One more question, and I'll be done. What about Buzz Rockwell, the young man who lived across the street? Did you know him well?"

"You mean, Peepin' Buzz. No, I didn't care for him. He was George's reclamation project."

"Okay, Mary Jane, one more question."

The woman pulled her gloves on and waved her spade in my face. "I'm getting sick of your one more question crap. Leave me alone."

"No, seriously, this is my last question. Back before Mindy died, did you know a young man named Wayne the Drifter?"

Mary Jane grunted. "I knew *of* him, but as a drifter, he was more myth than real to me."

"One last question," I said. "I promise."

Mary Jane dropped to her knees and started viciously chopping the dry dirt with her spade. "I got nothing else to say."

Maybe she didn't, but Nic Knuckles did. I had one wild-ass opinion to give her something to think about after I left. It was what Kate had said about jealous females and how far they'd go to take down a competitor.

"I wondered if you were envious of Mindy's freewheeling love life. Did it bring back memories of your misspent youth, a youth then shriveling right before your eyes? As terrible as it sounds, could you've been bitter enough to have your daughter killed?"

Mary Jane kept her head down, the dirt clods flying high and far as she repeatedly slammed the spade into the ground.

"I know the idea of a mother beheading her daughter sounds sordid, but didn't Willie Shakespeare get famous for writing such a storyline? If that kind of evilness could happen in Merry Old England, why couldn't it have happened in small town, Indiana?"

Mrs. Bauerman now assaulted the ground with such vigor she could've widened the Suez Canal. My words surely made her blood boil, but she maintained her silence. I wondered if holding in rage was a Bauerman family trait. George vibrated before he blew and offered me a great deal on a used car. His wife seemed to channel her fury into pulverizing hard soil.

"I'm not leaving until you answer me, Mary Jane."

Boy, was I wrong about sticking around until she answered me. Short, plump Mary Jane Bauerman rocketed to her feet with eyes ablaze and white foam boiling out of her mouth. She screamed and slashed her spade through the air like a plane's propeller. I shrieked, took off, and didn't look back until I crossed the railroad tracks six blocks from the Bauerman property. Once again, Nic Knuckles had pushed a suspect too far, almost costing me some flesh.

I waited an hour before sneaking back to the Bauerman residence to get my car. I didn't want to be ambushed and cut to pieces by a spade-wielding maniac. I didn't see Mary Jane, but I heard her. Around the back of the house, coming from the garden, was the rhythmic sound of grunting and digging, digging and grunting.

Chapter Thirty-Nine

Tuesday morning, after an overcooked breakfast prepared by Kate Crumble, I sat in the kitchen of Sandi Fliminsky, nibbling a pastry and sipping hot tea. I swore I'd gain fifteen pounds before finishing this investigation.

"Thanks for letting me come over, Sandi," I said. "Climbing your back fence wasn't as challenging as I thought it might be."

"Sorry about you ripping your pants. Maybe Miss Crumble can sew that tear."

"Oh, no doubt my landlady would love an excuse to mend my pants."

Sandi slipped me another cinnamon bun before explaining why she'd asked me to sneak in from the back of the house. "I don't want my neighbor seeing you coming here. She now has a pair of binoculars trained on my front door. You understand my concerns, right?"

I told Sandi I understood and that entering through back doors was a common practice for private eyes. Nic Knuckles also appreciated wanting to keep the redheaded neighborhood fiend in the dark. I never liked being closely monitored as a kid, so I knew how Sandi felt.

"I need you to clarify my understanding of a mysterious salesman," I said. "How did Mindy learn about him?"

Sandi rested her teacup on the table. "I think Mindy didn't know too much, or if she did, she never shared. All we knew was the rumor that before she was born, her mother had been involved with a salesman named Tommy."

I mentally checked off Miss Kate Crumble's boozy accusation as probably valid. Mary Jane did steal away her man.

"Did Mindy ever wonder if her mother's so-called involvement with this Tommy guy included sex?"

Sandi snorted. "Of course, she did. Mary Jane Bauerman's reputation as a tart was part of Kleinstadt oral history. Her phone number is still scrawled on the walls of the town's men's rooms."

I felt my eyebrows climb, and Sandi must've noticed. "I mean her *old* phone number. You can't hold a person's youthful indiscretions against them forever."

Boy, she was right about that. The memories of my youthful indiscretions swept through my mind like a backed-up toilet overflowing, and I cringed. How embarrassing. I was a middle-aged man, and my lifetime of recollections consisted of only a few saucy experiences. I fought a wave of self-recrimination for being such a dweeb and returned to Sandi.

"Knowing the possible outcomes of carnal engagement," I said, "did Mindy wonder if that Tommy could've been her father?"

Sandi looked at me and snickered. "Oh yeah, Mindy was obsessed with that possibility. She created a three-column table where she compared her physical features with George and Mary Jane. In the third column, she recorded the features she shared with neither of them. We'd spend hours scrutinizing her parent's faces and bodies and comparing them against Mindy's."

I admired the analytical approach shown by the teenage Mindy, which suggested an intelligent kid who used a classic scientific investigative technique of observation, comparison, and conclusion. I bet she could've scored a gold ribbon if she's entered her project in the school science fair.

"And what did Mindy finally decide?"

Sandi's lips thinned, and her gaze edged toward the ceiling. "After hours of finely detailed analysis, Mindy no longer addressed her father as Dad. She called him, George."

I retrieved my notebook and recorded the salient points. One, Mindy didn't think Daddy was her daddy. Two, how angry would George Bauerman get over his daughter's assumption? And, three, if she'd lived to adulthood, Mindy could've been a star actuary for some life insurance company with her analytical skills.

"Did you know the kinds of wares this Tommy guy sold? Was it kitchenware, auto parts, encyclopedias, stuff like that?"

Sandi's lips slowly parted into a smile. "He sold shoes, women's shoes."

Holy Gruyere, that explained it all, didn't it? Nic Knuckles never understood the power shoes had over the female gender, but I'd seen more than a few crimes committed for a pair of Jimmy Choo. Tommy Lyle could've been as ugly as a toad and still seduced Kate and Mary Jane, and, as a shoe salesman, had the means to get Mindy those new dancing shoes quickly.

I opened my notebook and scribbled in a formula: Lyle + shoes / canoodling with MJ = Mindy.

"When we last met," I said, "you mentioned following Mindy into Stickerbacker's Woods and hearing a man singing. You swore it was a song about Daddy's little girl."

Sandi nodded.

"We also know that George had ordered Mary Jane to keep Mindy from going to dances. I confirmed that with Mrs. Bauerman, who also claimed she'd tossed Mindy's dance shoes."

Sandi lifted her teacup to sip. "So far, so good," she said. "You take excellent notes."

"You reported Mindy told her mother she had someone in her life who loved her and Mary Jane would not ruin Mindy's fun. Did you not?"

Sandi emptied her teacup and smiled. "Yes, yes, keep going. You're getting close."

"Now, we know Mindy was a clever girl with an obsession to find her birth father. Doesn't it make sense that somehow, she made contact with Tommy Lyle in the hopes he could replace those dancing shoes."

"Oh, you are talented, Mr. Knuckles," Sandi said. "I am impressed."

"Most likely, Mary Jane heard about it, and she shared Mindy's threat with George. Figuring Lyle wanted to make amends for being out of Mindy's life, George knew the shoe peddler would be delighted to bring Mindy a new pair of dancing shoes."

Sandi clapped her hands. "A brilliant deduction of the obvious, Mr. Knuckles. Wouldn't you have to say that no one was as motivated to commit murder as George Bauerman?"

"Yeah, probably no one had a greater reason," I said, "but George would've never gotten his hands bloody."

"Right," Sandi said, "so who would have been his eager supplicant willing to commit murder?"

Not that I hadn't already given that theory a good workout. John Brown was married to the law, and George hated him for his Wednesday night hold on his daughter, so he was out. Insecurity neutered Buddy Lee Hoot; he would've gotten lost wandering in the woods. Buzz Rockwell had the means and a motive, and George could've manipulated the lonely lad, but his devotion to a living, breathing Mindy was unassailable.

"I always thought the drifter named Wayne was a strong possibility, but I've never met him. All I have is rumor and innuendo, nothing I could see with my eyes, hear with my ears, and smell with my nostrils."

"Didn't I tell you Mindy and Wayne had dinner two days before the crime?"

"Yeah, and all you said was she didn't like the food."

"Mindy also told me she and Wayne argued and that he got nasty with her."

"I know you said that, but she never gave you the details. We don't know if it was a squabble or a full-blown, rolling' in the dirt, screamin' cage match between them. I don't know if he was angry enough to commit a crime."

Sandi jumped to her feet. "Okay, we'll never know that for sure, but check your notes. What else did I say?"

I looked back at my Sandi Fliminsky entries, and my eyes swept across my scribbling until I found what Sandi wanted me to read. "You swore you saw Wayne the Drifter, a machete hanging from his belt, spying on Mindy and her mystery man."

"Right, Nic, right. Don't you see? Wayne must've been scouting out the location."

"Okay, that makes sense, but I can't visualize how it all played without more facts."

Sandi reached across the table and grabbed my hands. "Nic, you're being too analytical. This investigation needs a woman's intuition."

Nic Knuckles didn't like that suggestion. I was once romantically involved with a psychic named Madam Vue Due. She read the bumps on my skull and told me I'd be coming into great wealth, and all I needed to do was give her my bank account number and password. I believed her, and, of course, she drained my life savings. However, she dumped me when she realized I only had a hundred and six dollars in the account.

"I don't know, Sandi. Facts are the lifeblood of what I do."

"Just hear me out," she said. "We can find the facts later."

I agreed to listen, and she spun a tale that made a lot of sense. On that Thursday, when Sandi followed her, Mindy asked Lyle for new shoes, and he agreed. As promised, Tommy showed up the next night, and Mindy swapped out her sneakers for a nice, shiny pair of patent leather shoes. Then George's thug, Wayne, showed up and started swinging his machete and beheaded Mindy.

"Whoa there, Sandi," I said. "We agree that George Bauerman had the motive and Wayne's weak moral fiber made him the perfect accomplice, but was Wayne depraved enough to actually kill a young girl?"

Sandi held up her hands and nodded. "Okay, I hear you. How about Mindy sees Wayne swinging the machete at Lyle and she screams. Wanting to protect her shoe-bearing daddy, she jumps between the two men. Wayne, not being particularly coordinated, swung his blade and *accidentally* severed Mindy's head."

"Yeah, and Lyle, being the sleazeball that he was, high-tailed it out of the woods and disappeared for good."

Sandi kissed me on the cheek. "You're brilliant, Nic Knuckles."

No investigator liked having some civilian who learned their crime-solving techniques reading cozy mysteries lead them to a solution, but I had to admit what Sandi said made sense.

"George may have been upset that Wayne botched the job," I said, "but he couldn't do anything about it without implicating himself."

Sandi clenched her fists and cheered. "Right, Nic. Now you need to go out there and convince John Brown to do his duty and arrest that bastard George Bauerman."

I rolled my head to the side. "Oh, I don't know, Sandi. Of the four people involved in that incident back on October 5, 2005, one is dead, two have long disappeared, and the fourth is perfectly happy to let Timmy Hanlon take the heat."

Sandi blew a raspberry. "If you're half as smart as you claim, you'll find a way to nail George Bauerman with what we know."

The flaw in Sandi's high opinion of me was how easily I could persuade John Brown to look more closely at the Bauerman murder case. She didn't know how much the sheriff despised me.

"Sorry, Sandi, I still don't have everything I need to connect Wayne and George, but thanks for the pastry, tea, and an interesting theory."

The woman reached over and pulled my plate off the table. "I expected you to take me seriously, Nic. I left my crew unsupervised digging a koi pond to meet with you this morning, and now you're being dismissive."

"Oh, I do take your theory seriously, Sandi. But I have only one chance to get this right, and I can't rush it."

Miss Fliminsky settled into a pout and escorted me from the kitchen to the living room, where something on her credenza caught my eye. "Wow, those are beautiful," I said, pointing to a vase overflowing with flowers.

Sandi's frown flipped to a smile. "Yes, yellow roses are my favorite."

"Someone must really care about you to send something nice like those."

The smile on Sandi's face flipped back to a frown. "What are you talking about? Those came from my backyard rose garden. I *wish* I had someone in my life that'd send me flowers."

"Oh, I'm sorry. Well, wherever they're from, they're beautiful."

Sandi and I must've been too enthralled with the roses to realize she led me out through the front of the house. The door closed behind me, and after I'd stepped off the porch, that toxic-mouthed ginger from across the street ran out, screaming incoherently.

"And good morning to you, sweetheart," I replied, which sent her into a spasm of obscene hand gestures. Why I seemed to set off that old gal was a mystery to me. Being one of America's premier private investigators, Nic Knuckles would've typically felt compelled to learn the woman's motives. However, I needed more time, and I wasn't getting paid to do so. I ignored her and hustled around the block to my car. Before starting the engine, I pulled out my favorite tome, my notebook. I entered the latest data from Sandi Fliminsky, especially her theory on the who, what, why, and how of Mindy's murder.

As much as I liked Sandi's plotline, there were still too many holes. I needed to talk with the two men who could confirm or deny the validity of her thinking. I'd gotten nowhere finding Wayne, so that left Tommy Lyle. For all the speculation about the man, I knew nothing substantive other than he sold shoes and could charm a woman off her feet.

Learning more about Lyle depended on the two women in town who knew the man best. Since Mary Jane Bauerman wanted to cut out my gizzard with her trowel, I couldn't approach her. That left my landlady, Miss Kate Crumble. I might have to sacrifice my virtue to get her to talk, but I needed to determine if Tommy Lyle was more than an errant lover boy and an absentee father. For all I knew, he might be the sole witness to what happened in Stickerbacker's Woods the night of Mindy Bauerman's murder.

I also wondered if I could locate him, would he get me a nice pair of leather oxfords for my feet? My puppies have been taking a pounding lately.

Chapter Forty

I'd barely sat down for breakfast when Kate Crumble appeared and placed a hot plate of eggs, hash brown potatoes, and toast in front of me. The speed of her service surprised me, as did the tone of her greeting.

"Good morning, Nic," she said. "I haven't seen much of you."

My response was deliberately concise. "Lots to do."

Kate hovered for a movement and then spoke. "You must be close to cracking the case since you no longer badger me with questions."

I looked at her and grinned. "Oh, I still have questions, but I don't need to bother you anymore. I've found someone else."

Kate's polite inquisitiveness went up in flames. "Who are you talking to? You can't trust people in this town. They'll lie through their teeth, and if they're toothless, their gums."

I nodded as my mouth was too full of eggs to reply. Inside my head, I was snickering because I knew Kate would flip out if she suspected I had a new rumormonger in my stable of sources.

"Who is it? Please don't say Mary Jane Bauerman. You wouldn't dare trust her after all I've told you."

My mouth was busy chewing, so I couldn't answer. I shrugged and beamed instead, which further cranked up Kate's temper. "It can't be Molly Spear because she's dead, and I don't have any contemporaries worthy of your time. You're messing with me, aren't you?"

A swig of drink from my coffee cup freed my mouth to answer her. "I thought it was time to employ a younger person, someone whose gossip would be fresh and more in tune with the times."

"Oh my God, you're not using Sandi Fliminsky. She should be your number one suspect, you fool, not your prized confidential informant."

"You're being sexist, implying that only a woman could provide me with valuable insight and information." I scraped up a forkful of potatoes and shoveled them into my mouth. "Think about it."

"Who, who is it then?" Kate jittered like she'd stepped on a frayed lamp cord in her bare feet. "Buddy Lee Hoot, of course, a damn bartender. I should've known."

"It may not be Buddy," I said. "Buzz Rockwell sees a lot of people passing through his store. The man has his finger on Kleinstadt's pulse as much as anyone."

Kate let loose a profanity as she pulled on her hair. Since I first checked in, I'd seen her in various stages of emotional distress, but nothing like what I saw before me. I almost felt guilty stringing her along.

"Stop toying with me, Nic. I can't take it."

Fortunately for Kate, I had my fill of breakfast and was ready to cash in on my little manipulation. I knew it would bother Kate if I stopped working her as a source, and maintaining the silent treatment into its fifth day made her ripe for the plucking. After swiping a napkin across my mouth, I plucked.

"Okay, I'll give you another chance, but you better be thorough and truthful."

Kate clapped, squealed, and dropped into the nearest empty chair. "I will, I promise. What do you want to know?"

"Start by telling me everything about Tommy Lyle, and I mean *everything*."

The gleeful expression disappeared from Kate's face. I guessed she thought I wanted more dope on John Brown or Mindy Bauerman, not on the man who caused her immense heartbreak. I took my notebook and pencil in hand as Kate gathered her courage. She lowered her head, drew a breath, and talked. "I was living with my auntie, helping her run the lodge, when Tommy showed up a few days before my twenty-first birthday. He was so handsome and sophisticated, unlike the yahoos walking the streets in this town."

I asked her to expand on what she'd previously told me about Lyle's business, and she confirmed what Sandi had said. The man pitched shoe samples to stores throughout the Midwest. At that time, Kleinstadt had Brinkman's Shoes and over on Oak Street, Tony's Shoes, and Socks, so Tommy had reasons to visit the town often. Those were the good old days, according to Kate. Now, most locals drove fifty miles to the big box store to buy footwear, although I knew the Speedi Food Mart sometimes sold cheap Chinese-made cowboy boots.

"When Tommy heard it was my birthday," Kate said, "he surprised me with a beautiful pair of slippers. After learning I had turned twenty-one, he asked me to dinner. It was heavenly."

The day I turned twenty-one, no one treated me to supper. No, old Nic Knuckles had stopped celebrating the day of his birth long ago, and I had my mother to blame for that. It was my eighth birthday, maybe the ninth one, and she announced I'd gotten too old for cake and presents. She started a new tradition where I sat in a chair and looked at graphic color Polaroids taken during her eighteen-hour labor. Yeah, Mom's idea of a birthday celebration stunk. Even today, I couldn't see a frosted cupcake with a candle without getting the dry heaves.

"Tommy introduced me to whisky and how to drink from a flask while riding a bicycle. He taught me a lot about nature, and I never knew how much you could learn lying on your back with your eyes closed." Kate's history report went on for ten minutes and got so steamy I worried the wallpaper might separate from the wall.

The dreamy look of pleasure on Kate's face suddenly evaporated, and her eyes squeezed tight, and her nostrils pulsed like an angry bull getting ready to charge. "Then Mary Jane Bauerman ruined everything," she said, "and forever changed my life."

"Tell me about it, Kate," I said. "Let it pop."

Miss Crumble unclenched her jaw and spun the tale.

"Mary Jane showed up one day, telling Tommy she needed a new pair of shoes, and asked him to stop by her house to take measurements. Later, Tommy told me Mary Jane planned to have a closet full of footwear, and it would require daily sales calls."

"I don't get it," I said. "George funneled his extra income into the widows and orphans charity. How'd Mary Jane pay for those shoes?"

Kate leaned on her elbows and snarled. "Exactly."

As she continued her story, Kate's voice became dry and edged with bitterness. "Tommy gave me less and less attention, and while he called me a fun girl, he said a man needed to be with a woman from time to time."

"It didn't bother him that Mary Jane was married?"

Kate shook her head. "We're just talking about the latest fashions, he claimed; there's no hanky-panky going on." Kate hacked her disgust. "Trust me, Nic, more than shoes were being tried on over there."

"How long did that go on?"

"I ignored my suspicions for a couple of weeks, but when Tommy could no longer pay for his room, I realized he was a cheater and a liar."

"Is that when you told George about Mary Jane's infidelity?"

A million-dollar facelift couldn't have pulled Kate's mouth any tighter. "Yes. One afternoon I went over to the car lot and told George that he needed to get home because Mary Jane had fallen ill. He rushed to their house and found his wife in bed with a fever. But her high temperature wasn't because of a virus. Tommy Lyle's filthy hands were responsible for raising it."

I brought up Miss Crumble's previous narrative about how Tommy immediately departed town, George forgave Mary Jane, and poor Kate was left older and wiser from the experience. She agreed I'd remembered correctly.

"So, how'd you get over such a painful experience?" I asked. "When Nic Knuckles suffered humiliation at the hands of cruel lovers, I'd leave town, start fresh, and remake myself." Somehow, I always remade myself as a private eye, but I did live in Massachusetts, New Jersey, and Delaware before settling in New York City. "Why'd you stick around Kleinstadt?"

"I didn't stay around long. My auntie told me I needed to pick myself up and get on with life. She found me a job at a camp in Michigan, and I worked there for about a year."

"Doing the camp leader thing didn't work for you, huh?"

"No, the camp job wasn't bad," Kate said. "My aunt fell ill, and I had to return to help run the lodge. Eventually, she retired, I took over, and that's how I got trapped."

I thumbed the pages of my notebook until I found the entries for Molly Spear. She'd once hinted at a bigger scandal involving Mary Jane and a salesman, and I hoped Kate could add some details and turn a rumor into a fact.

"I want to ask a sensitive question without being crass," I said. "Several reputations are riding on what I'm suggesting, so please don't be offended by my wording."

"Yes, Tommy knocked up Mary Jane. Mindy Bauerman was born less than nine months from the time Tommy last measured Mary Jane's feet."

"Oh boy," I mumbled. Looking again at my Molly notes, I marked her claim that George might not be Mindy's daddy with a big, fat check. "Did you ever bring up Mindy's questionable paternity to George? You must've been tempted after suffering so much humiliation."

Kate spat out her words. "I tried, but it was a waste of time. George got some sick sense of religious superiority by forgiving his wife's indiscretion, and Mary Jane took on the role of happy mother and housewife. They both disgusted me, and I went out of my way to avoid either one of them."

The bitterness of Kate's recollection drained her enthusiasm for reminiscing. She stood and cleared my plate, but before she left the room, I asked her if she'd ever seen Tommy Lyle again. Kate looked down at the dish in her hand and took a beat or two before answering.

"I never saw him again, but for about fifteen years around my birthday, I'd discover a box of new slippers on my porch."

Whoa, flap my arms and fly me to Costa Rica. The old shoe salesman *did* continue to slip into Kleinstadt from time to time. Maybe Sandi had it wrong, and it wasn't Mindy who located Tommy Lyle, but he contacted her. And Sandi's doped-out memory of Mindy's daddy singing in the woods now seemed feasible. That must've been when Mindy begged Tommy for new dancing shoes. Yeah, he'd need a day to pull a pair from inventory and get back to her. Could they've agreed to meet in Stickerbacker's Woods that Friday night?

I flipped the pages of my notebook to John Brown's descriptions of Mindy's corpse. There it was in my handwriting; Mindy was found dead with an un-scuffed pair of shoes on her feet. If they'd examined those shoes closely, they'd discover they were ideal for dancing.

Chapter Forty-One

I swung by Buddy's Tavern for what was now my noontime meal. We had our ritual where I inspected the cold cuts for discoloration, and Buddy made the sandwich according to my specifications. It would never be a New York City deli sandwich, but his accommodating manner made it easy to give him my lunch business. Another benefit of eating at the tavern was the more time I spent with Buddy, the more we trusted each other. I guess he'd replaced Molly Spear as my local confidant and oracle.

"I have to say, Nic, you helping me and Buzz work out our misunderstanding has improved my business. My foot traffic has increased a hundred and fifty percent since Buzz started encouraging his customers to stop here for a beer."

Quick activation of my brain's math function generated some interesting numbers. If Buddy's average crowd was two older men slowly sipping their drinks, he now had four full-timer tipplers, with another customer coming in every other day. I didn't hear the cash register ringing up big numbers, but I guessed every day was now Black Friday for Buddy.

"And to reciprocate," Buddy said. "I've been sending my customers over to shop at All Things Sharp."

The idea of Buddy's drunks buying Buzz's knives and axes made me uncomfortable, but not enough to keep me from switching the topic to my other troubling issues.

"What's the problem, Nic? Maybe I can help."

With Buddy's offer, I floated Sandi's theory about George Bauerman being behind Mindy's murder. I wanted to see if he could sink it.

"I've been thinking about George lately. He's a big guy with a volcanic temper, but even after I'd provoked him, he never blew. He'd tremble and once pushed me out of a parked car, but his hands never delivered any serious violence."

"I hear you," Buddy said. "Like I told you, Mindy was afraid of him, but she never said he laid a hand on her."

"Did he ever physically threaten you back then?"

Buddy dipped his head. "He'd ask me if I was living in a way that ensured a place in the Lord's Kingdom, if something terrible happened to me. I suppose that could've been read as a threat, but he never raised a fist."

"Did Mary Jane ever complain about being abused?"

A streak of pink colored Buddy's ears, and he dry-swallowed before responding. "She once said she *wished* George would unclench his big hands from prayer and put them on her body. But other than that comment, she never mentioned him touching her."

I reached over and scooped a handful of salted nuts from a bowl as Buddy sliced tomato for my sandwich. "There's my dilemma, Buddy. I believe George had a powerful motive to harm Mindy, yet I can't see him committing such a heinous crime."

"Maybe he had someone help him get it done?"

Geez, Buddy, I thought, you're making this too easy. Let's see if he comes to the same conclusion as Sandi and me.

"I thought about that," I said. "But, but…." My response stalled as my mind shifted to the nuts I was chewing. They were so delicious that I wondered how long a man could live just by eating salted peanuts. Maybe that's something I'd research after I retired from investigating crime.

After a strenuous swallow to clear my mouth, I returned to Buddy. "But George didn't seem to have much of an inner circle, and in fact, the only circle he had was his prayer group on Wednesday and Friday nights."

"I doubt one of his fellow congregants would've been involved," Buddy said. "Several of them come in here from time to time, and if they'd done something wrong, I'm sure I'd heard a boozy confession by now."

"Can you think of anybody back in 2005 that might've been willing to do

George's dirty work?"

Buddy lifted his gaze toward the ceiling and hummed. "One afternoon about a week before Mindy's death, I was at the house with Mary Jane when George pulled into the drive. I remember because we were surprised he'd be home that early. We peeked out the window to judge his mood and saw an older kid get out of his car."

"Did you know the young man?"

"I wasn't sure who he was. He didn't look like any of the kids from school."

"You had no idea who he was, huh?"

"No, but Mary Jane knew him, and she said she knew his daddy."

"Okay, don't keep me waiting. Who'd she say he was?"

"She called the kid trouble."

I reared back in disbelief. That's an odd name. Why hadn't this Trouble guy ever come up before? Good Lord, I removed one potential murderer from my suspect list, and now I have to add another. I'll be stuck in this town forever.

"Did Trouble come into the house?"

"No, when the front door swung open, only George came in. He growled at me and snapped at his wife before going into the basement. I took the hint and left."

"Did you ever see Trouble again?"

Buddy placed a parsley sprig on my lunch plate and slid the meal in front of me. "Nope, I never did see that guy again. Do you want a beer with your sandwich?"

I told Buddy to draw a glass of whatever he was trying to unload. I didn't have time to think about his different offerings because Mary Jane Bauerman was now on my mind. I would have to go back and learn more about the mysterious juvenile. Hopefully, the woman had gotten over our last heated meeting. Otherwise, I might never know about a kid named Trouble and his possible role in the murder of Mindy.

Chapter Forty-Two

About an hour after I'd finished my lunch at Buddy's Tavern, I stood on the porch looking into Mary Jane Bauerman's face. Her rounded features did nothing to soften the scowl, and her pawing the porch floor didn't make me feel any more welcome. However, all her snarling and intimidating behavior didn't stop me from asking my question.

"Years ago, right before Mindy's death, your husband came home unexpectedly. According to Buddy, you both saw a young man get out of George's car. He wasn't anyone Buddy had seen before, but you said he went by the name of Trouble. What can you tell me about him?"

"Why should I help you? All you've done since arriving here is dig up old dirt, and for what? Tell me, for what?"

"Well, actually, Mary Jane, I appreciate your interest in my progress. My client can't give me two minutes, and it's discouraging. You know what that's like, right? Simply wanting someone to listen about your daily tribulations and validate your feelings."

It was like heating a stick of butter in a microwave the way Mary Jane's face went all creamy. Nic Knuckles was conversant in the language of lonely people, and I knew I'd eventually break through Mary Jane's hard-crusted defenses if I found the right words.

"Yeah," she said, the brittleness gone from her voice, "sometimes you just want to be heard."

I apologized for creating more discomfort in her life, and when I complimented her hair, a hint of a smile showed on her face. I sealed her transformation by commenting on how nice she smelled, unlike when I last visited, and she was sweaty from weeding her garden.

"Okay, what'd you want to know?" she asked.

I repeated my question.

Mary Jane shook her head and mumbled. "I can't believe someone's paying you. I probably said the kid *was* trouble, not that his name was Trouble."

I pulled out my notebook, flipped to Buddy's section, and crossed out my last entry. A good investigator was always happy to correct his errors and avoid wasting time chasing a misunderstanding.

"I appreciate the clarification," I said. "So, who was this young man?"

Mary Jane's eyes narrowed, her head turning slightly to the left. "This conversation is confidential, right?"

"Of course. Once I hear what you have to say, I may yip, but that's all anyone will hear from me."

Mary Jane looked around before settling her eyes on mine. "The father of that kid can still create problems."

I swore I'd write whatever she said in a secret code that only I, and the CIA, could decipher.

"Okay, the kid was named Wayne."

I yipped. Well, turn me upside down and ride me like a pogo stick. "Did you say, Wayne, as in Wayne the Drifter?"

Mary Jane threw her hands up. "Yes, it's Wayne, the delinquent who wandered. There's only been one Wayne in this town."

"Who was his father?"

"His daddy was Barney Feif."

I yipped again, only louder. "How come this is the first time I've heard that Barney's son was Wayne?"

Mary Jane raised a finger to her lips. "Not so loud," she said. "Barney was deeply embarrassed that the town's biggest hooligan was his own boy, and believe me, back then, you didn't want to embarrass Sheriff Feif."

As stunning as Mary Jane's revelation was, my relief was greater. Now, I didn't have to think about some enigmatic character named Trouble. I could only handle so many men of mystery, and Wayne and Tommy Lyle were enough.

"Why do you think George gave Wayne a ride that day?" I asked. "From what I've gathered so far, your husband never thought highly of any of the young men of Kleinstadt."

"The kid was a troublemaker, so I wouldn't be surprised if my husband wanted to try his hand at saving his soul. George was big in helping the misfits and underprivileged of this town."

"Did you ever see Wayne and George together after that day?"

Mary Jane's mouth folded into itself, and her eyes went hard. "No, I don't recall. Mindy was murdered soon after, so my memory gets somewhat cloudy thinking about that time." She lowered her gaze and seemed to shrink in front of me. Her willingness to share was closing fast, so I asked one last question. "Who do you think killed Mindy?"

Mary Jane slowly shook her head and cranked her shoulders around her ears. "I dunno."

The woman turned away and reached for the front door knob, and I figured the conversation was over—no use pumping a woman with a broken heart because you'd get nothing but tears. "Thanks, Mary Jane," I said. "I appreciate you answering my questions."

I'd stepped off the porch and was halfway to my car when Mary Jane called out. I turned and looked at her. "Next time you see Buddy," she said. "Tell him I miss him."

"Yeah, I will."

It took time to drive back to the lodge before the gloominess I felt from my conversation with Mary Jane faded. Even a crusty private eye like Nic Knuckles got thrown off stride by a sudden display of human neediness. Mary Jane might've been a hellion set loose on Kleinstadt, but beneath the saucy attitude and loose morals was a person who only wanted to be seen and heard.

Once in my room, I stuffed my sentimentality, pulled out my notebook, and compiled my latest notes. There's a last name for Wayne, and his pappy was none other than the jelly-headed Barney Feif, the sheriff responsible for putting Timmy Hanlon behind bars. Throw in his first cousin, John Brown, the man working hard to end my investigation, and this case was suddenly a tangled family drama.

I wished Molly was still around, sucking down her coffee so I could see what she knew about the old sheriff and his wayward son. Per my notes, she once said Barney would do anything to save a kid. Then she corrected me, claiming she said that a *father* would do anything to save a kid. Now that comment made sense.

I turned to the back of my notebook and updated my suspect ranking. I moved Wayne to the top with George right behind him. Then I drew a dotted line from Wayne to Barney Feif and John Brown, with an arrow pointing at Kate Crumble. I crossed out Buddy Lee Hoot, Buzz Rockwell, Mary Jane Bauerman, and Sandi Fliminsky. My list was the cleanest since I arrived almost three weeks ago.

I closed the book and fell back onto my bed, feeling the hundreds of questions, the angry threats from suspects, and the physical abuse I endured were paying off. I'd finalized the order of the key players, and tomorrow I'd start bringing everything to a grand conclusion by squeezing who I thought was the main cog of this criminal machinery, George Bauerman. It was time to show the IRS that Mindy's daddy didn't deserve their saintly Citizen of the Year citation. No, all he earned was a lifetime sitting behind prison bars.

Chapter Forty-Three

The next day I stood in the middle of the Kleinstadt's Auto Emporium lot, cogitating. I'd learn from Buddy that locals preferred that term instead of contemplating or thinking. When in Rome, Nic Knuckles liked to do as the Romans did.

I appreciated the arc of my visits with George Bauerman. He was cold-eyed and near-mute when we first met, then talkative and overly friendly as he tried to sell me both a car and some fiction about Buddy Lee Hoot. His true maniacal nature appeared after I exposed his lies and possible motivations for targeting Buddy. I loved being a private eye; you could meet multiple exciting people, and they'd all be in the same body. Which George Bauerman personality would greet me today?

It was grumpy George. "What do you want?" he said, his mouth twisted in a familiar snarl as I stepped through the office door. "I'm tired of hearing your slander."

"Now, Georgie, please," I said. "We both know I won't stop hounding you until I get my answers. We've played that game too many times to think otherwise. So, here's what I've been thinking."

Bauerman groaned and covered his face. Maybe he thought if he couldn't see me, I'd disappear. Playing peekaboo might work with an infant, but not with Nic Knuckles. It didn't matter if he crawled under the desk because I'd still be there, trying to break him.

"I have a theory on what happened the week Mindy was murdered," I said. "It all began when Mary Jane tossed out Mindy's shoes to keep her from dancing with John Brown. Your daughter told your wife it didn't matter, that she knew someone who'd replace those shoes. Fearful what Mindy might do, your wife told you. Of course, you assumed the person Mindy was talking about was a shoe salesman named Tommy Lyle. That's when you concocted a plan to confront Lyle and fulfill your long-simmering need for retribution."

George removed his hands from his face. His eyebrows hung low on his forehead like a heavy morning fog, and I couldn't tell what he was thinking. Nonetheless, he was listening.

"As a man of God, you would never bloody your hands, but Buzz Rockwell might. The sad loner, befriended by the father of the girl he secretly loved, would do anything. How could Buzz not want to impress you by doing what he did best, chopping things apart?"

George cried out. "That's a horrible thing to say. I only wanted to help Buzz to be a better person, not use him to commit sin."

I slowly nodded. "I know, George. Young Rockwell would've never done anything to frighten Mindy. Why ruin his tiny chance of winning her heart someday by playing her Daddy's goon?"

George seemed confused that I backed off so quickly. The poor fool had probably never fished before, or he'd known I was slowly reeling him in.

"But you knew from your interactions with Buzz, that he had a friend of questionable character. Yes, a drifter named Wayne, who might be happy to make a little money scaring people."

"No, no, I'd never think of something like that."

I stepped closer to Bauerman and waved my finger at him like an admonishing school teacher. "Oh, I think you did, George. The long-buried pain of being humiliated by a traveling shoe salesman drove you to execute your plan. Regrettably, things in the woods that Friday night didn't go according to your design. Wayne showed up and threatened Lyle and Mindy. Neither one of them were afraid, so your henchman grew more aggressive and started swinging a machete. Mindy must've thrown herself between the two men and was killed. Maybe Wayne had no intention of harming anyone, but it happened. Lyle, being the snake that he was, ran away, never to be heard from again. Wayne reported back, you paid him off, and demanded he leave town."

I pushed my nose inches from George's. "And you've been trying to cleanse your soul of that horrible guilt ever since."

George's face turned the color of tapioca, and tears dribbled from his eyes. He pounded the desk and cried, "Okay, I was afraid Mindy was seeing Lyle, and I wanted Wayne to find out when and where they were meeting. But everything else you said was completely wrong."

I dropped into the chair in front of the desk with my pencil poised over my notebook. "If I'm so wrong, big guy, why don't you dry those tears and educate me."

"There isn't much else to say."

"I'll help you with my usual array of probing questions. How'd you cover Wayne's expenses while he did your dirty work? Did you divert some of your charity money?"

"No."

"Did you make a cash sale that week and kept it off your books?"

"No, no." Bauerman folded over and started mumbling. "All I can say is that it wasn't my money or my idea."

Now, it was my turn to be knocked off stride. "Are you saying you had a partner in all of this?"

George nodded. "I was approached by a person who was interested in breaking up Mindy and John Brown. Since Mary Jane was failing miserably at keeping our daughter in the house at night, I said yeah."

"What did this man want you to do?"

"He wanted me to hand off a wad of cash to Wayne and then, the following Wednesday night, let Mindy sneak out of the house."

"That was all you did; there was nothing else?"

George took a tissue from a desk drawer and dabbed his eyes. "Yeah, well, there was a little more. I thought that as long as Wayne was spending time with Mindy, I'd use him to get some important information for me."

"Let me guess. You wanted Wayne to learn where Mindy was meeting Tommy Lyle, right?"

"Yes, but that's all Wayne was supposed to do for me."

196

"Is that how you knew she was going to be in Stickerbacker's Woods the night she was murdered?"

George hunched and dipped his head. "No, no, no, I made the mistake of giving Wayne the cash upfront. I never saw him after his supposed dinner date with Mindy."

"So, you didn't know where Mindy was meeting Lyle to get her new shoes?"

George nodded his shiny dome of a head. "That's what I'm telling you. I never knew she would be in the woods, and I never had a chance to confront anyone."

My bullshit meter was clicking pretty loudly despite George's appearance of transparency, but I had nothing to refute his assertion. I decided to hone in on the mysterious financier.

"What can you tell me about your partner who paid for Wayne and Mindy's epicurean escapade?"

"Sorry, I'm saying nothing. That man still has ways of hurting people who cross him."

I folded my arms and cocked my head to the side. Where had I heard that sentiment spoken before? I didn't have to consult my notebook because I remembered Mary Jane said the same thing about Barney Feif. George looked determined not to budge, and I figured my relentless grilling might take hours to work, so I'd play upon his weakness to get him to reveal his collaborator.

"I saw that Chevy Nova on your lot when I came in. I always had a soft spot for that model. Is it still available?"

George raised his head, and his watery eyes sparkled. "Would you like to give it a test ride?"

"I wish I could, but until you tell me who was behind your little plot to scare Mindy straight, that vehicle will have to sit out there, undriven, unloved, and unbought."

"Ah, come on, don't be that way," George said in a singsong manner that I found irritating. "I really need a sale this month."

No matter how much he whined, I wasn't going to give in. I sat there, not moving, for another ten minutes as George fidgeted. Finally, he broke and gave me the answer. He looked surprised that I wasn't.

"Why would Barney Feif use his son," I asked, "to break up his nephew's relationship with a sixteen-year-old girl?"

George shrugged. "I don't know. Feif gave me the money, introduced me to Wayne, and I told Mary Jane to ignore Mindy's escape from the house. That's all I did."

I closed my notebook and squeezed it against my chest. If George were truthful, which was not a guarantee, I'd have to drop him from the upper echelons of my suspect ranking. Was the Mindy Bauerman case nothing more than a low-rent family drama that got out of hand? Did half the town want to forget the murder of a sixteen-year-old girl because half of Kleinstadt was somehow involved?

For the first time since I arrived in Indiana, I felt exhausted.

Chapter Forty-Four

I sat outside the Kleinstadt Auto Emporium in a used Chevy Nova, my mind and the engine idling. I'd gone into Bauerman's sales shack determined to score a confession and got nothing but another suspect mucking up my investigation. My notebook only had so many pages, and I couldn't handle any more suspects.

After taking the Chevy car keys and telling George to draw up financing paperwork, he coughed up more details. He said Feif approached him about two weeks before Mindy's murder, claiming John's dancing dates with Mindy threatened the boy's future law enforcement career. He feared his nephew might run off and join some dance company if there wasn't an intervention. Since George wanted the same results, he didn't question the logic of Feif's motivations. A few days later, the old sheriff dropped off an envelope with several hundred dollars in cash, and not long after, George picked up Wayne. During the short ride, George gave Wayne the money and instructions. That was when Mary Jane and Buddy saw them outside the Bauerman residence.

As far as the dinner date, George had heard nothing about it. Playing the fooled parent, he couldn't ask Mindy how her evening went, and she wouldn't have volunteered anything. Wayne failed to connect with George, and Bauerman never learned about his daughter's plan to be in Stickerbacker's Woods. Or, so George claimed.

With the chaos of Mindy's murder days later, George and Feif never spoke about their scheme. I wondered why Bauerman wasn't more troubled by that fact. How could Feif have been an impartial investigator in his daughter's murder, what with his son hired to create problems between his nephew and the eventual victim? Add in Wayne's disappearance, questionable history, family loyalty, and the crime-screaming coverup, why was I the only person hearing it?

I did what I always did when overwhelmed with confusing and conflicting data. I pulled open my notebook and studied my notes. The exercise, however, failed to bring any clarity. Too bad Molly wasn't alive because she'd help me sort things and inscrutably point me in some direction. Man, I missed her impatient demeanor and acidic-smelling breath.

Resisting the urge to drive over to The Next to Last Supper for a nostalgic cup of bad joe, I pushed the pages of my notebook to Molly's section. The drawing of a skull drinking coffee still looked cool, but something else grabbed my attention—Molly's mysterious inscription -*Kleinstadt Klarion, 1998, issue 27, page two.*

It seemed like an obvious clue, and one might wonder why Nic Knuckles hadn't acted on it by now. The reason, sadly, had to do with my childhood. When I was a kid, I was one of the city's famous newsies, selling copies of a tabloid called The Daily Screed. The publishers knew skin and sin sold, so on Tuesdays, the paper ran a photo of a nearly naked woman, and Thursday, one of a criminal hauled off to jail. It was the third week in August, when I was eleven, maybe twelve, when my mother showed up in the Tuesday edition, and the Thursday paper highlighted my old man. I never read a newspaper after that horrible week.

"Come on, Nic," I barked, like a Rottweiler with a sore throat. "Molly died while trying to help you solve this case. Get over your trauma, go to the library, and find that old edition."

"Okay, I will," I shouted just as loudly. "Now stop bugging me."

I slammed the Nova in gear and tooled over to the public library. The afternoon spent sneezing and coughing while digging through dusty boxes of the defunct Kleinstadt newspaper paid off. I found the article Molly wanted me to read, and the old caffeine guzzler came through. After recovering from the shock of what I had learned, I went to the county courthouse.

"You're back again," the woman sitting inside the records administrator's office said.

"Hi, Grace, yes I am."

She asked if I'd been able to put to use what I learned about the town's rules and regulations from my first visit.

"Not yet," I said, "But my knowledge of the restaurant sanitation rules came in handy."

Grace's lips parted like a question was forming, but she held back. As the person in charge of the town's legal minutia, I assumed she was used to never getting a sensible answer from anyone who spent time in her storage room.

"Okay, what can I do for you today?"

"I'd like to see the county census records from around 1988 and 1989. Could you pull them for me?"

The woman laughed and jerked a thumb toward the basement door behind her. "Knock yourself out, mister investigator from New York City. I'm not going down there."

My asthma was in a full-blown, mucus-producing Armageddon by the time I finished searching Grace's file cabinets, but it was worth it. My carefully constructed suspect pyramid would have to be dramatically rearranged, with George Bauerman going from prime guy to a simple tool of the real mastermind. I felt guilty knowing in a half hour. I'd disappoint George when I returned the Chevy to his lot and back out of buying it. He'd be so upset with me.

My concern over Mr. Bauerman's anger lasted but a minute because the greater fear was whether Kate Crumble would throw me out of her house when I accused her of being behind the murder of Mindy Bauerman. She'd already shown a temper that scared me.

Chapter Forty-Five

It wasn't until late the following day that I could confront Kate Crumble. Yesterday's asthma attack forced me to spend most of last night sucking steam from a hot shower. I finally could fully fill my lungs with air around two in the morning, so I slept until about ten. I found Kate in the kitchen, where she'd finished hand washing and drying a load of dishes.

"Okay, I'm ready," Kate said, a wet dishtowel in her hands. "What's gotten you so all excited that we had to talk?"

"A question or two about John Brown, that's all."

"Good Lord, Nic, haven't I answered every dang question by now?"

"You'd think so, wouldn't you?" I said, "But with your inability to tell me the full story, I keep having to come back."

Kate's lips thinned and started wiggling. I knew that was her tell, and she was probably wondering how she might finesse anything I asked her. But today, she'd have no defense because Nic Knuckles had done the research, and I'd soon have Miss Crumble crying for mercy.

"How close were you with John's mother?"

Kate shrugged. "I told you several times. We were like sisters."

I felt a smile push the stubble on my face to one side. "Did Jean ever talk about her pregnancy? You know, like sisters would."

"No, I only met her years after John was born. Why would we discuss her pregnancy?"

One of the best parts of an investigation was when the private eye already had the answers to the questions they were asking. Poor old secretive Kate Crumble would be stunned when learning what a few hours in a dank library basement and a moldy courthouse records room could reveal.

"I did some investigation at the county courthouse and learned that John Brown wasn't born in this county. Yet, he shows up in the local census as an infant child of Jean and Mike Brown."

"Maybe his folks moved to the area after he was born?"

I shook my head. "The property tax records had them living here a decade before John's birth. In fact, Mike Brown's family owned their farm going back two generations."

Kate cracked a smile. "I have to give you credit, Nic, you're a better gumshoe than I thought."

People who underestimated Nic Knuckles did so at their peril. I fooled a few criminal masterminds who thought I was a bumbling private eye, like that investigation of the local Postal Workers union and the missing spice-scented underwear. There are a couple of guys sniffing the stale air of Riker's Island right now because they thought they'd fool me.

"I think it's possible," I said, "that Jean and Mike Brown were not the birth parents of John."

Kate's lips disappeared from her face, and her hands squeezed the damp dishtowel.

"I also learned that Mike Brown died when John was ten years old."

"Yes, we talked about it," Kate said. "A farming accident, right, like I told you?"

I slid my hand across the tablecloth and picked up a tiny piece of burnt crust left over from someone's breakfast. "According to my notes, you said Jean and John moved into your aunt's lodge for four months until the widow found an apartment."

Kate hunched over and mumbled. "Yeah, that's my recollection, but it was a long time ago."

"Well, before my dear friend, Molly Spear, departed this earthly coil, she directed me to an old newspaper article. It was a feature in a 1998 issue of the Kleinstadt Klarion. The owner of a local boarding house was recognized as the town's citizen of the year. The woman had taken in a widow and her son and let them live there rent free while the widow went to school and earned her poultry inspection certificate."

A few drops of water fell from the dishtowel Kate held tightly in her hand. "Yeah, so what?"

"Apparently, Jean Brown was no genius, because she required three years to earn that certificate."

Kate melted like the Wicked Witch from *The Wizard of Oz* without steam coming from her body, which I appreciated because that scene always creeped me out as a kid.

"I saw the newspaper photo, and I must say, Kate, you 've barely aged a day."

I absentmindedly rolled the burnt toast crumb between my thumb and index finger. If I weren't so focused on exposing Kate's secret, I'd ask her why she tended to burn everything she cooked because it had to be more than accidental.

"Why'd you tell me Jean and John lived at the lodge for four months when it was three years? Why not tell me the truth about your long-standing relationship with John Brown and his mother?"

Rouge-colored splotches formed on Kate's neck and cheeks as she talked. "Maybe I'm modest?" she said. "Did you ever consider that, Mr. Knuckles? Perhaps I'm uncomfortable being lauded for my generosity."

"Oh, I know all about your generous nature, Miss Crumble. But I wonder if that summer camp your aunt sent you to years ago was more than a bunch of mosquito-infested cabins filled with bored kids."

Kate cried out. "It was a camp, and the kids swam in a lake and made potholders, and that's the truth."

"I don't believe you, Kate," I said. "I don't think you were honest when you said you and Tommy Lyle did nothing more than smooch. I think new slippers weren't the only thing old Tommy Boy gave you."

Kate's eyebrows pulled together, and she dropped into the chair across the table from me, the dishtowel in her hands wrung dry.

"Here's the timeline that I've pieced together," I said. "Tommy Lyle stayed at your aunt's lodge multiple times, up until 1988, when he left town after the exposure of his dalliance with Mary Jane Bauerman. Maybe four or five months after that, you left town as well for some camp in Michigan to sing songs around a fire. On October 27 1989, per the county birth records, a girl was born to Mary Jane Bauerman, and she was named Mindy. Less than a week later, Jean and Mike Brown showed up with a baby boy they called John."

Kate's eyes misted when I got to that point, and I didn't think she was nostalgic about the singing of a bear comin' around some mountain.

"Ten years later, after Mike Brown's tragic death, a broken Jean and her boy showed up as guests at your aunt's lodge. Auntie agreed to take them in for a few weeks, maybe a month, but she retired, and you took over running the place. It was you who decided to let them stay for three years without charging Jean a dime. You did that, and you did it because John was *your* child."

Kate lifted the bone-dry dish towel to her mouth and chewed the corner.

"There's no shame in admitting you'd gotten into trouble," I said. "Why don't you tell me what happened and save me from further exposing your sordid past?"

Kate pulled the dish towel from her teeth and threw it on the table. "Maybe nowadays, an out-of-wedlock pregnancy doesn't shame a woman, but back then, it was a scandal."

"Yeah, those were the days when closets held more skeletons than clothes."

Kate twisted in her chair. "Don't try and make me feel bad about falling for a smooth-talking salesman. Weren't you ever twenty-one?"

Kate nailed me there. Nic Knuckles' twenty-first year on the planet hadn't been stellar. I was three years out of high school, lacking direction and eating out of restaurant dumpsters. I was in a dismal space at the time. On the positive side, however, most of the leftover food tossed by the local eateries tasted better than what my mom made. I gained twenty pounds that year.

"Okay, Kate, don't get your feelings hurt. I'm not judging you. I only want the truth, the whole truth, and nothing but the truth."

Kate dropped her head and averted her eyes. Nic Knuckles knew the look of confession time, and my notebook and pencil quickly materialized in my hands.

"It wasn't a camp, and it wasn't in Michigan," she said. "It was a home for unwed mothers' two counties over. My aunt shipped me out when I started to show."

"That must've been tough."

"Yes, it was."

"How'd you know the baby Jean and Mike Brown adopted was your child?"

"When I got pregnant, the rest of Indiana apparently discovered either abstinence or birth control, because I was only one of two girls at the home. I birthed a ten-pound boy with a chunky head, and before I left, the other woman delivered a girl, so I knew very few male babies were available. I'd barely got home when I learned that some nearby farm family had taken in a strapping baby boy to live with them."

"That had to be difficult," I said. "You must've had some messy feelings."

"Messy doesn't say it all. Mary Jane got to have her love child in a hospital with her family nearby. She got flowers and cards from well-wishers and was celebrated., while I had to sneak out of town and have my baby all alone."

"I'm sorry, Kate, I really am."

"And it never got any easier. I had to watch some other woman be the mother to my son while Mary Jane strolled around Kleinstadt pushing a baby carriage. Even when Jean and John lived at the lodge, watching them together ate me alive."

Kate's eyes brimmed with tears, and even a hard-hearted PI like Nic Knuckles had to hug her. I walked over and wrapped her in my arms. "Now, Kate, Nic is here to soothe your troubled mind, and that's all."

Unfortunately, Kate's need for empathy only lasted a few seconds before she wanted more than her broken heart comforted. I pulled away when I felt her hand caress my right butt cheek because either she crossed a professional boundary or picked my back pocket.

"Okay, Kate, you've had your thirty seconds of Nic Knuckles' intimacy. Let's get back to my questions."

Miss Crumble crossed her arms, and her eyes turned beady. It looked like I'd disappointed her again.

"Jumping ahead to when John and Mindy were sixteen and out dancing, did you worry, as half-siblings, that they might inadvertently violate the laws of nature?"

"Of course I did," she said. "I knew where dancing could lead, and John and Mindy each had Tommy Lyle's promiscuous blood flowing through their veins. I reached out to Mary Jane and told her we had to break them up."

I didn't share with Kate that it was old news for Nic Knuckles, having heard it first from Mary Jane. I'd let her run her mouth, hoping I'd learn something more.

"That idiot wouldn't help me," Kate said. "She'd convinced herself that her fling with Tommy hadn't happened and claimed that Mindy was made of pure Bauerman DNA."

"What'd you do?"

"I went to Barney Feif. I figured as John's uncle and mentor, he'd want to do something about it."

Oh boy, that disclosure added credence to George's story about Feif's role. Now, to see if she'd reveal the level of her involvement. "Was Barney willing to do something?" I asked.

"He was dubious. I mean, I never had a one hundred percent proof that John was my boy or that Mindy was Tommy's child."

"How'd you convince him to help you out?"

Kate wobbled and shrugged. "He was the sheriff and knew who did the bad things in town. Mary Jane's promiscuity was no surprise to him. And since he cared so deeply about John and his future, he finally agreed to help me break them up."

"Did he arrest Mindy for chewing gum and gave her a night in the pokey to think about how miserable he could make her life if she kept dancing with John? That's what I would've done."

"No, nothing like that," Kate said. "Barney was afraid John would get upset with him if he knew he'd help break up him and Mindy. He suggested another way of making it happen."

"Involving George Bauerman, I'm guessing, and then Barney's drifter son,

Wayne."

Kate jerked her head sideways. "How did you know that?"

"What do you think I've been doing these last three weeks, Kate, taking those discounted Pilate classes at the Speedi Food Mart?"

I closed my notebook and settled my most serious expression on Miss Crumble. "Let me get this straight," I said. "You needed a way to break up John and Mindy because you feared as possible half-siblings; they'd grown too close. Mary Jane was someone you thought would be equally concerned, and she laughed at you. Then you asked Feif, and he agreed to find you someone who'd work with you. That's how George got connected since he had the same goal. Feif served as the middleman, introducing George to his son, Wayne. The drifter needed money, which you provided, and since he hated John, he happily escorted Mindy to dinner on that Wednesday."

"Your recap is impressive, especially when you basically repeated what we've just said to each other."

Nic Knuckles always appreciated a compliment, and I thanked Kate. But I wasn't going to let up until she told me everything. "So, what happened? Why did Mindy end up dead? Was that part of your plan?"

"Of course not. I only wanted Mindy to stop dating John, not die. I never saw Feif after I gave him the money to pay for everything. I was as shocked at the murder as everyone."

"Really," I said. "You only wanted to break the fever of two teenagers, did you?"

Kate brushed her hand through her hair and grumbled. "You're acting like you know something. Go ahead and take your best shot, Nic."

I smiled and leaned closer. "While it's true George Bauerman was just as eager to break up Mindy and John as you were, you both shared another all-encompassing desire."

Kate's right eyebrow flickered, but her pride made it impossible for her to ask what I meant. She'd wait and hear me out.

"You both hated Tommy Lyle."

Kate's head bobbled ever so slightly.

"I have to believe you and George wanted to maximize your investment in Wayne and have him settle an old hurt for both of you."

"You're being ridiculous."

"Am I," I asked. "I have you and George with the motivation, you financing a known bad boy, and George making it all happen. Two days after the dinner date, you knew where Mindy was meeting Lyle. I don't know what went wrong, but we have Mindy dead, and both Wayne and Tommy Lyle gone from the face of the earth."

"You should write crime fiction, Nic, with that imagination."

"Bauerman claimed he never heard from Wayne after that dinner date. Barney Feif's memory dissolved into a puddle years ago. Only you might know what was said between Wayne and Mindy on their date, and only you might know who showed up in Stickerbacker's Woods the night Mindy died."

"I don't know a thing."

"I'm not so sure, Kate, but I gotta tell you. The more I learn about your past, the less I want to eat your breakfast."

Chapter Forty-Six

I could've driven over to Kleinstadt's Sheriff's Department, but it was quicker to jaywalk across Main Street. Once I reached the other side, John Brown pulled his official law enforcement vehicle to the curb, the siren wailing.

"Okay, Knuckles, spread 'em."

Brownie roughed me up as he gave out his standard admonishment. It'd been several weeks since our last encounter, and I didn't intend to be the one squirming when it was over. I threw this question over my shoulder.

"Why do you think Sheriff Feif never considered his son Wayne as a suspect in the Bauerman case?"

Brownie's steel-tipped fingers halted their mauling of my soft flesh enough to allow me to turn around and look at him. I'd seen street mimes with more color in their faces.

"I'm telling you as a favor, Sheriff," I said, "everything I've learned points to Wayne Feif as Mindy's killer. Will you cooperate with me, or do I have to reveal your uncle, and maybe you, as being in cahoots to keep an innocent man in prison?"

That didn't go over well with the sheriff. He stretched to his maximum height, and his eyes grew wide. Dressed in his brown and tan uniform with an aggrieved expression, he reminded me of a Nature program on Grizzly Bears. When encountering one of those beasts, you never stared at them because it made them feel judged. With their claws and sharp teeth, the program's narrator suggested you should curl up and play dead.

I wouldn't give Brownie the satisfaction of watching me cringe, regardless of how much of a Grizzly he looked. "Maybe now you'll cooperate with me," I said, "or do I have to expose your dirty laundry for the town to see."

Much to my relief, the vibrating tension in Brownie's face dissipated as he chose to keep his laundry hidden from public view. "It's not like that, Knuckles," he said. "It's complicated."

"Why don't you help me understand?"

The man stepped back, and his eyes grew moist. "Okay, I'll talk, but you better not use what I tell you to hurt my Uncle Barney."

Brownie's willingness to finally open up jacked my heart rate, and I promised him Feif was off limits. Why would I go after a sad shell of a man wasting away in a nursing home, anyway? "Okay, John, I'd love to hear what you have to say."

The sheriff suggested we ride to a secluded area where he'd be comfortable talking. Ha, nice try, I replied. Having been dumped five miles out of town by George Bauerman and then hoodwinked by Sandi Fliminsky in some isolated woods, I told him we'd stay right there in the middle of the street. Even though he was far down on my suspect list, Brownie was still in the mix. There'd be no meeting in the woods where the only eyewitnesses were birds and squirrels.

"Gimme the backstory on you and Barney's family," I said as I whipped out my notebook and pencil and turned to the John Brown page. "Clear that up for me."

The sheriff leaned against his cruiser and tipped the brim of his hat upward. He heaved a sigh and began speaking. "After my dad was killed and my mom couldn't handle the farm, we moved into Kleinstadt. My Uncle Barney helped us out, but only for a few weeks. His wife and son didn't get along with my mom and me, so we moved into town." Brownie looked away. "You know you can't always count on family to help when you need them the most."

Boy, did Nic Knuckles know how unreliable relations could be? My cousin Winston needed a liver transplant, and we had an older relative born with two livers. You'd think the man would've donated one to Winston, but nope, not that guy. He swore his retirement planner told him to keep it in case his portfolio failed and he had to sell some organs on the black market. Thoughtful retirement planning, he called it. I dropped a little prayer in Winston's memory and switched my attention back to listening to John Brown.

"You have to understand that Wayne was five years older, and we already had a history before my father died. When the families got together on the holidays, Wayne wanted me to join him in soaping windows or setting small fires. I resisted, and when I finally dropped a dime on him with his dad, he never forgave me."

It sounded like Brownie was a stickler for the rules, even as a kid. I could see how a natural-born hooligan like Wayne would hate the snitching little Eagle Scout.

"What were the issues with Barney's wife?" I asked. "Why'd she disliked her sister-in-law so much she'd throw you and her to the streets?"

"Barney and his wife had a contentious marriage. She hated that he was too busy as the town's law enforcement, leaving her to raise Wayne. The idea of me and my mom sharing his limited time was too much for her."

"So, you lived at Miss Crumble's Cozy Lodge for a few years, right?"

"Until I was thirteen, and by then, Barney's wife left him for good, so he invited us to live with him."

"Wayne must've been very unhappy with that development. Is that when he started drifting?"

Brownie shook his head. "Naw, apparently, when Wayne started crawling as a baby, they never knew where he'd end up. I don't think me being in the house was the cause of his vagabond nature."

"How'd you feel about living with your uncle?"

"Oh, I loved it. By then, I was aware of his stature in town. I admired his uniform and how people jumped whenever he drove by and triggered the siren. I wanted to be just like him."

Nic Knuckles understood Brownie's feelings because my Uncle Spittle always inspired me with a larger-than-life presence. The man would walk into a room, and men and women would fall at his feet like he was some potentate. Not that they admired him. Poor bastard's feet were size 18 and laid at such an odd angle that he'd trip anyone near him.

"Later, after my mom died, I hung out at the Sheriff's Department, making a pest of myself. Uncle Barney took me on as an intern, and we grew especially close."

"I have to tell you, John, my long, dark history with siblings leads me to think Wayne was upset with his dad giving you the extra attention."

Brownie agreed with my assessment and said Barney and Wayne's strained relationship worsened. As Wayne got older, Barney tried to find the boy work, hoping he'd save enough to buy a one-way bus ticket out of Indiana. Not surprisingly, Wayne failed to keep any job to spite his father.

I wondered how much Brownie knew about his cousin getting hired to break up his romantic relationship with Mindy. I'd throw out an opening and see if he walked through. "Were you aware of Wayne having any sort of employment around the time of Mindy's murder?"

John Brown's chest rose, and then he loudly exhaled. "I recall my uncle fighting with Wayne about some work he'd procured for him, but I never learned the details, and I didn't care to get into their business."

I imagined Feif didn't want John to get into his business, either. Not with him as the middleman behind Wayne's date with Mindy.

"Why didn't Sheriff Feif take a serious look at Wayne?" I asked. "I'd only been in town a week, and your cousin quickly appeared on my radar screen."

Brownie shrugged. "I think he convinced himself that Timmy Hanlon might've, could've, would've done it, so why not focus all his attention on connecting those dots? He didn't have the resources to go after multiple suspects."

"I know you were only a teenager, but you had a supernatural sense for right and wrong. What'd you think as you watched things unfold?"

Brownie turned away from me, and the answer slipped from the side of his mouth. "I thought maybe Uncle Barney should've looked carefully at Wayne as well."

"Did you tell him that?"

"What could I say? I knew he carried a heavy guilt, being such a lousy dad. How could I point out all the reasons why his son might've done such

213

a terrible crime?"

"That doesn't sound like the incorruptible John Brown I've learned to fear."

"I know, but I was caught between loyalty to Barney and my affection for Mindy."

The mention of Mindy and affection moved me to ask a question that first came to mind when Mary Jane showed me Mindy's photo albums at my initial family visit. "I know you adored her dance skills, but you have to admit, she wasn't a good-looking girl."

A mouthful of air whistled through Brownie's lips. "Maybe she wasn't a beauty, but she put out some powerful pheromones. That's why all the boys liked her. I knew it was irrational, but I was drawn to her, like iron shavings to a magnet. Can you understand?"

Oh yeah, Nic Knuckles knew something about the witchy magic of women, and I'd learned that lesson when I was a young buck. Her name was Eldora, a seductress, a vixen, and a witch. How else to explain being attracted to a woman with a hairy wart sprouting off her beak? And her laugh, a gleeful cackle that turned heads and made babies cry. I could burn hours talking about that time in my life, but I had to listen to John Brown's testimony.

"More importantly than my affection for Mindy," Brownie said, "was my desire not to mess up my uncle. He was under tremendous pressure to find Mindy's killer, and if he thought Timmy was the one, why complicate his thinking? I did owe that man everything."

"Okay, I hear you," I said. "But other than your personal animosity for Wayne, why did you think he may have been involved?"

John Brown shifted his extra-large behind against the side of the car, signaling he was settling in for a long talk. "It was the Wednesday night before Mindy was murdered. Since I didn't have a partner, I wasn't at the Swing and Swoon, but home watching TV. About eleven, a noise out in our backyard got my attention. Looking out the window, I saw Wayne standing there with a fire going in the old barrel we used to burn trash. He was roasting wieners."

"That sounds strange," I said.

Brownie shook his head. "Not really. Our gas line was cut the week before when Barney used a backhoe to dig a new latrine. He was so embarrassed, you know, the town's top cop not asking the gas company to come out and mark their line. It hadn't been repaired, and we had to cook many a meal over the old burn barrel."

"Did you ask Wayne about why he was eating so late?"

"Yeah, I went out and questioned him. He laughed and said the lobster he had at dinner wasn't enough to fill him up. He whined he should've taken Mindy to a pizzeria and gotten better food for a lot less money."

Wowzer, so Brownie knew all about the date. "That must've hurt, him throwing it in your face that your dance partner preferred him over you that night."

"Yeah, it made me mad. But what really ground my gears was Wayne knew I always wanted to try lobster, and he didn't invite me along."

I didn't get it. A lobster was one of those things you believed might be fabulous until you ate it. To me, it was an expensive excuse to slurp down melted butter.

"Did he talk about what went on at the restaurant?" I asked.

"Naw, other than complaining how Mindy invited two friends and it cost him twice as much, he said nothing."

I stumbled backward, and if Brownie's cruiser hadn't been behind me, I'd be sitting on my butt. "Who in the heck were Mindy's plus two?"

"My feelings were hurt enough that I didn't ask. I went back in the house."

Brownie claimed he never saw his cousin after that late-night weenie roast. The next day, Wayne's disappearance didn't mean anything since drifting away for unexplained reasons had been Wayne's operating method for years.

"What changed to make you think Wayne should've been considered a person of interest?"

John Brown scanned the street before answering me. "Three days later, after I last saw him, I found a pair of badly burnt men's pants in the burn barrel. They were size 34, and that eliminated me and Barney, because I'm hefty and my uncle is slight. The only man in the house they'd fit was

Wayne."

"So, your cousin was not only catching a late meal, he was burning his clothing. Assuming you had a washer in the house, I have to believe he was destroying evidence."

"Yeah, it sure felt that way."

"And why'd you decide not to share that news with the sheriff?"

"While it was strange, I didn't know when he'd done it. Was it before I saw him roasting the wieners, after I went back to bed, or sometime late Friday night after Mindy's murder? With all that uncertainty, I didn't want to waste Uncle Barney's time."

Nic Knuckles was as cautious as the next investigator, but who sets their clothes on fire other than a clumsy pyromaniac? I felt my irritation with Brownie rising. "When Wayne failed to return after a year, didn't you think maybe he had a good reason not to come back to Kleinstadt?"

Sheriff Brown lifted his shoulders. "By then, Hanlon had been convicted, and I was finishing my senior year, preparing to go to the police academy. I didn't want to think about it. I guess that's why I've been working so hard to get you out of town. You were making me think that we all could've been wrong."

I pushed Brownie from several new angles and got nothing. I decided to give the interrogation a rest when the big guy mumbled. "You know, being a sheriff intern required me to maintain a stoic attitude during that time. But, man, I missed Mindy. No other girl excited me like her. After she died, I never danced another step with anyone."

As much as I didn't want to admit it, Brownie's performance convinced me he was a human with feelings. I crawled back into my car, my head and notebook overflowing with new details.

"Thanks for opening up, Sheriff," I said. "You've bumped my investigation forward with that information."

Brownie leaned into the open window. "What are you going to do with what I told you?"

I felt my mouth go tight, and I sucked on my teeth. "I'm going to bring some sunshine into a downtrodden family's dismal life, and then, I'll focus on finding Mindy and Wayne's dining partners. I suspect they might be able to fill in the missing pieces to what went on that night."

Sheriff Brown gave me a stern look, and a rumble came from deep inside his chest. "You better not surprise me, you hear?"

"Don't worry, Brownie. I suspect you and I'll be talking real soon."

Chapter Forty-Seven

It was twilight as I maneuvered my car along the country road, the windows down so I could feel the cool evening air. It wasn't too often that a private investigator got to deliver good news. Most of the time, I reported on cheating spouses, thieving children, and dogs that ate the homework. I tried to imagine the smiles of Pa and Ma Hanlon when I shared my latest thinking on the Bauerman murder case. It might be the most joy they've experienced in fifteen years.

As I pulled into the gravel drive to the homestead, a pair of junkyard dogs started barking up a storm. Fortunately, they were chained, and I got out of my car without having my leg mauled. I saw the light in the barn and walked up to find Timmy's father bent into the open hood of a pickup truck.

"Good evening, Mr. Hanlon."

"Well, look what just walked into the barn," he said. "It's that big city investigator."

A woman's voice came from beneath the truck. "What the hell does he want?"

"I'm here to share some encouraging developments," I said. "I think you'll be happy to hear what I have to say."

Pa Hanlon wiped his right hand on his overalls and offered it in greeting. Ma Hanlon popped up and gave me a second-degree stink eye. With the social formalities out of the way, I delivered my news.

"I've been working hard since I saw you three weeks ago, and I now believe your boy, Timmy, is innocent."

Ma Hanlon's eyebrows crawled together. "How's that good news?"

Most people would've been stunned by such an insensitive remark, but not Nic Knuckles. I grew up with a mother who had that kind of mouth, so it only upset me for a few seconds before I recovered. "I don't know," I said, "maybe he can come home and rebuild his life."

Pa seemed to like that idea. "Yeah, Ma, maybe he can start back up with his girlfriend. Who knows, he could marry and have a happy family, just like you and me did."

Ma laughed. "That boy never had no relationship with any girl. He was scared of them."

Pa appeared less confident. "Hold on a minute, Ma, don't you remember his high school sweetheart?"

"That wasn't no girlfriend, you fool. He had one date with her."

Pa scratched the top of his head and frowned. "Oh yeah, now I remember. They ate at a fancy joint out of town somewhere, and he got sick."

There's an old saying that it's better to be lucky than good, and Nic Knuckles didn't subscribe to that way of thinking. Successful investigators have their ears always perked to capture the misspoken word, eyes continuously scanning the environment for subtle clues, and noses sniffing for suspicious behavior.

However, if Lady Luck dumped something in my lap, I didn't push it away.

"Wait, wait, wait," I said. "Tell me more about Timmy's long-ago date."

Ma and Pa looked at me, then each other, before they rubbed the whiskers on their chins in contemplation.

"It was right before he done got himself arrested," Pa said. "He was so excited to be finally going out with a girl."

"All I remember is Timmy being out of sorts the next day," Ma said. "He didn't even want to tell jokes, as I recall."

"Yeah, yeah," Pa said. "He was all aggravated and snarky. I'd never seen him so cranky."

"Did Timmy say what happened that night to upset him?" I asked as my hand reached into my pocket to retrieve my notebook.

"Naw," Ma said. "I think he wasn't feeling well from the crawfish he ate at that fancy place."

Pa shrugged and said, "That boy always had a sensitive stomach. Remember his job at the slaughterhouse, where they fired him after two days? He kept passing out from the sight of blood."

"Oh boy, you're right," Ma said. "You couldn't crack an egg open without him goin' queasy on you. But, then again, he never had crawfish before that night."

Pa rolled his bottom lip. "Good point, Ma. That's why I only eat pork, chicken, and cow meat. If it ain't breathing air, then I don't touch it."

My eagerness to gather more data on Timmy's once-in-a-lifetime date went unacknowledged as the Hanlon's debated the merit of rabbit and squirrel as alternative protein sources. Stepping physically between the arguing husband and wife, I finally broke through. "You don't recall who Timmy went out with that night, do you?"

"Naw, I don't," Pa said.

"Does the name Mindy sound familiar?" I asked. "Mindy Bauerman?"

"You mean the girl he killed?" Pa shook his head and looked at his wife. "Ma, that don't sound right, does it?"

"I don't know. I just hope if Timmy does go free, he don't move home. That closet's no longer available to be his bedroom, you know."

I felt my shoulders sag as Ma Hanlon's continued insensitivity forced up memories of my mother giving away my bedroom. Why the big rush? I remembered asking. I was sixteen and still had two years to go before I graduated high school, but that didn't stop her. My new roommate was a mouth-breathing insomniac named Nightcrawler Finnegan, and even though I rarely got a good night's sleep, Mom was happy because he never missed paying his rent.

"If a name comes to mind, please contact me," I said and handed Pa my card. "Anything you can recall is important at this stage of my investigation."

"What's more important to me is how Timmy's getting a bed and three meals a day at the State's expense," Ma said. "That's better than him having to find a job around here."

Pa nodded. "You know, Ma, that's a good point. He's got a pretty good deal, right now, don't he?"

I retreated to my car and drove away, feeling depressed. Poor Timmy Hanlon, the guy, never had a chance with those parents. No wonder he was so excited fifteen years ago about a girl who thought enough of him to go on a date. Someone who saw his potential and found him somewhat attractive.

That thought, however, bothered me even more than his insensitive parents. There couldn't have been more than one or two girls who'd date Timmy, considering the man's reptilian looks and annoying personality. Buddy might know of a classmate desperate enough to accept a meal with Timmy. Yeah, I'd see what the old barkeep could tell me. I might even have a few beers to help drown my memories of Nightcrawler Finnegan snoring like a chainsaw cutting through a metal door at two a.m.

Chapter Forty-Eight

I approached the door of Buddy's Tavern and found it locked. What the heck? It wasn't much later than eight. Why'd he be closed during the prime bar hopping time? Inside, I saw Buddy mopping the floor, so I rapped on the glass, and he smiled and let me in.

"Why are you closed?" I asked. "Slow night and not worth keeping the lights on," was his answer. After complaining about needing something hoppy to lighten my mood, he poured me a beer. I sat on a stool while Buddy continued cleaning the floor, and a half of glass down, I felt more myself, which meant I asked questions.

"How come you never left town, Buddy? What kept you around Kleinstadt?"

Buddy paused his mopping and looked at me. "I don't know. Owning the tavern gave me something to do, and although I never made much money, my regulars depended on me. I have to admit I care about them as well."

"Staying for friends and the comfort of the familiar, huh? But doesn't it wear on you that everyone knows you and your past?"

Buddy swiped the mop across the floor once and stopped. "As much as I hated being judged, I think it's better than being ignored. I mean, if I didn't show up and open my tavern, people would call John Brown for a welfare check. I wouldn't lay hurt or dead for days until my stink alerted the neighbors. You wouldn't see that kind of caring in a big city. Knowing that people were watching out for me was worth something."

Small-town folk might think no one would care if Nic Knuckles got run over by a New York City bus. They'd be wrong. Many people would raise a ruckus if my broken body somehow delayed their commute. Heck, some of them might even kick my corpse free of the tires to get the bus back on schedule.

Buddy squeezed the mop dry and pushed the bucket aside. He kept up the conversation without me asking many follow-up questions, which was nice. Since I arrived, I don't think I've had a regular give-and-take chat with anyone in Kleinstadt.

"This may sound strange," Buddy said, "but knowing people's history makes me feel like I'm part of their lives. Buzz Rockwell may be a successful businessman, but he knows that I know he once was a basement-dwelling dweeb. That's the same with John Brown, Sandi Fliminsky, and Timmy Hanlon. We all grew up at the same time with the same memories in the same town, and so we have a bond."

Buddy's soliloquy impressed me. Some bartenders were actually booze-serving philosophers, but most of them that Nic Knuckles knew opened beer bottles with their teeth and had a ten-word vocabulary. Buddy Lee was more profound than I ever gave him credit, and now I understood why Mary Jane liked having him around.

"You're a smart guy, Buddy," I said. "You've given me a perspective about small towns that I didn't have before I came here."

Buddy smiled. "That's something I've discovered. When you listen to people, you learn things that make your life better."

Nic Knuckles liked the late-night bull sessions as much as the next amateur Socrates, but I was a private eye who still had unanswered questions. I hoped that gabber Buddy would fill the gaps in my knowledge.

"I understand that Mindy and Wayne Feif went out on a dinner date right before she died. I've learned since then that another couple joined, and I think Timmy Hanlon was one of them."

"You mean Timmy, the class clown who murdered my girlfriend?"

"Yeah. Do you know if, back in the day, any girl desperate enough to go out with him?"

Buddy chuckled. "The boys in my high school were all pimples and obnoxious personality, and yet, they felt they were superior to Timmy.

The girls were even more snobbish, so I doubt anyone in our school would voluntarily go out with Hanlon."

Hearing how poorly Timmy fared as a sixteen-year-old depressed me. I asked Buddy to pour me another beer, and he drew one for himself, and we saluted lonely boys who longed to be cuddled by a girl, any girl.

"Here's to finding the one, honest love," I said. Buddy tapped his glass against mine and added. "Yeah, if Mindy had stayed true to me, maybe she'd be alive today."

"Fidelity has advantages, doesn't it?" I said, and we both emptied our glasses.

Buddy poured two more beers, and we settled into a boozy state of speculation, wondering how our lives would've been different if certain females had treated us better.

"I suppose everyone wonders about that," Buddy said.

"Do you think Mary Jane regretted cheating on George? It must've been hell living with a man who held one indiscretion over your head."

"One indiscretion, you say." A grin flickered across Buddy's face. "Don't feel sorry for Mary Jane. She didn't let guilt ruin her good times."

"What does that mean?"

Buddy shook his head and turned away. "Nothing, never mind."

I wasn't letting him tease me, especially when I knew he'd make me pay for the beers. "Come on, Buddy, we're pals. I'll soon be back in New York, consumed by a new case, and I'll forget everything you told me."

"Naw, I'd feel bad sharing Mary Jane's secrets." He might've felt bad, but he failed to suppress a grin. "Boy, there were some whoppers."

I knew Buddy was dying to talk to me. After all, who else in this town ever asked his thoughts on anything? That's the curse of being a good listener like Buddy; they never had a chance to share their feelings. It might sound sad, but I was probably Buddy's best friend after knowing him for less than a month.

"Okay, if you won't tell me everything, at least confirm this. Was George Mindy's daddy?"

Buddy Lee chewed his bottom lip as he pondered. He finally shook his head and said, "Nope, George wasn't Mindy's father."

That was no surprise. Sandi, Molly, and Kate had implied the same thing. Now that Buddy opened the vault, I'd like to get him to confirm my hunch. "So, I guess Tommy Lyle was Mindy's poppa, am I right?"

Buddy's shoulders slid up and down as if the bones were trying to break through the flesh. "Am I right, Buddy? The traveling shoe salesman was the father of your old girlfriend, correct?"

"No, you're not correct. He wasn't Mindy's father either."

I almost dislocated my jaw when my chin fell toward the floor. "Are you kidding me? Kate Crumble swore it was true. Sandi and Mindy suspected as much. Hell, even George Bauerman believed it."

Buddy raised his shoulders. "What can I say? Mary Jane told me otherwise."

Dang, Nic Knuckles finally got Buddy to give him answers, and they led to more questions. If Sandi was right and Mindy met her father the night of her murder, it may not have been Tommy Lyle. Holy Pecorino, I didn't expect that twist.

"Buddy, I have to know the name of Mindy's father. He might have vital information about what went on in Stickerbacker's Woods that Friday night. You gotta tell me."

Buddy walked over to a switch and hit the buttons, shutting off the lights. "Come on, Nic, you need to get back to the lodge before Miss Crumble locks you out."

"I can't believe you're not cooperating," I said. "Don't you want justice for Mindy?"

The tip of Buddy's lips puckered. "Let's be honest, Nic. Mindy was a selfish girl and a terrible girlfriend. If I owe my loyalty to any female, it's Mary Jane. At least she liked having me around, so I'm saying nothing more."

"Oh geez, Buddy, don't go all mushy on me now."

Buddy told me he'd add the beers to my tab and hustled me through the front door. "Good night, Nic," he said as he gently shoved me toward Miss Crumble's Cozy Lodge. I turned and pinned him against the wall. "You want to talk about loyalty, do you? How can you ignore me after I ended your feud with Buzz? If it weren't for me, you two would still feed the town rumor mill, making people think you escaped justice."

For all Buddy's acquired wisdom, he still was suspectable to hyperbole. He pushed my hands off his chest. "Okay, but if you name me as your source, I'll poison the next sandwich I make you."

Shifting his eyes left and right, Buddy pulled me close and whispered a name in my ear. I grabbed his arms to keep myself from falling over.

"Barney Feif, no way."

Buddy shushed me. "Keep it down."

I twisted away from him and stumbled down the street toward the lodge. Three beers and the shocking news of Feif being Mindy's daddy was too much for my equilibrium. Did the old sheriff know he might've sired a little girl? Did George, Lyle, Mindy, Kate, or Brownie have any idea that was possible? That news would've had Molly Spear spinning in her grave if she hadn't been cremated. Yank me by my ears until I yipped; what was going on? How many secrets could one burg hold before exploding?

Chapter Forty-Nine

The chains on the porch swing groaned under my weight as I swayed back and forth. Sandi Fliminsky, not surprisingly, wasn't home, but I expected her soon. The rain that had fallen since morning had picked up, and I knew she and her crew would have to call it a day. My gaze swept across the neighborhood with its collection of tidy houses and their tidy properties. The gentle pattering of raindrops on the porch roof enveloped me in a strange sense of being soothed. Not since I was in my mother's womb had I felt such an all-encompassing comfort, even though that only lasted until she finished her break and resumed her job operating a jackhammer for the Public Works Department.

Could a guy like Nic Knuckles be happy living in a small town where nothing much happened? I found the idea of swaying on a porch swing and hearing nothing but my heartbeat very appealing. I might consider it once this case is over.

The sound of creaking door hinges alerted me to the redhead she-demon storming out of her house and onto her porch, her voice roaring like a leaf blower. "I'm watching you, you pervert!"

I waved and wished her a good day—what a nut job! Maybe living in a town like Kleinstadt wasn't a remedy for my frayed nerves. Sure, there were plenty of crazed, angry people in New York City, but they generally poured out their vitriol inside their cars.

My attention shifted from the lunatic across the street to the yellow pickup truck pulling into the driveway. It was Sandi Fliminsky.

"Good Lord Knuckles," she cried as she climbed out of the truck, her forearms covering her head. "What do you want now?"

"Just an answer or two about Mindy's dinner date with Wayne. Sit down here, and let's get this over with."

Sandi ignored me and unlocked her front door. "I'm soaked and cold, Nic. I've told you everything I knew about that dinner."

"Not so fast," I said as I jumped from the swing. "A highly reliable source told me that Mindy did not dine alone with Wayne. He claimed several of Mindy's friends were included and I wonder who that might've been."

"I don't have a clue," Sandi said, although her eagerness to close the door on me suggested she did. I slipped behind her, pouncing before she could take off her wet work jacket. "I realized that your cockamamie story about Mindy never telling you the details of her date with Wayne was just that, cockamamie. She never had to tell you because you were there."

I never knew what cockamamie meant, but I liked the sound of it. Growing up in New York City, I was more familiar with meshuggenah, but I figured Sandi had limited exposure to Yiddish.

"Come on, Sandi, it's time you told me everything you know about Mindy's dinner date with Wayne. And I don't want any game playing, you hear me? I'm tired of it."

Sandi must've been tired of it as well. She took off her damp jacket and cap and tossed them on a chair before dropping onto the sofa with a grunt. "Okay, you win. What do you want to know?"

I pulled my notebook and pencil from my pocket. "Start from the beginning and run to the end, and for once, do it without leaving anything out."

Sandi rubbed her face, freed a deep sigh, and began. "Of course, Mindy made sure I knew about her date. She bragged how Wayne was so much older and had money to treat her to a lobster dinner. She knew I'd never eaten lobster before. I mean, who could afford something like that?"

"Wayne had a bit of a reputation," I said. "Wasn't she at all worried about going out with a man known as a mysterious drifter?"

Sandi shook her head. "Mindy would never admit being afraid, but I knew she was. Wayne was very rough and had this sinister vibe about him. That's why she asked me to go along."

Holy Mascarpone, now I had an eyewitness at the dinner. I almost heard the Mindy Bauerman murder case closing and Timmy Hanlon's jail cell door swinging open.

"I wasn't happy about going as the third wheel," Sandi said, "so I told her I wanted to bring someone. Mindy agreed, but insisted on picking the boy."

"Why wouldn't she let you choose your date?"

Sandi's eyes narrowed as she explained how Mindy worried Sandi might bring a good-looking guy, and Mindy would then be too busy flirting with both boys to enjoy her lobster. I didn't need the cruel instincts of a teenage girl to guess who she selected as Sandi's escort.

"So that's how Timmy Hanlon was at the table that night," I said.

Sandi's eyes went cold. "Yes, Mindy thought it would be hilarious to have him there."

"And you weren't too happy, I imagine."

"No, I wasn't happy at all. That's why I didn't tell you about me going to the dinner. Timmy acted all foolish trying to make me laugh, and I just wanted to forget it ever happened."

"It sounds like you didn't find Timmy's humorous stylings to your liking back then."

Sandi cocked her head. "How many fart jokes can you hear before they stop being funny?" She answered her own question. "One."

I set an intense gaze on Sandi, suggesting a hard-earned skepticism. "What changed, Sandi? You once told me you found Hanlon highly entertaining at his murder trial."

Sandi lowered her eyes and shrugged. "Mindy said some nasty things about Timmy being from a poor family and how he smelled like a barn. I don't know. Maybe I felt sorry for him, knowing what it was like to be on the receiving end of Mindy's cruel remarks. Even though she was my bestie, she could be spiteful."

"Once you settled in with Wayne, Timmy, and Mindy, how'd the dinner go?"

Sandi's stellar recall from that evening seemed to falter. "It was okay," she said. "The lobster was rubbery."

"That's it? You remember nothing more than a chewy crustacean?"

"It's been fifteen years, and I was young. Give me a break, will ya?"

I turned on the woman like a mongoose on a chilidog. "From our first meeting, you tried to direct my attention toward Buddy and then Buzz. You implied George Bauerman had enough reason to kill his daughter that he'd hired a thug to do it. You threw in John Brown as a possible candidate. I swear, you've cast suspicion on every pant-wearing citizen of Kleinstadt."

Sandi rolled away from me and closed her eyes. "Leave me alone, Nic."

"I've spent hundreds of hours checking out alibis and running down rabbit holes, and they've led me to one conclusion," I said. "You're hiding something, something big."

I saw a slight tremor move across Sandi's shoulders.

"What are you covering up? Who are you protecting?"

Sandi sucked in a sniffle, and without turning around, she said, "I'm done talking with you, Mr. Knuckles. Please leave my living room."

"I won't leave until I know what happened at that restaurant. Did the fact Mindy brought you and Timmy upset Wayne? As a guy with limited resources, he must've been angry having to cover uninvited guests."

"Yeah, he wasn't pleased."

"What went on between Wayne and Mindy during the meal? Did they coo like two love birds, or did it have all the makings of an illegal cock fight?"

"Mindy complained about the lobster, and Wayne was irritated. He called her a name."

"What was the name?"

"It wasn't very nice, and I won't repeat it, but it rhymed with persimmon."

My memory spun for every cuss word I'd heard and came up empty. The expletive must've been something only a Hoosier would know, so I'd run it by Buddy later. I pushed on with my interrogation of Sandi.

"Did Wayne emit any evil vibes after Mindy complained about her food?"

"Yes, but nothing like his reaction when Mindy knocked the little boat filled with melted butter into his lap. That set him off."

An involuntary contraction swept across my nether parts. "I bet it did.

Were any threats made?"

"He told her she'd never see him again, and she laughed and said, 'I don't care if I ever see your ugly face.'"

"Mindy liked to mix it up. How'd Wayne react to that insult?"

"His eyes got really small, and he trembled like he wanted to reach across the table and strangle her. It was freaky."

"What happened next?"

"Timmy opened his mouth. He was uncomfortable with the tension and wanted to cool the emotions, so he told some jokes."

It appears Timmy Hanlon was a peacemaker, using his gift for comedy to soothe the angry beasts. I had to like that guy. Even though he looked like a snake in human form, he had a good heart. I hoped to exonerate him and get him his freedom.

"Did that work?" I asked. "Did Wayne and Mindy find Timmy funny?"

"No, Mindy was mean, telling Timmy he didn't have one funny bone in his body. He looked so dejected that I defended him, and she turned on me, calling me a pathetic loser."

"Wow, that girl had an attitude. How'd the evening end?"

"After Wayne paid the bill, we left and went to the parking lot. I'd ridden with Timmy, so we had two rides. I saw Wayne open his car door for Mindy, and after she got in, he saw me, and he did this." Mindy swiped an extended index finger across her throat.

Wow, fill my pants with angry groundhogs. What'd Sandi just imply?

"Did Timmy see Wayne's throat-cutting gesture?"

"Yes, but he thought Wayne was indicating it was time to end the date. Timmy said that slashing across the neck motion was the way comedians were told their time was up and to get off the stage."

I thanked Sandi for finally giving me a full accounting despite how painful it was for her to recall. Having an eyewitness who saw and heard Wayne threatening Mindy was better than her previous drug-induced observation of Wayne in the woods with a machete.

"I think with what you've told me, I might have enough to convince Sheriff Brown to take another look at who killed Mindy Bauerman."

Sandi offered me a weary smile and stood to walk me to the front door. "Goodbye, Nic," she said. "Don't let this hurt your feelings, but I hope I never see you again."

I chuckled. Having heard that comment so many times, I never let it bother me. But before she sent me off, my curiosity got the best of me. "I gotta ask, Sandi. Did you let Timmy give you a good night kiss?"

Sandi grunted. "Like I told you, I found Timmy unattractive and irritating, but after Mindy had been so nasty, I let him get close enough to shake hands."

"So, no smooch, huh?"

A shudder twisted Sandi's shoulders. "The thought of his lips on mine makes me recoil."

I jotted down her last comment in my notebook, thinking how Timmy was so dang unlucky. That poor guy's best chance to lock lips with a girl was that evening, and all he got was a handshake.

Sandi's front door closed behind me, followed by the lock clicking into place. The rain had stopped, and I detoured to Sandi's pickup truck as I strolled toward my car. Being a big city guy, I wanted to know what tools a landscaper used in their work. Sure, I'd seen Mary Jane's trowel, but what did a grass and garden professional like Sandi use?

Pulling up the tarp covering the truck's bed, I saw all kinds of tools that could dig, lift, and spread dirt. There were things with sharp edges that looked ideal for chopping stubborn vegetation and tools that could grind and pulverize. Sandi had two lawnmowers and some grinding thingy on small rubber wheels. I was impressed.

The grip of five bony fingers on my shoulder shattered my concentration. A woman's voice screeched in my ear, "What the hell are you doing, you pervert? Stop your dang snooping."

"Good Lord, you scared me," I said, my hand over my heart. It was that crazy old coot who lived across the street. "What's wrong with you?"

"What's wrong with me? What's wrong with you?"

"Nothing's wrong with me," I said. "I'm Nic Knuckles, Private Eye, and it's my vocation to find the truth, no matter where it's hidden."

The woman crossed her arms and stepped closer. "So, that's who you are.

I've been wondering what you were up to, coming over to the Fliminsky's house all the time, peeping into her windows."

Sensing a new source of information in front of me, I asked her, "How well do you know Sandi Fliminsky?"

"Oh, I know that girl. I've watched her since she was a baby, living here even after her parents moved out."

"That's interesting," I said. "Maybe you can answer some questions."

"I don't talk to perverts."

That was it. I let my temper take over, and I barked at the woman. "Why do you keep calling me a pervert? I find that so offensive."

The woman pulled her head back and laid a pair of contemptuous eyes on me. "You sneak around, don't you?"

"Yeah."

"You peep in windows, dig into people's sex lives, and make them uncomfortable, am I right?"

I nodded.

"In Indiana, my friend, that's what we call a pervert."

Chapter Fifty

I rose the next day, ate a filling breakfast at Miss Crumble's table, spent the morning compiling my notes, and joined Buddy for our lunchtime chat before making the most important phone call of the month. I recognized the gruff voice of my client when he answered, "Yeah."

"Mister Client, this is Nic Knuckles calling. I'm done collecting facts and fictions, collating and merging theories and bad guesses, and I'm ready to give you my Mindy Bauerman investigative findings."

"It's about time, Knuckles. Meet me in twenty minutes. I'll be at the corner of Oak Street and West Park Drive."

Holy Jarlsberg, Mister Client, was in town. I knew the man had once spent much of his life in Kleinstadt, but I assumed he'd moved away. What if he'd been living here and we frequently crossed paths? Did we bump elbows at the Speedi Food Mart, or was he one of Buddy's regulars? Did he drink coffee at The Next to Last Supper, watching Molly and me? Whoever he was, I was hyped to meet my secretive sponsor and conclude the investigation.

Not that I wasn't dealing with some anxiety. Briefing a client after a lengthy investigation could be tricky. Once, I told a woman her conjoined twin was swindling her of millions while cheating with her husband. That was one awkward meeting, let me tell you.

I hopped in my car and started driving. Although Kleinstadt was a small town, the streets were poorly marked, and I burnt time asking for directions. I finally arrived at the designated intersection and found the location vaguely familiar. My brain spun a sprocket before realizing I was across from the extended care facility where I visited Barney Feif. The old sheriff himself was standing on the corner looking all confused and agitated. He must've wandered away from supervision. I rolled down my car window and shouted. "Hey Barney, get back inside before you freeze."

Feif looked up at me, cursed, and then charged over. "Where in the hell have you been, Knuckles? You're fifteen minutes late."

I knew it was unprofessional for my tongue to hang out of my mouth, especially in front of a paying client, but I was flabbergasted. It was Barney Feif who'd hired me to examine his investigation. Was there no end to the surprises with that guy? What the heck was going on?

The old sheriff opened the passenger side car door and slid in. "Get going. I'll tell you where to go."

I did as he instructed, but only after asking for an explanation. "Is this a temporary moment of lucid thought, or were you fooling me when I first met you?"

Feif rotated his face around at me, sending his jowls flapping. "It was all a ruse, Knuckles. I wanted to avoid instilling any bias in your investigation. I disguised my voice and acted daft to force you to look at everything and everyone with fresh eyes."

I told Feif I admired his approach and guaranteed I'd looked high and low to draw my conclusion. "That's good to hear, Knuckles." He told me to drive ahead two blocks, take the next left, and then hang a right a block down.

"I do have to ask you, however, with thousands of PIs available, why *did* you hire me?"

Feif answered without hesitation. "Believe it or not, you have a reputation among the investigator community."

I said, *I do*, like a blushing bride at the altar. I couldn't help myself. That was the coolest recognition anyone had given me since my first therapist said I inspired her to change careers and become a New Jersey Turnpike Toll Booth operator.

"Don't get big-headed, Knuckles," Feif said, "no one said you were overly bright or that you had superior intuition. They swore you were a bulldog and wouldn't quit until an answer fell in your lap."

"A bulldog, huh? Rowl." Nic Knuckles the Bulldog would make a great Saturday morning kid's cartoon. That might be a lucrative side job to augment my income. My vision of fame and fortune as a children's entertainer stalled when I came to a stop sign and had to ask Feif, "Which way now?"

"Take a left. We're going to my old office. I want Sheriff Brown to hear your briefing at the same time I get it."

"You mean Sheriff John Brown, your nephew, the old dance partner of Mindy Bauerman, and the possible bastard child of Kate Crumble?"

Feif curled his lip and sputtered. "Good God, I hope you were as good at identifying the killer as you are getting the dirt on John."

If my last comment cut Feif down a notch, let's see how shorter he'd stand after my next question.

"Any chance your son Wayne might be joining us?"

Sure enough, that remark lit Feif's fuse. "You know damn well I haven't seen him in fifteen years. Why would you even ask that?"

Usually, Nic Knuckles would've buttoned his lip, but since Feif had played me as the fool and wasted my time, I let my smart mouth run wild. "I thought maybe Wayne would like to be there when I reveal who murdered his half-sister."

The heat from the profanity streaming from Feif's mouth would've set my head on fire if I hadn't forgotten to gel my hair that morning. He waved his fist in my face and screamed. "I didn't pay you to dig into my past, Knuckles. You better watch it."

I didn't back down. "You hired me because I'm a bulldog, Barney, and bulldogs can't let loose once they clamp those jaws. Unless you want me hanging around town longer, give me the back story on your love child, Mindy Bauerman."

The older man grumbled and threw out a few curse words I'd never heard before. Then he sagged in his seat and conceded I had him. "It was more than thirty years ago. Kate Crumble came over one afternoon in a fever about Mary Jane, claiming she was an adulteress who stole her man. I tried to explain that what might violate the Ten Commandments wasn't necessarily against the law in Indiana. She wouldn't take no for an answer and threatened to raise a stink."

"I'm familiar with the volatile Miss Crumble," I said. "In fact, I've found most women in Kleinstadt had hair-trigger tempers. It's amazing this place hadn't blown itself off the map."

Feif nodded. "Oh yeah, don't get me started on the number of altercations I had to break up that some local female initiated. There were bar fights, domestic disputes, church socials, charity fund raisers, baby showers, you name it, and Kleinstadt women have brawled."

"Finish your story about Mary Jane, Barney because we're almost to the sheriff's office."

"With an election coming up, I knew I had to contain Kate's anger, so I confronted Mary Jane. She gave me a woeful story about her loneliness, about how George left her alone at night while he did his good deeds. Being a sheriff and having talked people off an emotional ledge, I was skilled at listening. Low and behold, I discovered Mary Jane found empathic men very attractive."

"You're not the first person to tell me that."

Feif hung his head and whispered. "You have to understand, Mary Jane was some good-looking woman back then. I knew it was wrong, but my missus and I weren't getting along. I'm ashamed to admit it, but I found solace on Mary Jane's mattress that afternoon."

"Are you a hundred percent sure Mindy was your child? Mary Jane was involved with a number of men at that time."

"I was never a hundred percent sure, but Mindy looked enough like me that I thought it possible."

"Wow, Barney, you've lived a complicated life."

Feif let loose a dry laugh. "You don't know the half of it. Years later, when John and Mindy became dancing partners, Kate Crumble showed up again, all upset."

Nic Knuckles was able to fill in the rest of Feif's sorry tale. "Of course, she did. Kate thought Tommy Lyle had impregnated two of Kleinstadt's fairest maidens, and she worried that as half-siblings, John and Mindy might fall in lust and risk siring a genetic freak."

"I felt bad that I couldn't tell Kate the truth," Feif said. "But then again, Mary Jane might've been lying to me, and Tommy Lyle *was* the father."

I pulled my car into the visitor's space of the Kleinstadt Sheriff's Department. Feif reached over and grabbed my arm. "You gotta promise me none of this will get out," he said. "I don't want John to think poorly of me."

"Not to worry, Barney. Nic Knuckles has his own secrets, and although they're nothing like your depravity, I appreciate the importance of privacy. Right now, however, I have to debrief Kleinstadt's law enforcement dynasty. Are you ready?"

The old sheriff let out a wheezy sigh. "Okay, Knuckles, let's get this over with."

Chapter Fifty-One

The female deputy almost fell over, seeing Barney as he escorted me into the building. She squealed. "Sheriff Feif, it's so good to see you. How are you feeling?"

Feif gave her a wink. "I have good days and bad days, doll. Thanks for asking."

I followed him down the hall and into an office with the name Sheriff John Brown stenciled on the glass door. "Sit wherever you can find a seat," he said. "I swear that kid can't throw anything away."

I cleared a chair of its pile of knitting magazines and sat. It wasn't a minute before John Brown stormed in, all red-faced and agitated. He looked at the older man and back at me. "I knew it, Knuckles," he cried as he jabbed his finger in my chest. "I knew you'd do something so illegal that my predecessor would come out of retirement and arrest you, you jerk."

I had to smile, watching Brownie's gleeful expression evaporate when Feif told him to hold on to his shorts. My affection for that expression was growing.

"I hired Knuckles to investigate the Mindy Bauerman case," Feif said. "He was working for me."

Brownie's mouth dropped open, his voice whining like a car needing to shift out of first gear. "You'd caught the right guy years ago, Barney. Why go digging into a settled case? I don't understand."

The old sheriff went over and gently guided the new sheriff onto a chair. "As I wasted away in that nursing home, I had time to think critically about all my investigations. That Bauerman case stood out as my biggest one,

239

and I had to wonder if I'd done a good job, you know, did I look carefully enough at all the possible suspects? What if I'd missed something and royally screwed up?"

John Brown's eyes watered, and his voice went soppy. "Why didn't you come to me if you wanted to reopen the case? Why'd you hire an outsider? Didn't you think I could've done the job?"

"Now, don't go and get your feelings hurt," Feif said. "Your affection for Mindy and hate for Wayne would've kept you from being objective. I needed someone who had the mind of a Hoover vacuum, an investigator to suck up every bit of evidence associated with Mindy's murder and see if I missed anything."

I didn't appreciate Feif's comparing me to an electric sweeper, but he was close. I did collect a big bag of Kleinstadt dirt.

"What's Knuckles doing here, then?" Brown asked. "Is he going to rub it in my face that you thought he was a superior investigator?"

"I brought Knuckles here because I wanted you to hear his findings at the same time I did. If he proves I was wrong about Timmy Hanlon, then I'll need you to clean up my mess and arrest the guilty party, whoever it might be. You understand me, boy?"

"Yeah, I understand you." Brownie turned toward me with eyes slits, holding back two carbon-hard black dots. Whatever joy I had watching John Brown's comeuppance disappeared because I knew he'd seek revenge for making him look small in his uncle's eyes.

"Okay, Knuckles," Feif said. "Give us your findings."

I stood and cleared my throat, ignoring Brownie's hateful glare. I pulled my trusty notebook from my pocket and started.

"The triggering event for Mindy's murder seemingly occurred on the Wednesday before her death. On that evening, she went out to dinner with Wayne, aka The Drifter." I paused for dramatic effect, feeling I deserved the chance to show off my theatrical skills. I'd worked hard for nearly a month to get where we were, and I was going to enjoy my big moment.

"Of course, I wondered who'd be most upset knowing Mindy was stuffing her face with lobster paid for by an unemployed ne'er-do-well like Wayne?

Was it Buddy Lee Hoot? He'd never have the money to afford to treat his girl to such a fine meal, so why wouldn't he feel emasculated and resentful? How about Buzz Rockwell? It had to be a deeply felt hurt when his only friend, Wayne, dumped him and took out the girl he secretly longed for. How humiliating that must've been?"

I spun around on one foot and lunged at John Brown. "And there was our friend here, the young hoofer. How mad was he, knowing his favorite dancing partner had abandoned him, so she could go out supping with his waster cousin?"

I paced around the room and continued talking. "So, what do we have here? We have a trio of hormone-infused young men with motives to harm Mindy Bauerman. The Bad Boy B's I called them Buddy, Buzz, and Brownie. Did either one of those suspects have the evil intent and means to commit murder?"

I raised the notebook to my eyes and read from my conclusion page.

Buddy Lee Hoot had one basic failing that kept him from ever being a cold-blooded killer: he was too nice. And Buzz Rockwell, despite his peculiar nature and competency with an ax, was too much in love to even think of harming Mindy.

Barney looked up at me and gasped. "If Buddy and Buzz aren't the perps, surely you're not saying John did the crime?"

As much as I wished to throw shade Brownie's way, I couldn't. "No sir, I'm not accusing your nephew. Other than ignoring Mindy's underage drinking when he was a Sheriff's Department intern, Brownie has always been like a rusted mason jar of putrefied green beans. No matter how you tried, you'd never loosen his lid. Back then as now, he's impervious to corruption."

John Brown sat and patted his chest. "I take pride in that," he said. "Yes, I do."

Feif, however, could have been happier. "That's it? I paid you thousands of dollars, and you found your three prime suspects innocent? I can't believe that you swindled me."

"Keep those shorts on, Barney. I wanted to give you everything I learned, so we'd have no second-guessing going on. Please be patient."

The old sheriff's thin lips squirmed, and a low growl emanated from his throat, but he stayed quiet.

"Buddy, Buzz, and Brownie weren't my only suspects. There was George Bauerman, a cuckolder with a thirst for revenge. The man was able to keep it together for sixteen years," I said. "Then one day, in early October 2005, rumors flew that Mindy was meeting the man who might've sired her, Tommy Lyle. George decided he had to confront the shoe salesman and ensure he never returned to Kleinstadt."

Barney Feif chewed on a fingernail and stared at me with big, filmy eyes. He had to wonder if I'd expose his role in Kate and George hiring Wayne to treat Mindy to lobster. How would I explain broke-ass George having money to pay Wayne to cover an expensive meal without revealing Kate Crumble's participation? Would old infidelities be exposed and reputations ruined?

"What do we have here, gentlemen? George had to face Lyle, and to do that, he had to know when and where Mindy was meeting her shoe-buying benefactor. I believe he tried to hire Buzz Rockwell to work Mindy, but the boy was too uncomfortable and refused. He did, however, put George in contact with Wayne, who happily accepted the job."

Brownie must've sensed an opportunity to slam my analysis because he jumped up, yelling. "That's not right," he said. "I knew how poor the Bauermans were back then. I can't believe George had the money to pay Wayne hundreds of dollars to treat Mindy and two friends to lobster and still have cash to finance his departure from town."

I stepped close enough to Brownie to see the remnants of the chimichanga he had for lunch in his teeth. I opened my notebook to a blank page and read. "George Bauerman reported that he sold a Ford Fairlane and a VW Beetle that week fifteen years ago and made a tidy profit. He said he remembered because it was one of his best sales months ever. Therefore, Sheriff Brown, unbeknownst to you, George was flush with cash at that time."

From the corner of my eye, I caught sight of a smile creasing Barney's face. My little lie had worked, moving us forward without revealing Barney as the facilitator between Kate, George, and Wayne. Brownie, however, was still determined to prove he was more intelligent than me. "It sounds like after getting Wayne's information, George went into the Woods and confronted Mindy and Lyle. That puts him at the crime scene, hotly motivated to secure revenge."

"Nope, sorry, John," I said. "George had a rock-solid alibi that Friday night. He was leading a prayer marathon at his church that didn't end until midnight, hours after Mindy's murder."

Brownie's mouth sagged at the corner, and he dropped back into his seat. I felt sorry for the big lug, as his confidence must be crawling on the floor with his wrong guesses. To his credit, he took another swing at the ball. "How about George gave Wayne another job after that dinner date? What if he hired my cousin to slip into the woods, confront Mindy, and kill Lyle?"

Brownie's face took on a golden glow, and he raised his right index triumphantly. "And that explains the remnants of Wayne's pants I found in the burn barrel. He tried to destroy the bloody evidence that would implicate him. Oh my God, I did it. I solved the biggest crime in Kleinstadt history, Uncle Barney."

Feif grabbed his head and moaned. "Oh no, that was always my greatest fear. I must've been blinded by my regret of being a lousy father and avoided thinking it was my son." Tears poured from the older man's eyes. "I messed up. I messed up badly."

Brownie danced a jig and laughed at me. "I figured it out, didn't I, Big City Private Eye? I could've done your job."

"Ease up on the waterworks, Barney," I said. "And you, John, hold off on the celebration. You're wrong."

My comment wiped the grin off Brownie's face, and he dropped back into his chair.

"Let's look more carefully at your recollection, John. You said you found burnt pants in a barrel the day after Mindy's murder and two days after you last saw Wayne. Am I right?"

"Yeah, they were badly burnt, but I recognized them as something Wayne wore."

"When you pulled the pants from the burn barrel, we're they hot to the touch?"

"No, you know that."

"Warm?"

"Huh, no, they were cold."

"So, it's unlikely those pants were tossed into a fire the night of Mindy's murder. If they were cold, most likely the fire was lit two nights before at the wiener roast."

Brownie slumped into a slag pile of disappointment. "Yeah, I guess that makes more sense."

That's why Barney Feif hired Nic Knuckles instead of relying on the local talent; I wanted to scream. When you needed a professional job done, you hired an old pro. But I held back. I knew I'd yet to hit them with my best stuff, and I was confident they'd go off on me when I did.

"You're partially correct, however, as I believe Wayne most likely set those pants on fire. But not because they were blood-stained from a murder. What I've learned is that while eating lobster with Mindy, she'd spilt a tankard of hot melted butter on his lap. That's most likely why he did it. We all know you can't get a butter stain out, right?"

Like a champion fighter, Brownie bounced up from the canvas with a rebuttal.

"Okay, maybe I'm wrong about the burnt pants, but the rest of my theory is solid. Once George knew when Lyle was meeting Mindy in the woods, he paid Wayne to kill him. Lyle never appeared, and the only way Wayne could collect from George was to show him a bloody murder weapon. George wouldn't know whose blood was on it, and Wayne would be long gone by the time Mindy's corpse was found. Damn, I might not be able to arrest Wayne, but I sure can lock up that bastard, Bauerman."

"I'm sorry, Brownie, you don't have all the facts." I again turned to my notebook for the relevant Bauerman notation. "Wayne was supposed to meet with George Thursday night to report when and where Mindy was meeting Lyle on Friday. According to Bauerman, your cousin never showed up. Even you told me that Wayne disappeared after that Wednesday night wiener roast."

Barney Feif rose from his seat, a tearful smile pulling apart the wave of wrinkles on his weathered mug. "Are you now saying Wayne had nothing to do with Mindy's murder?"

"That's what I'm saying, Barney. Wayne might've been in George's employ, but not as a bloodthirsty thug."

"Halleluiah, my boy was a worthless use of lungs and a heart, but he wasn't a killer."

John Brown didn't share his uncle's good feelings and snarled at me. "Okay, Knuckles, if it wasn't Hanlon, Wayne, Buddy, Buzz, George, or me who killed Mindy?"

"I didn't say Timmy Hanlon wasn't there when Mindy died."

Feif spun around twice, cuss words flying from his mouth. Once he wobbled to a stop, he screamed at me. "Was I right or was I wrong, Knuckles? You're making me nuts."

"Hanlon didn't wield the weapon that sliced off Mindy's head, but he was there to see it."

Brownie's complexion soared through the color spectrum from ghostly white to deep purple. "I'm going to crush you like a walnut, Knuckles," he said in the most unfriendly way I'd heard from him since my arrival. "Tell us who killed Mindy Bauerman."

"Okay, hold on to your shorts. It was Sandi Fliminsky."

Both version 1.0 and 2.0 of the Kleinstadt sheriff became consumed by a fit, flapping their hands and shouting over each other. I deciphered Barney's screaming first. "What the hell are you saying? I can't believe Mindy's best friend did something like that." Brownie fired off an opinion as well. "Sandi was a skinny shrimp back then and couldn't hurt a fly. You're worthless, Knuckles, absolutely worthless."

I let the boys continue yelling until they exhausted themselves and fell back into their seats. "You two done with your tantrums?" I asked. "If so, grab a pair of handcuffs, and let's go over and arrest Mindy Bauerman's killer."

Chapter Fifty-Two

I bumped around in the back seat of a Kleinstadt official law enforcement vehicle as John Brown, Barney Feif, and I motored toward Sandi Fliminsky's house. The compartment smelled of the drunks once confined there on their way for a night in lockup. My suggestion that he might want to sanitize his car to make the ride more enjoyable brought a smirk to Brownie's face. Further evidence that he liked me being uncomfortable.

Barney sat in the passenger side seat and said little as Brownie came to a complete stop at *each* and *every* intersection. The only spoken words came after my phone chimed; I answered, had a short conversation, and disconnected. "My Confidential Informant reported that Sandi Fliminsky just got home," I said. "Once we get there, let me do the talking, okay?"

Barney turned around and sneered. "Don't worry. I want to see how you pin a murder on a woman who was a skinny little teenager and best friend to the victim." Brownie snickered but said nothing. It looked like the last two men to wear the Kleinstadt sheriff's badge relished the thought of me failing. Sheriff Brown pulled the car to the curb at Sandi's house, and we all climbed out. Before our feet stepped on the sidewalk, the red-haired demon from across the street appeared beside me. "Sandi left before six this morning, dressed to the nines," she said. "I don't know where she went, but something's up."

John Brown inserted his supersized frame between the woman and me and asked, "Who's she?"

"That woman is my Confidential Informant, so I can't tell you her name;

246

otherwise, she wouldn't be a CI, just a random stoolie."

The woman offered her hand to Brown and said, "I'm Mrs. Gertrude Steinhorst, and I live across the street."

Sheriff Brown thumbed at me. "You been helping that guy?"

Mrs. Steinhorst nodded. "Yes, but it hasn't been easy. He always seemed more interested in peeping into windows than talking to me."

Brown chuckled. "I know what you mean, a pervert, right?"

Not inclined to hear Brownie and my CI judging my investigating techniques, I said, "Come on, people, it's time we confront Sandi Fliminsky."

I pounded on the front door and yelled. "Open up, Sandi. I know you're in there."

The door swung wide, and Miss Fliminsky seemed more resigned than surprised to see me, two members of law enforcement, and a nosy neighbor.

"Your day of reckoning has arrived, Sandi, and I'm here to hand deliver it to you."

"Oh, Nic, don't you ever give up?"

I responded by leading my truth contingent into the living room. After instructing Sandi to sit in an armchair and the three others to squeeze onto the sofa, I began my summation.

"Okay, Miss Fliminsky, I'm through with your lies and distortions. Sit back and hear me out, because you're leaving in handcuffs."

Sandi moaned. "I'm tired, Nic. Please make this quick."

"I bet you're tired," I said. "It's a long day's drive to the Indiana State Penitentiary to visit your co-conspirator and lover, Timmy Hanlon."

Sandi must've not been too exhausted because she fed me her usual nonsense. "I was out running errands, not visiting Timmy Hanlon, you idiot. I have a business to operate."

I scoffed and pointed at her clothing. "If you were doing business locally, you wouldn't have dressed up in your Sunday best. It's obvious to me you wanted to impress someone, someone you owed your freedom."

Gertrude cackled. "He's right. Most days, you're wearing dark blue coveralls, tan colored work boots with alternating red and pink shoe strings, and a long sleeve cotton shirt manufactured in India."

John, Barney, and I all looked at Gertrude in wonderment. That woman was one hell of an eyewitness, and it was comforting knowing she was on our side. I moved on to my next point.

"You've been gone all day, and I know that trip is a good three hours both ways. But most importantly, your laugh lines look like they worked overtime reacting to lame jokes."

Sandi tried to keep a poker face, but her pair of deuces caused it to crumble. "You have no proof I visited Timmy today. You're just guessing."

I pointed to the green Penitentiary visitor's tag still attached to Sandi's suit jacket.

"Damn it." Sandi said and ripped off the badge. "Okay, you got me, but you're wrong if you think it's anything more than a woman befriending an old-school chum wrongly convicted of a crime."

I pointed over at the empty flower vase atop her credenza. "I'm surprised those yellow roses I saw last week have died, considering they'd survived a hard frost days before you claimed to have picked them from your garden."

Sandi's lips sputtered, but she said nothing.

"When Timmy told me the flowers were for someone, he owed his life, I figured he meant his mother. I'd probably kept that assumption if you hadn't forced me to make so many fruitless trips to your house. How many times would I see your street address before I connected it to that flower order?"

"Just because Timmy appreciated my kindness and sent roses doesn't mean I'm a criminal mastermind."

"Oh, I think you were more than kind to Timmy." I pulled out my notebook and flipped a dozen pages before finding the one I wanted. "Let's see. When you and I last talked, you told me you barely tolerated dining with Timmy, and at the end of the evening, the only affection you gave him was a handshake."

I raised my voice for dramatic effect. "And, you said, and I quote, 'the thought of his lips on mine makes me recoil.'"

John Brown grumbled. "That's cold, Sandi."

Sandi's eyes lit, and she rose out of her seat. "I think that shows how wonderful I am," she said. "I might find Timmy repulsive, yet I willingly visit him to lighten his loneliness. My actions are chaste and kindhearted."

Barney Feif offered his two cents. "You know, she has a point there. That is a very charitable spirit."

I looked at Feif and shook my head. "Don't be fooled, Barney. There is very little that is charitable about this woman."

I stepped next to Mrs. Steinhorst and opened my palms. "Let me introduce my informant, the neighborhood busybody Gertrude Steinhorst, aka, the red-headed she-demon. She has lived across the street from Sandi's house for more than three decades."

Gertrude pushed up her posture, a wide grin cresting across her face. I suspected she'd been waiting a long time for this moment.

"How well do you know Sandi Fliminsky?" I asked.

"I've known that girl since she wore diapers and have been watching her ever since her parents passed years ago."

"As a keen observer of her comings and goings over the decades, you have something to share with us, don't you?"

She nodded, rubbing her hands. "I do."

"Okay, let it pop, Gertrude."

Mrs. Steinhorst claimed it all started as a classic neighborhood tiff that got out of hand. Five-year-old Sandi walked on Gertrude's newly seeded lawn one summer, which evolved into decades of nearly constant monitoring of Sandi's movements.

"I never knew when she'd trod on my sod again."

"I assume you have memories of Miss Fliminsky as a teenager."

Gertrude bobbed her head. "Yup, I sure do."

"Any chance you remember the week in October 2005 when Mindy Bauerman was murdered?"

Gertrude hooted. "Oh boy, do I."

The woman may come across as an avenging crackpot, but what she said knocked Brownie and Barney back onto the sofa. She swore she saw Timmy Hanlon and Sandi parked in front of Sandi's house late on Wednesday, the night of the critical lobster dinner with Mindy and Wayne.

"Why would you remember something like that?" I asked. "It's been more than fifteen years."

Gertrude laughed. "The girl never went out in her life, so of course, when I saw a pickup truck driven by this beanpole of a teenager pulling up to her house, I knew something unusual was up."

"Tell us what you saw that's so relevant to my case."

Gertrude stood and snapped out her answer. "It was about ten o'clock, and the truck was parked under the streetlight. Sandi and the kid got out and climbed into the bed of the truck. I had my new, military-grade, nighttime binoculars, so I was able to clearly see what happened next."

Barney and John tilted forward with eyes distended, listening.

"That's when I saw Sandi tearing the clothes off of that skinny kid's body. I still blush, thinking about what I saw them doing."

Sandi jumped from her chair and yelled. "So, what, if I took his virginity, he was willing and damn happy. Give me a break."

Gertrude stepped toward Sandi, her fingernails exposed and ready for clawing. "It was right in the middle of the damn street, you pervert."

I stepped between the two women and ordered them to take a breath and return to their seats. Sighs of relief came from Brownie and Barney as neither appeared eager to intervene in an old-fashioned Kleinstadt brawl.

"Getting back on track," I said, "the important point isn't careless teenage sex or the fact Sandi lied about it. What's critical here is how messed up Timmy Hanlon became after he and Sandi did the genitalia tango. His parents noticed a distinct change in his personality following that evening, and they claimed a goofy, happy-go-lucky kid woke the next morning cranky and surly."

"It must have been bad sex," Gertrude said before giggling into her hands. Only my outstretched arm stopped Sandi from jumping her neighbor. "Watch it, Gertrude," I said, "or else I'll have to send you home."

My threat quieted Mrs. Steinhorst, and I continued, arguing that Sandi had gained mind control over a vulnerable young man with her sexual voodoo. I talked about how Mindy had humiliated Sandi and Timmy that evening, and while the young man had grown up disrespected by everyone,

CHAPTER FIFTY-TWO

Sandi hadn't. She needed her vengeance, and Timmy would help her get it.

"That, my respected sheriffs," I said to Feif and Brown, "was Miss Fliminsky's motivation for killing Mindy. And Timmy Hanlon agreed to be her cold-hearted instrument of revenge."

Sandi threw her head back in laughter. "Are you nuts? You're ignoring what else I told you about that night. How Mindy angered Wayne with her selfish behavior, cruel remarks, and dumping hot butter in his lap. It was Wayne who indicated he wanted to slice her throat. It was Wayne who disappeared soon after her death, never to be seen. Wayne Feif killed Mindy, and I won't let his father and cousin and some third-rated New York City private eye railroad me into prison."

Barney responded first. "Did you say Knuckles was a third-rated private eye? I swore he scored higher than that on Angel's List."

Brownie joined in. "Maybe we should arrest him for fraud, Uncle Barney."

That interruption by Feif and Brownie pushed me over the edge, and I yelled at them. "Stop letting her distract you, you dang knuckleheads. You both knew Wayne all his life and did he ever do anything violent?"

Feif and Brown looked at each other and shrugged. "Uh, come to think about it, he did mostly petty crimes," Barney said. "Maybe he threatened people, but I never knew him to throw a punch."

Brownie also failed to come up with an example of his cousin physically hurting anyone.

"That's what I'm saying, gentlemen. When Wayne was under stress, he didn't fight, he didn't attack, he wandered. After that lousy dinner date with Mindy, he fumed, he burnt his soiled pants, but he didn't hurt her."

Sandi must have seen that Barney and Brownie were falling under my spell and shouted her objections. "You forget, Nic, that I saw Wayne in the woods with a machete spying on Mindy the day before her murder. If he was prone to drift when upset, why was he stalking Mindy the day *after* the dinner date?"

"She got you there, Knuckles," Feif said. I heard a rumble of laughter come from John Brown. "She sure did."

"Not so quick, my fellow crime fighters. While Wayne had good reason to be furious with Mindy after her rude behavior, nothing happened to her that night, and she got home unharmed. No one reported Mindy being fearful the day after, and her mother said her daughter was her typical teenage self that Friday. My bottom line on Wayne is that he never intended to hurt Mindy. The only reason he was in the woods spying on her was to keep his commitment to George that he'd learn when and where Mindy was meeting Lyle."

Barney's face broke with a broad grin. "Are you saying my boy was a man of his word?"

"Yes, Barney, but after your son learned when Mindy was meeting with Lyle, he never showed up to share that information with George."

"Oh, so he wasn't a man of his word?"

"Not so quick," I said, thrusting my right index finger at Sandi Fliminsky. "It was her fault he failed to deliver the information. Sandi confronted Wayne as he was leaving the woods and demanded to know what he'd heard. I believe she threatened to report him to you, Barney, as the purveyor of her hallucinogens, so he talked. The fear of arrest was enough incentive for Wayne to immediately depart Kleinstadt."

Barney shook his fist at Sandi. "You were a nasty girl," he said with a thickened voice. "I haven't seen my boy in fifteen years because you scared him off."

Mrs. Steinhorst squeezed Barney's hand, and he quieted.

"Miss Fliminsky now knew where her victim would be the following night," I said. "She'd convinced Timmy that Mindy had to be punished for her nastiness and he agreed to bring along his never used meat cleaver. Sadly, things would get out of hand, and Mindy Bauerman would lose her life in the most brutal fashion."

Barney roared. "Well, at least I was half right. Hanlon was guilty."

Sandi jumped to her feet. "Barney's correct, and he did get the right man," she said, "but you have no proof I was there. For all you know, Timmy took it upon himself to avenge my honor. He was a crazy kid back then."

Spittle from Gertrude's mouth flew across the room as she screamed at Sandi. "You cheap tramp. You used that Hanlon kid, and now you're throwing him under the bus. You're shameless."

The hair on Sandi's head bristled. "You haul your ass up to the Indiana State pen and listen to his endless prattle," she said, "and then tell me I don't care about him."

I yelled loud enough to stop the wrangle between Gertrude and Sandi. What's wrong with those Midwesterners, anyway? Couldn't they follow cozy mystery protocol and hear me out? I bet Miss Marple never had to bang heads so she could finish her revelations.

"Please, everyone, stay quiet until I finish," I said, and the room went still. "Okay, thank you. Now, let's not forget Timmy was a comedian at heart and only wanted to make people laugh, not cry. He was the guy who lost an afterschool job at a slaughterhouse, because he couldn't stand the sight of blood. I'd wager that when Timmy whacked Mindy atop of her head, and she bled, Hanlon was done with the mayhem."

Barney let loose a whine that made my teeth vibrate. "I can't keep up with you, Knuckles. Are you now saying Hanlon did or did not kill her?"

"I'm saying Timmy delivered the first blow, but it wasn't what killed her."

My slow rollout of the findings must've gotten to Brownie because he jumped up and yelled. "Good God, Knuckles. Get to the point before I bust a button."

Considering how snuggly Brownie fit in his uniform, a busted button could be dangerous shrapnel, so I moved quickly. "Okay, John, tell me again the nature of Mindy's wound you discovered when you found her body."

"A deep cut to the top of her skull."

"Right, but you have to admit, as an untrained crime scene investigator, you missed the fact that Mindy had been beheaded."

Sheriff Brown shrugged. "Maybe I did, but the cleaver wound looked deep enough to do the job, so why consider any other possibilities?" Feif added his opinion. "And if we did realize she'd been beheaded, a meat cleaver could've been used."

"No, my incompetent friends, if a cleaver had been used, a closer examination would've shown the telltale signs of multiple chops. Instead, the autopsy report said Mindy's head was cleanly severed from her neck.

The killer used a very sharp tool like an axe or a machete."

Sandi screamed, "Yes!" and pointed her finger at me. "Look into your little notebook, Nic, and find where I told you about seeing Wayne with a machete in the woods. If you believe a machete was used, Wayne had one, and he wielded it to murder Mindy. It must've been Wayne and Timmy in the woods that night. Yeah, they must've hatched their plan after she'd humiliated them both at the lobster dinner."

"I have to give you an A plus for creativity, Miss Fliminsky," I said, "but it wasn't Wayne and Timmy. It was you."

Sandi folded her arms and gave a defiant flip of her head. "I don't think you have squat on me."

I never knew what squat was for sure, but whatever, I had it on Sandi. Licking the tip of my thumb, I quickly paged to the Buzz Rockwell section. "Here I have Buzz reporting Wayne had borrowed a machete to clear brush, but later Wayne swore he lost it. That event happened on the same day you confronted and demanded Wayne share what he'd heard between Mindy and Lyle. In addition to relieving Wayne of his information, you took the machete. The next night, it was in your hands when you confronted Mindy."

"That's ridiculous," Sandi said. "You can't prove I did such a thing."

Feif grunted. "Yeah, Knuckles. A machete was never found."

My face started to tighten as a grin stretched the flesh from ear to ear and halfway to my hairline. "I must tell you, Miss Fliminsky, I've always admired your manicured lawn and well-maintained shrubbery."

"If you think I'll give you a discount rate after all the trouble you're causing me, get over yourself."

I chuckled the knowing chuckle of an investigator about to apply the coup de grace to his suspect's freedom.

"As a city dweller more familiar with asphalt and concrete than vegetation, I was curious about the tools you needed to accomplish your art. Yesterday, after our talk, I happened to peek into your truck and was amazed at the assortment of shovels, saws, picks, and rakes."

"Where's this going, Nic?" Sandi asked.

"This is going to take you right to the slammer, because the tool that grabbed my attention was a machete securely displayed in the back window of your truck."

Gertrude giggled and softly clapped. "Here we go. He's got her now."

"So, what," Sandi said. "When the undergrowth gets out of hand, a machete is a standard tool for clearing. Every big-time gardener and landscaper has at least a couple."

I stepped up and placed my hands on Sandi's shoulders. "That machete in your truck isn't some Chinese-made hacker sold at the Speedi Food Mart. If I learned anything from my interactions with Buzz Rockwell, I know the difference between a cheap machete and a Jamaican Sugarcane Wacker Extraordinaire."

Sandi tucked her shoulders around her ears. "So what?"

"Buzz Rockwell still laments losing his Jamaican Sugarcane Wacker Extraordinaire all those years ago. He claimed there were only three in the world, and two were in the British Museum of Subjugated Peoples. That means the one supposedly lost by Wayne is the one in your truck."

Sandi's face emptied its capillaries, and tears pooled in her eyes. Her mouth gasped as if she were a fish stuck on land, wheezing between quickening breaths.

"There you have it, ladies and gentlemen. Sixteen years of being Mindy Bauerman's foil drove Sandi to commit the crime. Once she learned where Mindy was meeting Lyle, she had the opportunity. The tool for performing the lethal act was the rare Jamaican Sugarcane Wacker Extraordinaire. Finally, Sandi had an emotional hold over her accomplice, who'd live out his life in prison for one day a month sitting across from his beloved."

Gertrude bellowed. "Well, what do you have to say for yourself, Fliminsky?"

Sandi bent at the waist, tears dribbling from her eyes. "I was a desperate young girl longing to be popular, so I put up with Mindy's cruel behavior for years. But the way she treated me at that dinner was too much. It was my first date with a boy, and although Timmy was my last choice, he treated me nicely. When Mindy embarrassed me and taunted Timmy, I knew I had to put a stop to it."

"Did you plot your revenge that evening at dinner?' I asked.

"Yes, I schemed how I'd kill her while quietly eating dessert, a cherry jubilee."

"That's interesting," I said. "Barney, did you find most of your perpetrators had eaten a sugary dessert before committing their crime?"

Barney nodded. "In my day, it was more the bacon than the cake."

Sandi ignored Barney and me talking shop and continued confessing.

"You were right, Nic," she said. "I confronted Wayne in the woods that Thursday and asked what he'd heard. He said that information belonged to Mr. Bauerman, but after I threatened to accuse him of peddling dope, he coughed up the details. I took the machete, thinking if I used it, I'd drop it at the crime scene and implicate Buzz Rockwell."

Gertrude screamed a terrifying flow of vilification, calling Sandi pure evil for trying to ruin the lives of two young men. I felt tempted to tell her about my old girlfriend, Hannah, the Sociopathic Phone Solicitor, to show Gertrude what pure evil looked like, but I didn't want to take the spotlight away from Sandi.

"That Friday night, Timmy and I hid in the trees and watched this man, who I never saw before, helping Mindy put on her new shoes. She hugged him and called him Daddy, so I guess it had to be Lyle. He said he wished he could stay longer, but had some clients in the next county expecting personal shoe fittings that night."

I glanced at Barney and saw him blinking away a tear.

"Mindy spent a few minutes twirling and dancing," Sandi said, "enjoying shoes that probably cost ten times what I paid for my sneakers. But her gaiety ended when Timmy and I climbed out of the brush."

Sandi dipped her head and struggled to continue talking. "Do you need some water?" I asked. She shook her head. "I'd rather have a glass of wine, you know, to ease my tongue."

I excused myself and, two minutes later, returned with a full goblet of a lovely 2009 Pinot Noir I found in Sandi's kitchen. Gertrude mumbled about how rude it was not to offer everyone some wine, but I ignored her. My investigation was coming to a grand conclusion, and I wanted Barney and Brownie sober.

"After we stepped out from hiding," Sandi continued, "Mindy called me names and laughed at us. That's when I told Timmy to use his cleaver to give Mindy a haircut, if you know what I mean." Sandi slurped her wine. "Timmy swung his cleaver and struck her atop the head. She fell to the ground, still conscious, but blood was squirting everywhere. That's when Timmy dropped to his knees and heaved up his dinner. Mindy started screaming and said she was going to have us arrested. That's when I offered Timmy the machete to finish the job. He waved me off, so I took matters into my own hands."

"I'm guessing it took you one whack," I said.

Sandi nodded. "With a Jamaican Sugarcane Wacker Extraordinaire, Nic, that's all I needed."

Barney raised his hand. "Why didn't you leave the weapon like you planned? You were probably right; I'd definitely gone after Buzz Rockwell."

Sandi whimpered. "When I saw the superior craftmanship of that blade and how effortlessly it did the job, I couldn't leave it behind."

Ha, I thought, another criminal done in by quality.

Brownie stood and handcuffed Sandi, but before escorting her out of the house, he allowed her to finish her wine. He said she'd never taste booze again unless she drank jailhouse hooch. The handcuffs made it awkward, but Sandi was able to lift the wine to her mouth.

"Care to join me for a glass, Nic? Maybe to celebrate your success."

I turned her down, but I had to give her props. "You know, Sandi, you had me running around chasing my tail."

Sandi giggled. "When you tried to comfort me with a hug, I thought you had the hots for me, and I hoped I could steer you away from me and Timmy."

"Unfortunately, Nic Knuckles only has the hots for justice, Sandi, but you did help me book some serious billable hours."

The woman took another swallow of the wine. "You should give me a cut of your overtime."

"Not gonna happen, Sandi. But I might send you some yellow roses on your birthday."

Sandi emptied her glass and swiped the back of her hand across her mouth. She smiled and said, "I'd like that, Nic. I'd like that a lot."

Chapter Fifty-Three

I slammed the car truck lid after placing the last of my luggage. I was in a foul mood because Nic Knuckles could be such a tourist sometimes. Yesterday I stopped by All Things Sharp to say goodbye to Buzz Rockwell, and I let him talk me into an 18th-century double-bit axe. It was small enough to squeeze into my luggage, but explaining it to TSA would be a hassle. I had enough problems with those people. I once dated a woman who was an agent, and after I broke it off, my name suddenly appeared on a special Do Not Fly list. It was where they strip-searched you at the gate and made you count backward from 10,000 by seven.

Last night, the romantic intention of Kate Crumble reared its ugly head after the second toast to my success in solving the Bauerman case. By the third glass of the champagne knockoff, I thought I'd have to use my double-bit axe to extricate myself from Kate's clutches. Fortunately for me, she passed out and was still sleeping it off this morning, so I left without eating another burnt breakfast.

I took a gander up and down the street before climbing into the car. I could make out the sign hanging in front of Buddy's Tavern. I hoped the resolution of Mindy's murder would clear the name of Buddy Lee Hoot. Perhaps someday, he'd offer a Lady's Night special and attract a female clientele. Mary Jane Bauerman might find her way into the bar for a brew and conversation. That'd make Buddy happy, and probably Mary Jane, as well.

Although I couldn't see it, I knew further down the street from Buddy's place was The Next to Last Supper. I felt a pang of sadness thinking about the departed Molly Spear. She was crusty and played me like a cheap kazoo, but she'd been the only welcoming presence in a town full of hostile strangers. I hoped whatever heaven she now occupied, that they roasted higher quality coffee beans than The Next to Last Supper.

"So long, Kleinstadt, Indiana," I said. "You put catsup on your hot dogs instead of mustard and sauerkraut, but I learned there are a lot of good people living here."

I hopped into the car, punched the starter, and the engine fired to life. Pulling away from Miss Crumble's Cozy Lodge, I slowly rolled through the first stop sign I encountered. As if on cue, a siren sounded behind me, and the hulking figure of John Brown filled my rearview mirror.

"Good morning, Sheriff Brown. Are you here to see me off?"

The big man leaned into the opened window. "You just won't use your brakes to make a proper stop, will you Knuckles?"

"You got me, Sheriff, but hopefully, you'll let my indiscretion pass, since I'm on my way out of your town. You should celebrate because you'll never see me again."

Brownie didn't smile, but he didn't growl like he usually did. Hopefully, we'd finally forged a mutually respectful professional relationship.

"How'd the arraignment of Miss Fliminsky go?" I asked.

"Pretty smooth," he said. "She wouldn't give me a written statement of guilt, but she already has her lawyer talking a deal. I think we'll have a plea in a few days."

"What does she want?"

Brownie chuckled. "She'll go quietly if she can be in the same prison as Timmy Hanlon."

I laughed loudly. "Poor Sandi, at best, she and Timmy will be pen pals in the pen. Maybe she can get work in a prison garden and grow yellow roses."

The sheriff smiled, which was a significant change in demeanor for him. I decided to use the opening to do a good deed.

"I learned a lot about this town, John, and I know Kate Crumble was there for you and your mother when you were younger."

The smile slipped from the man's face. "Yeah, she was."

"I think Miss Crumble would appreciate a call from time to time, you know, just to let her know her kindness wasn't forgotten."

Brownie grunted. "Yeah, you're right. I'll make an effort."

Sheriff Brown elevated and threw back his shoulders, which signaled an end to our conversation. I guessed he was letting me off with a warning since his ticket book remained in its holster. If I had an ounce of sense, I'd been on my way, but I couldn't help myself. I had to ask him one more personal question because that's what Nic Knuckles did; I queried people.

"What about you, big fella? Do you ever think about getting back into dancing? It's an excellent way to meet a woman who might smooth your rough edges."

Brown refused to react to my helpful suggestion. He pointed his stubby finger at me and said, "Barney Feif wanted you to stop by before you left town. You'd better not disappoint him or I'll smooth your edges."

"I'll do that," I said. "You take care, Sheriff John Brown."

Brownie turned and took three steps before breaking into a soft shoe routine worthy of a vaudevillian. The big oaf still had happy feet. For the first time since I arrived in Kleinstadt, I felt good interacting with the town sheriff, yet I still wouldn't miss him.

Fifteen minutes later, the nursing home staff led me to Barney Feif's room. I'd learned from Kate why Feif was in an assisted living facility. His condition had eight syllables, and it'd turn his soft tissue into stone before his heart would shut down. He might have less than six months to live, so I took it easy on him.

"I'm heading out, Barney," I said. "I wanted to stop by and thank you for sending me your business."

"Yeah, sure, I guess in the end, I got my money's worth."

"Better yet, did you feel I brought you some peace of mind?"

Feif looked at me all doe-eyed and sad and admitted my findings helped. Previously, while doing the old-man looking at the end-of-life thing, he wondered if he'd blindly pushed the Timmy Hanlon narrative. Had he done it because he was crazed with grief over the murder of his possible love child? Or had he secretly feared it was Wayne who'd done the crime?

"I have to tell you. Wayne rode the number one spot on my suspect list right up until the end," I said.

Feif nodded. "My son always struggled to fit in with people. As a toddler, he exhibited the classic sociopathic behaviors, like lying, setting fires, and eating pickled eggs. His mother and I worried it was only a matter of time before his true diabolic nature would emerge."

"Did you ever consider getting him evaluated and into therapy?"

Feif shook his head and looked at his shoes. "I didn't believe in that therapy stuff back then. I just encouraged him to leave town. The week before Mindy's murder, I jumped at the chance to connect Kate Crumble and Wayne, hoping the money he earned doing her dinner date task would get him on his way to California."

Before I could ask why California, Barney explained. "They have more serial killers per capita than anywhere in the US, and I thought he might be happy living with his kind."

"I guessed you never thought that Wayne wasn't capable of killing."

Feif lowered his head and whined. "Not until you pointed out that he'd never actually hurt anyone."

What else could I say to a dying man filled with regret? I was about to offer my hand when he added one more bit of remorse to his list.

"Another thing that bothered me was when you said George believed Tommy Lyle was Mindy's father." Barney sucked in a breath and turned his wet eyes toward me. "I secretly thought that if Mindy ever confirmed her father was me, she'd be proud, and she'd feel special knowing her papa was a pillar of local law enforcement and not some hawker of shoes who never looked in on her."

I looked away so Feif wouldn't see my lower lip trembling. His anguished words got me thinking. Would my piece of crap father ever wonder how I felt about him? I got a hold of my weepiness and patted Feif on the back. "I'm sure she would've been proud to be your daughter."

"I sure hope so," Barney said, the words chunky in his throat. "That might make up for me failing Wayne."

I glanced at my watch and then turned to my fingernails, unsure how to end a suddenly uncomfortable farewell. I didn't want to end up hugging it out with a former client who was no longer paying me.

"I have to go, Barney, but I have one favor before I do. I understand your terminal condition will soon incapacitate you, so please give me a five-star rating before you kick off, okay?"

Feif nodded. "You got it, Knuckles."

My departure to the Big Apple was a cluster of delays, cancellations, oversells, and the third-degree by the friendly TSA folks. When the plane finally lifted off the ground and climbed into the sky, I looked down at the flat Indiana countryside. Thinking about everyone I'd met in the last month, I realized we all shared two common denominators. Whether you were from Kleinstadt or my New York borough of Queens, we all wanted to be appreciated. You could be a hard-crusted big-city private eye or a small-town loner peddling axes in a desolate downtown, but we all needed to be loved. Yeah, being appreciated and loved made life worthwhile.

I quickly grabbed the barf bag from the seat pocket and covered my face. The woman seated next to me leaned away into the aisle, but she needn't worry about me getting stinky sick. I'd pulled that bag over my face to block out the sobs I couldn't stop from escaping my mouth. A world-class private eye like Nic Knuckles couldn't cry like a baby just because he wanted more love and appreciation. If a photo of me all red-eyed and tear-streaked got out on the internet, my career would be over.

I wiped my face, closed my eyes, and rested my head against the window. I'd be landing at LaGuardia Airport in less than two hours, and if the subway lines were operating, I'd have time to get carryout from Kung Foo Eatery. It might not be the best Chinese food in New York, but the MSG headache that'd kick in later would make me happy to be home.

Acknowledgements

Harriette Sackler, for taking a chance on probably the quirkiest crime fighter in her stable of crime-fighting protagonists.

Also by William Ade

The Man Who Fixed Things (2023)

The Inevitable Failure of Jonathan Golding (2022)

Do It for Daisy (2021)

No Time for His Nonsense (2019)

Art of Absolution (2019)

About the Author

William Ade was born and raised in a large family in small town Indiana during the fifties and sixties; an experience that strongly influences his writing. While attending graduate school at the University of Illinois, he met and married his wife, Cindy and following graduation, they headed to the East Coast. After settling in Northern Virginia, they raised two children into adulthood. Those years of love and life also influences many of his stories.

Ade's latest novel, written as Nic Knuckles, is *Big Scream in a Small Town* and is the first in the Nic Knuckles Collection published by Level Best Books (LBB). LBB also published his crime novel, *Do It for Daisy* in 2021. Other novels by the author includes, *The Man Who Fixed Things* (2023), *Art of Absolution* (2019), and the serialized *The Inevitable Failure of Jonathan Golding* (2022). His short story collection, *No Time for His Nonsense* was released in 2019. His short stories have appeared in *Mysteries Unimagined*, the *Rind Literary Magazine*, *The Broken Plate*, *Black Fox Literary*, *Mindscapes Unimagined*, and the 2018 and 2019 *Best New England Crime Stories*. His short story, *Punch Drunk*, will be part of the 2023 *Chesapeake Crimes: Three Strikes – You're Dead* anthology.

SOCIAL MEDIA HANDLES:
  TikTok: WmAdeAuthor@williamade945
  Instagram: williamade87
  Facebook: william87

As Nic Knuckles
  Website at Nicknucklespi.com
  Tiktok.com/@nic.knuckles

AUTHOR WEBSITE:
  Eclectic Stories for the Humans at billade.com

www.ingramcontent.com/pod-product-compliance
Lightning Source LLC
Chambersburg PA
CBHW050150120726
47903CB00002B/566